Citizens Ununited

Steven —

You are the winner of a free copy of this novel out of 719 people who requested a copy on Goodreads' Giveaway book program.

I hope you enjoy it. If so, I'd greatly appreciate you posting a review on Goodreads.

Also, I am adding and editing a chapter at a time of a new historical fiction novel on Goodreads' Creative writing section. Any comments would be greatly appreciated.

Oliver

Citizens Ununited

A Novel

P.R. Oliver

To order additional copies of this book, contact:
Xlibris
1-888-795-4274
www.Xlibris.com
Orders@Xlibris.com
756117

Fascism should more appropriately be called Corporatism because it is a merger of state and corporate power.

—Benito Mussolini

Acknowledgments

I am grateful for the help in writing this novel from my friend Mike Brown and my legal assistant, Pam Santy. But particular thanks go to my wife, Patricia, who put up with hours of my inattention while I wrote this book and who critiqued my writing from time to time.

Thanks also to my siblings Vincent Oliver, Julia Oliver and Janis Oliver and my brother-in-law Bob Hammer for their comments and suggestions.

Finally, thanks to my friends George and Nina Fink for their help.

To those who oppose the oligarchic rule of our country by the wealthy and their corporations. History shows us that oligarchies often turn tyrannical. Those who resist oligarchy, tyranny, and foreign interference with our government are heroic, but they need the help of many citizens. Oligarchy is upon us. Tyranny is not close behind, whether it is called fascism or some other name. Persevere in your resistance like our heroine, Alex Pipe, and return our country to democratic rule.

Prologue

Russians visit, confirm Malmstrom ICBM launchers eliminated under treaty

By John Turner, 341ˢᵗ Missile Wing Public Affairs / Published April 21, 2014

<u>0</u> Share

<u>PRINT</u> | <u>E-MAIL</u>

MALMSTROM AIR FORCE BASE, Mont. -- Inspectors from the Russian Federation visited Malmstrom Air Force Base on April 9 to verify that 18 demolished Minuteman III Intercontinental Ballistic Missile launch facilities assigned to the 341ˢᵗ Missile Wing have been eliminated in accordance with the New Strategic Arms Reduction Treaty.

This confirmation will immediately reduce the number of ICBM launchers that the United States is accountable for, and bring the inventory of deployed and non-deployed launchers closer to the Treaty's limit that must be met by February 2018.

The launch facilities inspected were formerly operated by the 564ᵗʰ Missile Squadron and are located within a broad complex between Choteau and Shelby, Mont. The 564ᵗʰ MS was inactivated in 2008.

All 50 of the squadron's LFs are deactivated and will be permanently demolished.

The verification was accomplished by a Type Two inspection, a limited visit that gives the Russian inspectors 12 hours to set foot on the eliminated sites and confirm that each LF's launcher closure door has been removed, and that the launcher tube is filled with earth and gravel.

This was the first inspection of this kind at Malmstrom, said Richard Bialczak, 341st MW treaty compliance office chief.

"The inspections we usually have are a Type One, and that's when we go out to the sites and verify warheads and missiles," Bialczak said. For this inspection, the Type Two, the Russians came to "verify launchers we say were eliminated, and check on the processes that we used," he said.

Under treaty protocol, Type Two inspections cannot be used to verify deployed LFs at an operational ICBM base or to confirm the number of re-entry vehicles on top of deployed ICBMs. This type of inspection is normally reserved for storage and test facilities or to verify conversions or eliminations of strategic delivery vehicles. Russia is limited to eight Type Two inspections of U.S. facilities each year.

The 341st MW was notified April 8 that Malmstrom was selected for the inspection, Bialczak said. The inspection teams and their escorts from the Defense Threat Reduction Agency arrived on base the following day at 9 a.m., and began the site inspections at approximately noon.

Because the sites are spread across a wide network of back roads, and time was restricted, the inspectors were divided into two teams; each team would visit LFs until either all 18 sites were accounted for. The groups travelled on buses provided by the 341st Logistics Readiness Squadron and were led by vehicles from the 341st Security Forces Group. Bialczak escorted one group while Greg Aderhold, 341st MW compliance office superintendent, accompanied the other.

"From the time we started, we had to be completed in 12 hours," Bialczak said. "We were able to get all 18."

At each LF, the Russians used a GPS to confirm they were standing on a launcher and then walked around the site to verify the demolition had been completed. Each site only required a few minutes to check off.

"The sites are demolished," Bialczak said. "There's lots of dirt everywhere, dirt covering things that used to be operational missile stuff. And so it was just walk on site, and then off the site we went."

Bialczak said the inspection was completed 'in record time,' and that it would have been possible to inspect more sites if any others were ready for verification.

"DTRA seemed very impressed with our ability to welcome the inspection teams and take them to inspect so many sites in one short visit," said Col. Marné Deranger, 341st MW vice commander. "Overall, we felt the process ran smoothly, as testament to the preparation and experience of Rick and Greg. Our wing is fortunate to have them as part of our team."

As soon as the inspectors departed, Bialczak and Aderhold went back to work readying more eliminated LFs to be removed from treaty accountability. Within days the 341st MW treaty compliance office reported 16 more LFs as fully demolished.

"We can't have anybody go onto those sites," Bialczak said. "They're to remain undisturbed for that 60-day period. After the 60-day period, they come off our books."

Russia may choose to send another inspection team to Malmstrom within the first 30 days of this window to look at these 16 sites, thereby expediting the removal of these launchers. Otherwise, these additional sites won't be cleared from accountability until June.

Chapter 1

Clancy was not a usual name for a girl. But Clancy McCleary was not a usual girl. She was a tall redhead, and it was said she favored Nicole Kidman, both in height and in looks. She was single and lived alone in Georgetown, Virginia, in an upscale apartment with luxurious decor. After graduating from Holy Cross with a degree in journalism, she worked for a news service but then began freelancing after only a couple of years. Her clients were news services or anyone that would pay her for her investigating prowess. Clancy McCleary, Freelance Investigative Reporter Service, was in high demand. She had her own website and a long list of satisfied clients.

Clancy had a stellar reputation in journalism in the DC area. She had many contacts that helped her business considerably, and she was a driven woman. Clancy dreamed of future fame from a major exposé of equal or greater importance than Watergate. She was gorgeous, with pale white skin, long red hair, and clear blue eyes. She wanted to be a real-life duplicate of comic-book reporter Brenda Starr with all of her glamour, intrigue, adventures, and steamy romances. However, her dreams about romance were just that—dreams. She was busy and had never met a man she really liked, except a few gay men. To Clancy, men were competition as she strived to reach her goal of becoming a famous journalist. She had had far more relationships with women than she did with men, but she did not consider herself a lesbian. Her recent interest was an on-again-off-again relationship with a female weight lifter by the name of Marie.

The business line phone rang in Clancy's Georgetown apartment. It was midmorning, and she was still in her tattered white bathrobe, typing on her laptop with a cup of coffee sitting nearby. She tossed her hair back and picked up the phone.

"Hello. Clancy McCleary, reporter. May I help you?"

"Senator Randolph's office calling. Please hold for the senator."

She had met Senator Jennings Randolph at a cocktail party put on by a former employer for select members of Congress. The senator had not hesitated to tell Clancy how pretty he thought she was. She had given him her card and carried on a pleasant chat with him, but she could tell he was much more interested in her as a woman than as a professional reporter. Naturally, she had wanted to make a good impression on the senator but did not want him to think her interest in him was sexual. She had felt cornered by him and tried to plot several ways to get away from him in a polite way. A congressman who interrupted to speak to the senator had saved her. Clancy had carried out several minor assignments for the senator and, for the most part, managed to escape his persistent hands.

"Clancy. How good to talk to you again."

"Hello, Senator Randolph. Good to hear from you."

"Clancy, I have a job for you and would like to see you in my office tomorrow afternoon at 1:30. Can you be here?" asked Jennings.

"I'll be there."

US Senator Jennings Randolph was a handsome, distinguished-looking gentleman with graying temples from the state of Virginia. He was born and raised in Bedford, Virginia, went to Washington and Lee University in Lexington, and studied law school at "The University." In that day and time, the students and faculty at the University of Virginia spoke of the school as The University, as if there were no other. They also spoke of Mr. Jefferson in the present tense as if he were on campus. Jennings was somewhat of a celebrity on "the Grounds," given that he was a descendant of Thomas Jefferson. Randolph considered himself a middle-of-the-road Democrat. He had been a longtime champion of campaign finance reform.

Clancy was escorted into Senator Randolph's office promptly at 1:30. She was dressed in a conservative gray business suit with a bright green neck scarf, contrasting her flaming red hair. The senator was in short sleeves, wearing the obligatory power-red tie. Clancy noticed that Senator Randolph seemed quite serious and business like—no flirting. *This must be for real.*

"Clancy, as you know, I am chairman of the Senate Campaign Finance Reform Committee. We investigate complaints about unlawful political spending. The source of a large amount of political spending is from political action committees, better known as PACs. After the Supreme Court's *Citizens United* decision, a huge wave of money flowed to the PACs, and many have been dubbed 'super PACs.' For some time, we have gotten complaints about one super PAC called United Patriots of America, usually called UPA. I usually refer to them as Cobra because a coiled cobra is their symbol."

Clancy was aware of the famous *Citizens United* decision but had never heard of UPA.

The senator continued his narrative. "UPA was formed as a nonprofit organization under the Internal Revenue Code because it was, according to its founders, a social welfare organization. As a social welfare organization, it is supposed to spend its donations for activities promoting a social cause. In UPA's case, their social purpose was to promote patriotism among the American people; at least that's what they claim. Donations to UPA and many other super PACs are tax deductible, and its donors do not have to be disclosed. The problem is that we think only a small percentage of the money goes for promoting patriotism. We are not sure where most of the money goes or what it is really used for."

Clancy leaned forward and made a gesture that she wanted to ask a question. However, the senator kept talking.

"We have received unconfirmed allegations that massive amounts of money from God knows where have flooded their coffers. We are talking billions—enough money to fund an army. But we don't know where the vast majority of the money goes. It disappears. Then it resurfaces. Then some of it goes back to contributors or goes to other PACs."

"Why would one PAC give money to another PAC?" asked Clancy.

The senator leaned forward. The question was obviously a sore point for him. "Some lawyers have found loopholes in the Internal Revenue Code regulations and argue that a social welfare group can give away all of its donations to another PAC organization, even one that spends all the money for political purposes, without losing its tax-exempt, nonprofit charitable status."

"So exactly what is my assignment?" Clancy asked.

"We don't know where all the money is coming from, and we don't know where it is going. Primarily, we want to know what the money is being used for because we do not believe it is for a social welfare purpose. That is what I want you to find out. The Senate committee will pay you your normal rate and all expenses, and you can buy whatever you need to do the job."

Hmmm, thought Clancy. *My hourly rate just went up.*

"Thank you, Senator, for this great opportunity. I'll get on it immediately. Who will give me the briefing?"

"Butch Butler, my chief of staff. He's expecting you in his office now. I need to tell you first that this is highly confidential and that you need to take great care in covering your tracks. When large amounts of money are at stake, things can sometimes get dangerous."

Clancy was escorted into Butch's office. He was a short, outgoing southerner. He sounded like one of the good ole boys with his heavy southern accent spoken in the cadence of a country preacher.

"Hi, hon. Sit right down. Make yourself comfortable."

He asked Clancy to tell him all about her. He often interrupted her to get more details about her parents, phone numbers, e-mail address, former residences, and other details.

It seemed to Clancy that he would never stop asking about her personal life. He had not told her anything about Cobra. She was expecting a detailed briefing. Finally, she asked him about UPA. "Could you tell me some things about Cobra?" she asked. What she received from Butch was not much more than their address. He handed her a folder with a symbol of a coiled cobra on the front.

"You will probably need some office space and perhaps some contract employees. We have some storefronts in a place where no one would expect an office. Here is the address. There are tables and chairs there, so you won't have to buy any.

"I want you to report to me on your progress at all times," Butch told her. "Here is my direct line and my cell number in case you need to talk after hours. You keep in touch, ya hear?"

His secretary appeared and escorted Clancy out of the office. *I had better look at the offices first,* she thought as she left the Senate Office Building.

It was a rough, rundown area of DC. Many of the storefronts were boarded up. Everything looked dingy and in disrepair. The place was in the 900 Block of H Street. *My God, what a crummy part of town.* She looked around cautiously before getting out of her car.

There were three stores in a row in a single building, all vacant. The middle unit matched the address given to her by Butch Butler. There was an alley on the right side of the building and one behind it. The alley looked like a place she did not want to go. She went back to the front and put the key in the door. Clancy opened it with caution. The inside was nicer than the outside. The space just inside the door was vacant and clean. The back room was clean and freshly painted. There were electrical outlets and controls for the HVAC. A door labeled "Toilet" opened off the left wall. As Butch had said, there were tables and chairs throughout the room. On the back wall, there were high windows covered by blinds, and there was a back door.

Clancy's eyes roamed the room, checking out the details. She headed to the toilet door. *Wonders will never cease! It is clean. And there's a shower. Why do they have such a clean place in a dumpy neighborhood?*

The toilet room area did not lessen the size of the back room. It was a large back room, perhaps 150' x 150'. Clancy reasoned that the bathroom must take up space in the neighboring unit; either that or there was a fake wall from the bathroom to the alley wall.

Clancy was observant and had an eye for detail. Perhaps it was the reason she made a good investigator. She would ask herself "why" after her observations. Why would there be a fake wall in the unit? Why would the unit be so clean and yet in a rundown neighborhood? Why would a senator have such a place at his disposal?

Clancy returned to her apartment in Georgetown and immediately began to think about what she would need to do her job. Senator Randolph's words about the job being potentially dangerous concerned her somewhat. She had done stealth work before but nothing that could be called dangerous. She decided she needed secure communications that could not be traced back to her. She walked to a nearby electronics store and bought several cell phones and several prepaid wireless phone cards. She could use one cell phone and then the other to keep off balance anyone who might want to listen. No one kept track of who bought the cell phones or the cards, so no one knew who the user was. No identification was required for the phone or the cards for minutes of usage. If she was going to keep secrets, she did not want to use her personal cell phone.

Also, she determined she would have to hire a good computer specialist if she was going to find out financial information on Cobra. She called a recruiting firm for computer personnel called Technical Professional Recruiting and asked if there were any security specialists available. She was transferred to a Jim Dearing. Dearing asked Clancy to describe what kind of specialty she was looking for. She said, "A hacker."

"How good a hacker are we talking about here?" the recruiter asked. "A kid out of MIT, an experienced white-hat hacker, or a black hat with a record?"

"I don't want anyone finding out about what I'm doing," Clancy replied.

"I would not put a white hat in a black-hat job," he said.

"I'll go along with that. Do you have such a person, and if so, when can she start?"

"Today if you wish. The person is a he. His name is Carl Jones, and he is available right away. But you need to come by and fill out some forms first. We need to make sure we get paid."

Back in the apartment, Clancy took off her clothes and headed for the shower. She had a habit of undressing anywhere in the apartment, and her clothes were often scattered about. Walking around the apartment in the nude was second nature to her; she never gave it a thought. She went into the shower to plan what she needed to do for her investigation. Standing under the hot water was her favorite thinking place. *I need to get an interview with the CEO of UPA, sign the contract with Technical Professional Recruiting, and then meet the hacker, Carl Jones... I wonder what Marie is doing tonight.*

Chapter 2

Clancy opened the front door of the storefront office on H Street at 11:20 a.m. and strolled toward the back room. She turned on the light and realized with a jolt that there was a man sitting at one of the tables staring at her. Startled, she yelled, "Who the hell are you?"

"My name is Carl Jones. I thought you were expecting me," he said, as if nothing was abnormal.

"I was expecting you, but why didn't you knock on the door and wait until you are were invited in? And sitting there in the dark is weird. You scared the hell out of me."

"I didn't mean to scare you, but aren't you being a little oversensitive?" he asked.

"No, I don't think so," she blurted out, her blue eyes flashing.

Clancy looked at him and turned around and then back around to face him.

"Why don't we start over, Mr. Jones? My name is Clancy McCleary." She held out her hand. Carl accepted her hand and shook it.

He was in his late thirties with black-rimmed glasses and lenses that looked like the bottom of a Coke bottle. The comb-over of his diminishing brown hair went from right to left. There was nothing attractive about him, his body, or his clothing. However, his ego was as big as a barn. He had a slight smirk on his face, and the right corner of his mouth turned up slightly. Clancy could feel his disdain for her as she sat down.

"I studied under Adrian Lamo," were his first words, said with the expectation of a groveling response from her.

Clancy looked at him and did not know what to say. She had no idea who Adrian what's-his-name was. She could tell he was expecting her to know and respect this person.

"It is helpful for me to know your credentials," she replied. With that, he smiled.

"I can do everything that Adrian accomplished and more. I am the best cryptanalyst you can hire."

Clancy felt that he was rather odd and egotistical but felt no immediate fear of him. She wanted to get down to business and told him about the Cobra project.

"I need to know about every secret, every dollar, and every situation they are involved in. I want bank account records, wire transfers, telephone conversations, the works."

"This will be a piece of cake for me," Carl bragged. "Unlike others, I use a variant of DES called Triple-DES where the plain text is encrypted three times with three different keys and is almost universally accepted as a very strong encryption method. Most of the pinheads out there use their own secret ciphers for encryption. The mind-set of these weak-minded people is that if the internal workings of the cipher are kept secret, it would be hard to break. Over and over again, I and a few others have proven them wrong, and yet they keep committing the same costly folly. Two such idiocies in recent times are the large-scale adoptions of the GSM cipher and the DVD cipher. Of course, the GSM people or the DVD people could have just used any of the hundreds of well-known, publicly available ciphers—instead of building their own. They chose not to, for unknown, possibly lunatic reasons, and they proved to the world, once again, that code making is a very complex art. I can break them all and crack into any so-called secret information that you want."

Clancy was puzzled. She had only understood his last sentence. *Whatever the hell he said sounded good. I sure hope he knows what he's talking about.*

It occurred to Clancy that Jones was taking control of the situation. Shifting her attention, she looked down, tossed her red hair for dramatic effect, and then looked back up at him.

"Consider yourself hired, Mr. Jones. You will do everything I tell you. You may only charge your discounted government rate, and you have to work out of here under my supervision."

"I work better alone, but I guess I can live with that if I have to," he said sheepishly.

He decided to try to take control again. "I can tell you are on subcontract to some government agency or office but not the CIA or FBI; they have their own people that do what I do. It has to be a government office that does not want anyone to know they are snooping. Right?"

"Mr. Jones, I cannot and will not tell you who we are working for. Let's change the subject. We need to buy a couple of laptops. Which laptop is best suited for your work?"

"The only laptop for the job is the Alienware Area 51 laptop," he responded. "I thought everyone knew that," he added arrogantly.

Chancy ignored him. "Let's buy a couple of those laptops and get started."

"No. You have to order them online from Dell. Don't you know anything?"

Clancy bit her lip so she would not say anything inappropriate. She felt like firing him on the spot. "Okay. Okay. I'll do that and have them shipped express. I'll let you know when they get here, and we can get started. In the meantime, see what you can find out about United Patriots of America and give me your phone number." *How am I going to put up with this arrogant son of a bitch?*

Clancy drove back to her apartment. *It is still early. I should go to the gym.* She ran up the stairs, grabbed her workout bag, and jumped back in the car. Her car was a light gray Honda, several years old. She had picked it because it was the most inconspicuous car she could find. Many assignments required that she draw no attention to herself. Unfortunately, many drivers didn't pay attention to her either, so she had to be on the lookout for people pulling out in front of her.

Her workout was satisfactory but short. As usual, she spent more time under the hot water in the shower than she did in the exercise room. After her shower, she went to the weight room. Marie, her Latino friend, was talking with a group of women weight lifters. Buff and hot were the best terms to describe Marie. Clancy thought she was the best looking of the group by far. She had always been attracted to her even though Marie was much shorter than Clancy.

"Hey, girlfriend," Marie yelled at Clancy across the room. Marie walked away from the group of girls and got Clancy off to one side near the door. "I've missed you. You don't return my calls."

"I've been busy, but I miss seeing you too. I've been thinking about you lately, particularly when I'm in the shower. Maybe we should get together again sometime."

"I'll call you, maybe later tonight, and we will set something up. I better get back over there. Someone will be very mad at me if I'm over here with you much longer."

After she left the gym, Clancy stopped at an all-night convenience store and bought TV dinners, Pop-Tarts, microwave popcorn, and other items that required nothing but heating in the microwave. Clancy was not a cook. She stuck a Hungry Man Salisbury steak dinner in the microwave and changed into her white bathrobe. *I really need to buy a new bathrobe. This one is falling apart.* She took a beer from the fridge and sat down with the TV dinner.

The next hour she spent at her laptop, ordering the new laptops from Dell, searching the Internet for information on United Patriots of America, and making notes. About eleven o'clock, there was a knock on the door. Clancy looked through the peek hole and saw Marie.

Clancy opened the door. "That was quick. You keep your promises."

Marie stepped through the door and closed it behind her. "You looked too hot at the gym for me to pass up on my promise." She reached out to Clancy. Clancy stepped toward her with a smile.

The tattered white bathrobe slowly slipped to the floor.

Chapter 3

Lt. General Preston White (Ret.) sat at his desk in Washington, DC, lost in thought. His office was impressive—leather couches and chairs, a conference table for eight people, and a small wet bar. The desk, conference table, and trim work were Brazilian rosewood. The hanging paintings, ceramics, pottery, and other decorations were, even at first glance, extremely expensive. The colors of the walls blended with the rosewood and paintings very tastefully. It was an office that would impress a king. If one word could describe it, the word would be money.

Behind his desk was his trophy wall with several awards and a copy of *Time* magazine with a picture of Preston White on the cover. White was not smiling in the picture, but then he rarely smiled. The story in *Time* presented former Lt. General Preston White as a hard-nosed leader of industry. He reasoned he could not be deemed a hard-nose if he were smiling on the cover. The former division commander was portrayed as a leader, regardless of venue. He was on the board of directors of four major corporations, all of them defense contractors, active in the US Chamber of Commerce, and a host of other accomplishments.

White looked like a general. He was in his midsixties with a gray flat-top haircut and the bulging arms of a weight lifter. He carried himself in an erect military manner. He was in perfect shape. His suit and tie were expensive, and he had manicured fingernails. Other than his gray hair, it would be difficult to believe the general was in his sixties. He had an old scar near his right eye that gave him a sinister look.

A female voice came over the intercom: "General, your 10:00 a.m. appointment, Clancy McCleary, is here."

Clancy had called the general several times before she was able to talk to him. She told him that she was an investigative reporter and that she wanted to do an article on him and UPA. General White loved favorable publicity and made the appointment.

"I am glad to finally meet you, General White. I have heard so much about you." Clancy actually had never heard of him before this assignment but viewed it as a little white lie.

"Sit down, Ms. McCleary. Can I call you Clancy?"

"That would be fine, General."

He asked her if she would like a refreshment, and she said she would like coffee. The secretary she had met out front quickly brought it in. Clancy was on the edge of her chair leaning forward toward the general. She had a notebook and pen in her hands. Her beautiful red hair was shoulder length. She was dressed in various shades of green. The dress she wore was short, accentuating her long legs. She crossed one leg over the other. The general did not miss it.

The general wanted to comment on her expensive clothes and beautiful looks. However, he had an image to keep up and felt that comments like that were unnecessary maudlin remarks and a sign of a weak man. Despite his attempt to cover up his feelings, Clancy knew she had made a big impression on him. She could tell it in his eyes. She felt herself smiling inside. *This outfit always works.*

"So you want to write an article about me and my organization. Who do you think will buy it?"

"I have lots of media as customers. I don't think I will have any problem selling it quickly."

She asked the usual background questions about him and his accomplishments. She pretended that she was extremely impressed with his picture on the cover of *Time*. With each compliment given, the general seemed to open up even more. *You are doing a good job. Keep it up.* She then switched to questions about UPA. "Tell me about UPA, General."

"We are the largest super PAC in the country. We receive millions of dollars in contributions, particularly from corporations, now that they can give us unlimited funds due to the *Citizens United* decision by the Supreme Court. You are familiar with that decision, aren't you?"

"Yes," replied Clancy. "It has caused quite a lot of controversy. It is one of the reasons I wanted to interview you. But aren't you restricted by other laws?"

"Yes," replied the general. "Due to legal restrictions, we cannot directly send money to political candidates. We are a 501(c)(4) organization dedicated to the promotion of American patriotism. In case you don't know, 501(c)(4) is a number in the Internal Revenue Code. It is a quick way people use to identify our types of organizations, which are commonly referred to as social welfare groups."

"What does social welfare mean?" asked Clancy. Clancy had to continue to remind herself to ask questions that a journalist would ask. The wrong kind of question could unmask her true identity as a political spy.

"In order to be a 501(c)(4) organization, the group must have a social welfare purpose," replied White. "Our purpose at UPA is to educate the public about the benefits of patriotism and the American way of life, particularly about free enterprise. Recently, we started a campaign about the benefits of corporations to society and how corporations are in the best position to run this country.

"We favor conservative candidates for public office because they are friendly to corporations and our causes, but we cannot give money directly to them. We have to educate the public about the faults of the opposing liberal candidates. We can tear down the liberals, but we cannot give money directly to their opponents. You remember the Swift Boat group that caused the defeat of Senator Carey?"

"General White, who are your typical contributors?" she asked.

"Big corporations, banks, businessmen, Wall Street. You name it, both foreign and domestic. The Supreme Court opened up the floodgate, thank God. Many people believe in our cause. Those that don't will be taught to believe in it later."

"How do you distribute the money, General? Do you do anything else other than media advertising? I heard you get billions in contributions."

"Yes, we get quite a lot of money, but I won't tell you how much. We give money to promote patriotism, free enterprise, and conservative causes—rallies, conventions, debates, education on issues from a businessman's point of view, to name a few. After all, it was free enterprise and business that made this country great. We can give money to other PACs that we believe support our causes."

"I heard that you give money to other PACs who directly contribute to political campaigns, a way to get around the restrictions on direct contributions."

"It sounds like you know more than you led me to believe. Yes, there are some lawyers for super PACs who take that point of view," replied General White.

"Also, I read that you don't have to disclose the individual names of the businesses and businessmen who donate to UPA," said Clancy.

"What's wrong with that? We are allowed to keep that secret by virtue of the fact that we are a social welfare group under the tax code."

"That does not seem fair. Doesn't everyone else involved in receiving political contributions have to disclose their donors? What are you hiding?"

"There is a certain tone in your question that I don't like," the general replied. "You must be a liberal or socialist." The scar on his face became bright red.

"I am a nothing," replied Clancy. "This allows me to write impartial articles about any person or group. I just lay out the facts."

It was clear that Clancy's questions agitated the general. His voice grew louder. "The fact is that this country is going into the tank. This county achieved greatness because of free enterprise. We want to take our country back from the liberals and socialists who have ruined the country, who have no experience running businesses and who can't run the government worth a damn. We want to restore the greatness of our country. We need to be winners again. Brave men and women settled this country; we did not have Medicare or social security or health care or welfare. The men and women believed in God and provided for their own needs. The county is turning into a group of nonbelieving weaklings living off the government. We need to turn that around. Only business leaders have the capability of getting this country back on its feet."

"The economy of this country is doing very well, and many of your contributors have gotten rich during the last few years. Why is this so critical?"

"The fact is, Clancy, we are running out of time. In just a few years, the minorities, Hispanics, Muslims, and blacks will outnumber white people in this country. White males built this county; they didn't."

"Can I quote you on that, General?"

"It is time we patriots stop trying to be politically correct and tell it like it is. Yes, you can quote me on that because it is true. Soon you will hear lots of people in this country telling it like it is."

"General, I've heard rumors that you don't spend all the money you get."

"That's not true. Everything on our books balances. We have at times given money *back* to some of our corporations who have contributed large sums. Sometimes they need cash and want some of it back for their own cash flow purposes. In the end, we get a lot more money from these companies than we give back. We take it off our books, and they put it back on their books. It's all legal."

"Do you send the money back using a UPA checkbook?"

"No, we have an affiliated company do that to keep the books straight."

"How does using an affiliated company check help you keep the books straight?"

"It's too complicated to get into right now."

Clancy started to ask another question, but the general cut her off. "We have run out of time, Clancy. It was good to meet you, and I am looking forward to your article. My secretary has some material about us that may help you. If you need addition information, let my secretary know."

Clancy left feeling that she had not accomplished much, except listen to a bigoted old man. But the more she thought about it, the more she wondered why some of the contribution from a corporation would go back to the contributing company. *That's what the senator meant by money appearing, disappearing, and reappearing. And why do they need a separate company to keep their books?*

Shortly after Clancy left, the general received a call. "General, you have a call from Mr. Butler on the encrypted line." He had instructed his staff to always address him as "General" and gave anyone who slipped and called him "Mr." a stern look. His stern looks were classic. Most people wilted when he glared them down.

"Put him through," commanded the general.

"Butler, it's about time I heard from you. It is nice that for once you could get off your lazy ass and give me a call," he said. The general's words were meant to be humorous. However, his humor never came out sounding humorous.

He then listened to Butler.

"Are you telling me they hired an investigator to check us out?" the general asked.

The General listened intently and then said, "McCleary? She was just here. Why are you so late in reporting this?"

After listening, he said, "Okay, I know you're busy. Her questions were pointed, but I don't think she got anything out of my answers. On the other hand, she suspects too much, and we have to be careful. Where are her offices?"

"I put her in the Zahir building on H Street," replied Butler.

"Good. Let me know anything else you learn."

White reached into his desk and pulled out a small binder. The cover on the binder was stamped "Top Secret." He opened the binder and scanned a list of phone numbers.

Clancy was still stalling with White's secretary under the pretense of needing more information. She saw the general on the phone but could not hear what he was saying. As she was leaving the office, she glanced back over her shoulder as he pulled out a book from his desk. Her glimpse caught the words "Top Secret" and she mentally noted the drawer it came from.

Using his encrypted cell phone, White punched in a number. A voice answered.

"General. How are you today?"

"No time for chitchat, Zakhar. It looks like we are being investigated. I just heard from Butler."

"What are you doing about it?"

"That's a stupid question. Right now, I am talking to you. That is the first thing I am doing."

"Calm down, General. I meant what are you going to do?"

"I need you to call everyone in TXA around the country, particularly the control center in Palo Alto, and find out as much as possible about an investigative journalist named Clancy McCleary here in DC and anyone else snooping around. I must make sure there are no leaks. We are so close to our objective."

Dmitri Zakhar spoke up. "As a matter of fact, I have very recently been notified of another possible breach of security here in Massachusetts. We are working on it now and will keep you informed as soon as I know something."

"One final question, Dmitri. Who is the best computer/phone security guy you know about? I need to upgrade security in this office."

"He lives right there in DC. He is an arrogant prick by the name of Carl Jones."

Chapter 4

Clancy received the two laptops and accessories by FedEx. She called Carl and told him she had them and to meet her at the office. Clancy arrived at the office first and waited for Carl. She was still waiting a half hour later. *That passive-aggressive prick.* Finally, Carl arrived, and they unpacked the new laptops and got them online. Carl began downloading software onto the laptop. He could not do anything without acting arrogant and disdainful toward Clancy, who hated him more every minute she was around him.

"Carl, I need to break into the UPA office and look at a book in General White's desk. Can you help me out? I need to be able to get in and out without being caught."

"You are out of your league, girl. I can do it by hacking into their computer system."

"Well, I need to get in General White's desk, and I don't think I can do it alone. You could get the information off their computer right there in their office while I am going through his desk. It might not be as hard to hack in from there."

"Clancy, I am sure that you can't do it alone. I doubt you ever broke into anywhere. Anyway, even in their office, it will be just as difficult to hack through their security. I don't think it is a good idea. It is much easier to get caught."

Clancy had about had it with Jones. "Are you with me or not?"

"Okay, it's your neck," he said with his typical sneer.

UPA's offices were located in the Square 54 office complex on Pennsylvania Avenue in the Foggy Bottom neighborhood. Clancy was excited about its location because Foggy Bottom was also the home of the Watergate Complex and site of the notorious Watergate burglary that had elevated two journalists to sainthood. Carl brought along a laptop computer installed in a briefcase. It was impossible to tell whether the briefcase held paperwork or not. It was an unusual-looking laptop. It had a regular keyboard but also a digital pad like a cell phone and a variety of holes to plug in electronic probes.

They went to a sublevel in the building. It was 4:45 in the afternoon. They mixed in with the people moving around the floor, pretending to know where they were and where they were going. As they headed down a hallway, Jones put a Bluetooth listening device in his ear.

"These newer buildings have centralized burglary systems. I need to determine its location."

They walked the halls until Jones stopped next to a steel door. "It's in this room. Watch the halls for a minute for me." He reached into his pocket, brought out a couple of pieces of metal, and in fifteen seconds, he had picked the lock and was inside. Clancy followed quickly and closed the door. Carl placed his briefcase on a steel table and opened it. He walked across the room to what looked like a burglary alarm controller and looked closely. He returned to his computer and typed in commands and then the brand of the alarm system. A minute later, he said, "I'm in. I now have complete control of this building's security system. I can monitor and turn off and on the systems in each office."

He asked Clancy for UPA's office number and typed it in. "There are still people in the office. I hope there are no gung-ho types that want to work tonight. We'll have to wait. The security guards won't be patrolling this room until after dark, so we can wait."

At 5:45 p.m., the last employee to leave the UPA offices activated the alarm system. "They are leaving. I'll turn off their alarm protection, and let's go upstairs."

Clancy and Carl got off the elevator on the tenth floor and proceeded down the hall to suite 1028. They walked by causally to make sure no one was still there. Carl put his briefcase down on the floor and turned on his computer again. "They don't have a backup alarm system." He closed the computer and reached in his pocket for the tools to pick the door locks. They went inside quickly, closing the door behind them.

It was not dark outside yet, so there was no need to turn on a light. They walked to White's office. Before Jones tried to pick the lock, he ran his fingers around the inside edge of the door. "Ah, I think we have a low-voltage silent alarm on this door hooked into a phone system." He grabbed his briefcase again and turned on the computer. He then grabbed an electronic device the size of a cell phone from his briefcase and turned it on. He used the device to retrace the inside of the door where moments ago he had his fingers. Both the device and his computer gave out small beeps. Jones then used his lock-picking tools and opened the door to the office. They went into White's office, and Clancy tried to open the desk. It was locked. Jones went through the same routine with the device and the computer and then picked the lock to the desk.

Clancy reached into White's desk and grabbed the book stamped Top Secret. She reached into a pocket and pulled out a tiny camera and began taking pictures of each page in the book. In the meantime, Jones said he was going to find the main server for the UPA network and walked away. He picked several more locks and finally found the server computer. He grabbed a computer cord with what appeared to be a USB connector on each end. He plugged one end into his computer and the other into the server. When the server asked for a password, he started a password hacking program on his computer. It took five minutes for the hacking program to figure out the password. In the other room, Clancy continued to take pictures of the book on White's desk. Once inside the server, Jones began to transfer the contents of the server to his computer. There was considerable information on the server, and Jones knew it would take at least ten minutes to complete. The disk on Jones's computer was large, and there was no need for additional storage for uploading data.

Clancy was close to being finished taking pictures. The room was getting dark as dusk settled on the city. Out of the corner of her eye, she saw a flashlight scan the lobby. This could only mean that the security guards were making their rounds. She froze. The flashlight soon stopped. She quickly finished the job and put the book back in the desk. She went back into the lobby and looked down several hallways. There was the glow from a computer monitor coming from one of the rooms down the hall. She walked into the server room and told Jones about the security guard. He was unplugging his computer from the server. The transfer was complete. He began to wipe down anything that he had touched, particularly the server and its keyboard. Clancy and he went back around the offices wiping down everything they had touched. Carl then reset the alarms for White's office door and desk. All the doors locked as they closed them. When they left, nothing looked like it had been touched; nothing looked out of place. They took the elevator down to the lower level where Carl reset the main alarm system for UPA.

Clancy and Carl walked back though the main lobby as if they had done it a thousand times before. To the guard on duty, they looked like a couple of staffers who had worked overtime for one of the lobbyists in the building.

Clancy kept looking back over her shoulder as she and Carl walked away from the TXA building. "Don't look back," Carl said without looking at her. "That just draws attention." Clancy put her head down and did not look back. It seemed like Carl was going too slow.

Walking at a normal pace, Jones, his arrogance taking a repose, started talking to Clancy like she was an intelligent human being. "People welcome all the new technology and electronic gear but do not know the downside. The government and large corporations within a year or two will be able to do what I can do. Some of them are almost as sophisticated as I am today. They will be able to watch you through your web cam, even when you are not signed into your computer, or the security video camera if you have it. They can already turn on your cell phone remotely and listen to any nearby conversation. For some time, they have been able to look at your bank accounts, e-mails, telephone calls, credit rating, cell phone calls, and credit card purchases. They will know what you scan on the Internet, what TV shows you watch, what music you listen to, and even the books you read if you use Kindle or Nook or buy them with a credit card at a bookstore. Many people help these spies by disclosing everything about themselves on Facebook. Big government and big business will soon be able to have computer files on each of us, which reveal everything about us, including who we are having sex with. The end result is a total lack of privacy."

Clancy slowed her pace a bit and looked at Jones. "As a journalist, I would love to be able to get the total inside scoop on people. But it sounds like only governments and businesses have enough money to do all that."

"That is true. You would need a room full of hackers working diligently at gathering information in order to have an impact. And if you did have them, you could zero in on the people you want to blackmail and thereby have control of whatever you desire."

"That part sounds dangerous," said Clancy.

"It is. It is power through intimate information. I am sure that Stalin and Hitler would have loved to have the ability to monitor whoever they wished. Someone could come to power in this country and become a dictator if he or she could coordinate the snooping activities of all the branches of the FBI, the CIA, each branch of the military, and the hundreds of different spy agencies within each of those."

"Why hasn't that taken place?" asked Clancy.

"First, the technology is not quite there yet but almost. And even if it were, the politics of forcing each of these groups to cooperate is impossible. Nobody wants to give up their turf, and each group fights to stay in business."

"When did you get political?" asked Clancy.

"I have worked for all those government agencies undercover at one time or another. They battle each other fiercely for increased funding for their pet project. However, it is not the government that is the real threat to privacy in this country; it is the corporations. They have the ability to keep everyone and all their departments and divisions in lock step. They won't waste money on duplicate or overlapping spy agencies. They are beating government to the punch in high-tech snooping, and quite honestly, they have more money, a lot more money."

Back at the offices, the two transferred the pictures of White's book into Jones's computer. The book was a huge list of people's names, addresses, and phone numbers, each with a code next to the name. The people were all in a position of power in business and government all over the country. They included names of people within the FBI, Homeland Security, police departments, sheriff's offices, legislators, both state and federal, border patrol, the military branches, and National Guard units in every state.

Jones and McCleary worked diligently for the next several weeks. From the information gathered, he found at least ten corporations that were associated with UPA. They were all shell corporations, legally incorporated, but their addresses were vacant buildings. No one listed in the corporate papers was a real person, except the incorporator, who was also a lawyer in Arlington who acted as the agent for service of process. Each company had the same incorporator and agent. The lawyer also represented UPA. Each corporation had bank accounts, most of them offshore. Carl was able to trace the transfer of funds between UPA and the companies and transfers between the companies. The transfers were numerous, apparently to confuse anyone who might want to snoop. There were billions in transfers to UPA directly from outside sources, including foreign. About half of the transfers were then transferred to the shell corporations that kept the money moving around.

"All the shell corporations' names began with the letter Z: Zafir, Zabar, Zaad, Zabeeb, and so forth and so on. With the money moving around quickly from say, Zafir to Zabar to Zaad and then back to Zafir it gets confusing. It looks like there are thousands of transfers between these corporations, and then one transfer suddenly goes to TXA or one of the other defense contractors who were original contributors. The real question here is why does the money go back to the original donor corporation?

"I can't think of any other reason they would name them beginning with the letter Z other than to the confuse people about what is going on. I think these are Russian names, but I will check into it," said Carl.

Clancy's job was drafting a report to Senator Randolph about UPA based on the data she and Carl accumulated. On a Friday morning about three weeks after Clancy had met Butch Butler, she called him and reported their progress. She did not mention that they had broken into the UPA office, just that they had accumulated a large amount of data about UPA's money transfers.

Clancy said to Butler, "Despite the large amount of data we uncovered, we have not yet determined their purpose in sending money back to the original donor corporations or why many shell corporations located in Virginia names begin with Z. We were able to determine that only the donor corporations doing work for the Pentagon get money back—the defense contractors. None of the other contributors get back a dime. There are invoices from defense contractors like TXA to the Z corporations that are paid, but we can't figure out if the Z corporations are actually buying anything. There are part numbers on the invoices with no verbal descriptions and no ship to addresses. But I am confident we will figure it out. I want you to assure Senator Randolph of that."

"The senator needs a report immediately. When do you think ya'll get finished?" asked Butler in his southern drawl.

"By Monday morning. Right now Carl is looking at some data on funds transfers between the Z corporations and one of the defense contractors, TXA. He is trying to figure out what, if anything, the Z companies are buying, and if they are buying something, what is it and where is it being shipped?"

"Why did you become suspicious?" asked Butler.

"General White told me that sometimes the contributors need money back for cash flow purposes and that it is entirely legal and the money is all accounted for. But I don't believe him. The only contributors who get money back are defense contractors, and I doubt that defense contractors are the only ones with cash flow problems. And White told me that UPA uses the subsidiary companies to send the money back to the contributors because it is easier to keep track of the flow of money through the subsidiary. If you ask yourself why would it be easier, there is no logical answer. Actually, it would be more difficult because it involves multiple sets of books."

"That may well be the case, Clancy. But how is concentrating on TXA going to solve the question?"

"We will look for TXA shipping records on transactions with the Z corporations. We may have to hack into TXA to get those. From that, we may be able to determine the end game."

"Any records you obtain from a corporation won't be admissible evidence without a search warrant, so you better be careful."

"We can manufacture probable cause with a very small amount of incriminating, illegally obtained information and use it to get a search warrant. That way it looks like we obtained everything legally even though we already had the data."

"Good work, Clancy. I am sure the senator will be pleased. I'll talk to you on Monday."

Butler immediately called General White. "She knows too much. Way too much, General."

It was Saturday night, and Carl stood looking over Clancy's shoulders as she typed. She was going as fast as she could, sweat beading on her forehead, and in rapid jerky movements, looking down from time to time at her handwritten notes. She was tired. "I don't think that part you typed is correct," he said. "As I remember, that company is a second-tier shell corporation. It is owned by this corporation," he said as he pointed to the screen. He continued: "The money flowed through those two companies on its way to Zabeeb, LLC. As best I could tell from my hacking, the money is still held by Zabeeb in one of the offshore accounts. Many of those accounts for the other shell companies were emptied. The transactions between Zebra and TXA are interesting. Zabeeb is issuing purchase orders to TXA for some products that have only serial number designations, no product descriptions. Further, TXA is issuing billing statements to Zabeeb for the products on the purchase orders. Is TXA selling nonexistent products to Zabeeb to justify getting the money back and increasing their sales or are they really selling something?"

"Carl, I don't know," said Clancy. "If that's all we know by Monday morning, that's what we'll go with. I think Senator Randolph was hoping for more, like illegal campaign contributions directly to candidates or direct ads in favor of one of their conservative candidates. We did not find anything like that coming from the Z corporations or UPA. But let's keep working."

"There's one other thing I've thought of. These Z names sound Russian to me. Is TXA selling defense products to the Russians?"

"Good thought, Carl. I'll put it in the report."

Carl went back to his laptop and continued working. The two worked without talking well into early morning. At two o'clock Sunday morning, Carl suddenly got up and ran to the toilet room. Clancy heard noises from the room that sounded like Carl might be sick. Carl emerged and said, "I've got to go back to my apartment. I forgot my medicine."

Clancy got up and locked the door behind him. A minute later, she thought she heard a noise in the office next door. She froze and listened intently. She heard it again. Then nothing.

Chapter 5

Dmitri Zakhar stressed his point to United States Air Force General Thomas Jackson. Both stood in front of small groups of military personnel from the United States and from Russia, which were the START treaty teams of inspectors for silo missile sites in the United States. "The Russian inspectors do not have very much time for this second inspection." He continued speaking at length about the reasons for the short inspection time. "The only way we can accommodate their schedule is to skip the inspection on the silo in the Charles Russell Wilderness."

The general paused for a moment and replied, "Tell them we will accommodate them in any way that we can."

The general did not feel comfortable around Zakhar. Zakhar had been present during the initial inspections of silos a few months ago in April, and the general had spent considerable time observing Dimitri. The officer felt that Zakhar had a sinister look; his dark, dead eyes had no truth in them. But the general was acting in accordance with Defense and State Department orders. He saw no choice other than to trust in Zakhar's translations of the Russians' desires.

Dimitri, speaking in Russian, turned toward the Russian inspection team and directed his attention to the Russian general in charge. "I spoke with General Jackson, and he suggested that in the interest of time you could skip going to the farthest silo located near the Charles Russell Wilderness. I agree with him since I personally observed that location when I was here in April." Since no one other than Dimitri spoke both English and Russian, he could tell either side any interpretation he wished. He continued talking to the Russian general. "General Jackson and I visited the site together previously, and the demolition of the silo was ahead of schedule at that time. He says it is now completely filled with gravel. I have every reason to believe him. Regardless, there will be future inspection teams that can visit that location." The Russian general nodded and seemed satisfied with Dimitri's statements.

Dimitri had the unusual position of being both an American and Russian citizen. He had been born in the United States after his Russian parents immigrated to the United States. When Dimitri was a teenager, his parents' American dream became tarnished when his father was fired from his job; they moved back to Russia with Dimitri in tow. As a result, he spoke flawless English and Russian. He now lived in Massachusetts working as vice president of TXA, a large defense contractor that manufactured missiles. Due to his prestigious position in this country in the missile industry and his language abilities, he had been chosen by the Defense and State Departments to be the liaison between the Russian inspection teams and the air force for all START treaty inspections.

The Russian general spoke with his staff, and they agreed it would be best for their schedule not to inspect the missile silo in the Charles Russell Wilderness. It was, after all, a considerable distance from their present site. He personally knew Dimitri and believed that, despite the position Dimitri held in the United States, he was loyal to Mother Russia. Dimitri had been educated and trained at the Moscow Engineering Physics Institute and had secretly worked for the Russian military for years before moving to the United States. There was no reason for the Russian officer to have any doubt about Dimitri or what he had to say. Likewise the United States Air Force had no reason to doubt Dimitri. After all, he was appointed by the Defense Department, and he was well known in the US missile industry.

Where did Dimitri Zakhar's loyalties lie? What master did he serve? Only Dimitri knew, and he was not telling.

The inspection was taking place at a missile silo location near Great Falls, Montana, an area in the United States known for its wind. The weather helped everyone make up their minds to cut the conversation short and leave. In addition to the wind, it was very hot. The group moved quickly to the air-conditioned air force bus that would take them back to Malstrom Air Force Base. The Russians talked more about the weather than they did about missile silos.

A Russian military jet awaited the inspection team at the base. After it roared down the runway, Dimitri was escorted by an airman to a waiting Learjet 35 arranged for by the Defense Department for his trip back to Logan International in Boston. When safely in the air, Dimitri sat back and smiled and congratulated himself on his adroit handling of both the Russian inspection team and the U.S. Air Force.

"Out in the middle of nowhere, Montana," he said under his breath. "That silo will never get inspected by anyone." He paused. "Anyone." And then he smiled. Things were going well for him at various missile silos all over the country, those previously abandoned and subsequently purchased and those in the process of being abandoned.

A flight attendant interrupted Zakhar's reverie as she stooped to offer him a beverage. "He sends shivers up my spine," she told the other attendant when she returned to her station. "The way he looks at me with those cruel eyes is scary."

Chapter 6

Alexandra Pipe was in anguish. She could not concentrate on her work. She sat at her computer and stared vacantly at the screen. She had just learned that her coworker Cal Cummings had been abducted while at a shopping center last night. Cal was more than a friend; they had been lovers.

She was interrupted from her reverie by a man who flashed a badge and announced he was a detective. He walked into her small beige cube without waiting for permission, followed by a woman.

"Ms. Pipe, we have a few questions for you about Cal Cummings," he said. "I'm Detective John Biggs. This is my partner, Sheila Jones." The two pulled up chairs at Alex's desk. "We're with the Southborough Police Department."

"We're conducting interviews with all your coworkers here at the Massachusetts TXA plant, Ms. Pipe. This is just routine. We are trying to learn anything we can to find out what happened to him. When was the last time you saw Mr. Cummings?" Biggs asked.

"Yesterday at about five," Alex answered. "I was here at my desk still working. He said he had to leave early as he passed by my desk and said he'd see me tomorrow. We usually don't quit at five. We have more work than we can get done in eight hours."

"Did you notice anything unusual about the way he acted when he left?" asked Detective Jones.

"Nothing. He acted perfectly normal. He said he had some errands to run and would see me tomorrow."

"Were you friends with Mr. Cummings?" asked Biggs.

Alex hesitated for a second and glanced down at her desk.

"We were coworkers," she replied.

"We are aware of that, Ms. Pipe. Were you also friends with him?" asked Jones.

Alex was reluctant to give a quick response. Cal had been her lover for six months. He was new on the job when they first began dating. He was married, but she did not know about it at the time. When Alex learned about Cal's wife, she broke off the relationship. Communication with him after that had been icy at best. But recently she and Cal had been assigned to projects where they had to work together; in the process, they had renewed their pre-affair friendship.

She looked up at the detectives and said, "Yes, we were friends."

Alex and Cal had tried to keep their affair secret at work, but Alex was suspicious that there was some gossip in the office. She wondered if office gossip would make her a suspect in the case.

She did not see how she could be a suspect; Alex had learned from others in the office that Cal had been forced into the back of a car by two men when he came out of a shopping mall. His car had been in a dark, isolated part of the parking lot. A witness had been some distance away but had called the police because the actions of the two men were violent. She probably was not a suspect but was uncomfortable sitting before the two detectives.

"Friends? Were you close friends?" asked the woman detective as she scooted her chair closer to the desk.

Alex did not want to lie. She could become a serious suspect if they caught her in a lie. She tried to think of ways to present their relationship in the best possible light. Alex took a deep breath.

"Yes," she said. "At one time we were lovers, although that is not supposed to be common knowledge. Recently we have been strictly coworkers and have been working together."

"So you had an affair with Mr. Cummings. Did you know he was married?" asked Detective Biggs.

"Not at the time. When I learned, I broke it off."

"Any animosity?" asked Sheila Jones.

"I was not very happy about him hiding his marriage from me, but there were never any fights or arguments. It was more like no communication at all."

"What were you doing last night about 9:00 p.m.?" asked Biggs.

"I was at home in my condominium in Southborough."

"Can anyone confirm that?"

"Well, no. I'm not married and do not have a roommate. Am I a suspect?"

"No. We've asked that question of everyone in the office. You mentioned working with Cummings. What had you been working on?" asked Biggs.

"I think the answer to that would involve giving you classified information," answered Alex. "You know we do work for the military, and some of what we do is classified. You would have to talk to my boss, Phil Frane, before I could answer that."

"Okay, we might have to talk to him about that. Who is his boss?" asked Jones.

"Phil Frane reports to Dimitri Zakhar," answered Alex. "He runs this plant for TXA."

"That's right," said Biggs. "I heard some Russian was running this place now. What happened to Zimmerman... yeah, Bill Zimmerman?"

"I don't know," answered Alex. "One day he was gone. No one seems to know what happened to him. That same day, Mr. Zakhar showed up and announced he was the new boss. Things haven't been the same since."

"Is Mr. Zakhar in today?" asked Jones.

"No, he's flying back to Logan this afternoon from Montana. He will be here tomorrow I believe."

"Montana? Who the hell goes to Montana?" asked Biggs. "There ain't nothing there."

"Well, Montana is my home state," said Alex indignantly.

"Sorry. I meant no offense," Biggs apologized. "I mean not too many people go there."

"He's on official business for the Defense Department having to do with our treaty with Russia regarding reducing the number of missile silos. There are many silos all over Montana."

"Thank you for your time, Miss Pipe," said Jones. "We might be back in touch. In the meantime, here's my card. Call me if you think of anything that could be important."

The detectives stopped down the hall around the corner. Biggs turned to Jones. "Secretary what's-her-name felt there was a lot more animosity by Pipe toward Cummings than Ms. Pipe led us to believe."

"You mean Blanche Ruines?" asked Jones.

"Yeah."

"True, but I got the feeling that Blanche doesn't like Pipe to start with and may have exaggerated a bit much," responded Jones.

"Well something was going on between Cummings and Pipe!" exclaimed Biggs. "We better ask around a little more and also see what her boss says about the projects Cummings and Pipe were working on."

The detectives stuffed their notepads away and ambled toward the door into the statistics department. They told the secretary they would be back the next day.

After the detectives left, Alex became even more distraught. What she had failed to tell the detectives concerned a project she and Cal had worked on together where she discovered some unusual information in a database they were working with. She and Cal had discussed it at length. Data in one of the computer files had led both of them to believe that military products TXA manufactured were perhaps being sold to terrorists. Earlier yesterday, Cal had told her he was going to tell Frane about it. But Alex never saw Cal go in the direction of Frane's office, so she wasn't sure if he had met with Frane or not.

If Cal was abducted because he knew about the information in the database, that means terrorists have captured Cal, she thought. *But how would the terrorists know Cal was looking at the information in the database? Was Cal's office wired? Is Frane involved somehow? Do these men know that I know the same information?*

A feeling of anxiety swept over Alex. However, the feeling of anxiety would have been much worse if she had known Cal would be murdered that night; the feelings sweeping over her would have been pure panic.

Chapter 7

It was a two-stoplight town. Tonight, like any other weekday night, there were no people or cars on the streets. It was 3:00 a.m., and a low fog hung in the air. The few streetlights radiated halos of light struggling against the black of the moonless night. The brick facades of the town's century-plus-old buildings were sentinels standing guard for the little town that refused to die. It was quiet, so quiet that anyone new in town would notice the overwhelming lack of noise. A dark Hummer drove into town. Even slowing down, it bluntly cut through the normal peace of the morning.

There was a blindfolded man in the backseat, his hands tied behind his back. Anyone on the street, if there had been any, could easily have seen him. The man in the backseat screamed at the two men in the front.

"Where are we going? Why are you doing this? I did nothing wrong."

The bearded driver turned around. "Cummings, for the millionth time, shut up!" he yelled. "You will find out soon enough where we're going. It don't matter where we are; it's the middle of nowhere, so it don't matter. If you don't shut up, I'll ram that gag down your throat."

"What did I do wrong? Nothing. I did nothing wrong. I have told you again and again that I did not see any of the information in that computer file. Well, yeah, I opened it, and I mean I looked at it, but I didn't see anything. It was all gibberish. I really didn't. You have to believe me."

"Well why did you look at all? You know that you can't look at classified files. But no. You had to go and open it up, and now you say you didn't see anything. That's hard to believe. And if there was nothing to it, why did you go to your boss?"

"You have to believe me; I didn't see what was in that file. I swear on my mother's grave I didn't see anything," he sobbed.

The second stop light turned red, and the Hummer inexplicably stopped. There was no one there to see him run the light. The two men in front looked out the open windows. "Why the hell did you stop?" the man on the passenger side asked. "Ain't no cops in this Podunk town."

"You never know; we have to be careful. A cop asking about a tied-up man in the backseat would not be too cool, dude."

The Hummer turned onto a gravel road on the far end of town and headed east. The sun would be coming up soon. They had to hurry. The road narrowed and curved into some trees. The car stopped, hidden from view by the trees, tall grass, and the night.

The two men from the front seat got out of the vehicle and walked to a large lake near the road. The older one had a beard, was medium height, and heavy with a weight lifter's build. He went by Harry. The younger was skinny and short. Everyone called him Johnny Boy. The two came back to the Hummer, and Johnny Boy pulled Cummings out of the backseat and slapped him across the face. "Well, you wanted to know where we were goin'. This is it, pal. You gonna be here a long time." Johnny Boy's voice and manner of speaking made him sound like he was stupid. In fact, he was as stupid as he sounded.

Cummings pleaded with Harry. "What are you going to do to me? Am I going to die for something I didn't do? Look, I'm a family man with a wife and kids. They need me. Slap me around, kick me, whatever, just don't kill me. I'll do anything you want. I don't deserve to die." The two men guided him by the arms toward the lake.

"I think I'm going to call the boss," Harry said suddenly as he turned away slightly and pulled out his cell phone. Just as he raised the phone to his ear, a 9-mm slug entered Cummings's brain, blowing out the other side of his head. The noise, so close to Harry, was deafening.

"Christ!" the older man yelled. "You were supposed to wait for me to tell you when to shoot. I think the guy was telling the truth, and I was just going to tell the boss. And, look, you got blood all over my suit and tie, you trigger-happy fucking idiot." The shooter looked dejected and started to pout. Harry stared at him until the ringing in his ears was tolerable. Harry dialed his cell phone.

"Boss. It's me, Harry. I think the Cummings guy was maybe tellin' the truth. Johnny Boy just shot Cummings, and I think he mighta killed an innocent man."

The voice on the other end of the phone was loud enough for both to hear. "You wake me up to tell me this shit. By now, you ought to know we don't take any chances. He had to be killed. Our mission is headed for one of the biggest events that's ever taken place. To achieve our goal, there will be collateral deaths."

The voice paused and then continued. "Cummings looked at those files; they had enough information in them to expose our cause. Even if he didn't remember anything in the file now, he might remember something later. Just on suspicion, he could go to the cops or those FBI guys who are not allied with our cause. Think about that. And he knew something was wrong because he went to Phil Frane. In the meantime, you have to hide the body and think twice about waking me again at this time of the morning."

"We have a row boat, and we'll dump him in the lake with plenty of weight to hold him down. Nobody will ever find him."

"Keep up the good work," the voice said on the other end. "Soon it will all be worth it. One more thing. We might have a problem with yet another TXA employee. So stay in the area."

Chapter 8

Several weeks had passed since Cal Cummings disappeared. Alex had learned nothing new about his whereabouts and was deeply concerned for his safety. Although she was not a religious person, she prayed for his safe return to the higher power she believed in. At the same time, she was becoming less concerned about her safety. When she first left the office for home on the day she learned Cal was missing, she watched every car that followed her. When she got home, she turned off all the lights and made sure the doors were double bolted. But nothing had happened that night or since. Just as an added precaution, she hid one of her pistols in her car. This helped alleviate her concerns.

Nobody at work knew anything new about Cal, and nobody seemed to blame her for his disappearance. Even though the detectives still came around, they seemed to have lost interest in her. Her boss, Phil Frane, had been on vacation, which always improved her mood. In addition, a handsome guy at work had asked her out, and she made sure he was single. Alex was feeling good about herself again.

The weather for her date was perfect. It was a comfortable late summer evening. The sun was angling down toward the horizon, casting long shadows of trees across lawns and streets. It was that time of day when the trees, grass, and shrubs were a rich green. It was a perfect Saturday night for dating and romance.

A young man knocked on the door of Alex's upscale townhouse in an apartment complex in Southborough. Alex, looking stunning, appeared at the door, and they walked to his car. They were laughing as they drove away. The world was their oyster, and they were at the center of it, as if life did not exist beyond them.

The couple was not gone for long. The automobile returned, but it was only 10:30, early for a Saturday night date. The man and Alex got out of the car and walked to the townhouse. They were quiet—no laughter. She did not invite him in and did not give him a peck on the cheek before she closed her door. The man sauntered slowly back to the car and left.

Alex was disgusted. *I sure know how to pick the losers. When am I ever going to find a guy that I can at least like, even if there's nothing more? I should still be out there having fun.* She put on her bathrobe, popped some popcorn, and sat down to read her latest detective thriller. She loved mysteries and thrillers. In particular, she liked women detectives and strong heroines. Some of her favorites were Kay Scarpetta, Stephanie Plum, Bess Crawford, and Lizabeth Salander. She liked willful, intelligent women who could solve mysteries and escape danger. She often wished she had become a detective.

Although she felt justified in her disgust of her date, she sometimes wondered if there was something wrong with her. She always seemed to attract the wrong guys. Cal Cummings was a perfect example. He was married. *I ignored clues that anyone should have picked up on.*

Her history with men made her insecure. So tonight, as happened other nights, she stood looking at herself in the mirror, wondering if her looks were adequate. Her hair was dark brown and long. She had a smooth complexion that could not be called dark but could not be called light either, and it was difficult to tell whether she was of Hispanic, Italian, or some other nationality. In fact, she was half American Indian. There was not a flaw on her face. Her teeth were bright, and she had a Hollywood smile. Her eyes were brown with a twinkle. She was tall, about five ten. Most of her height was in her legs, which were long and beautiful.

I think I look okay. After all, the guys at work are always hitting on me. Lots of people tell me I'm beautiful, so why do I have so many problems with finding a boyfriend, one that's not married?

The guys always seemed okay until after she went out with them. At dinner, some would have terrible eating habits and table manners. Some were very immature, like teenaged boys. Some were too aggressive and started coming on to her before they even started eating. Some were braggarts. She hated those that were full of themselves, and it seemed to her there were too many of those in Greater Boston. Jimmy

Montgomery, her date that night, had been a total bore, asking questions about her job and politics. There was something wrong with every single man who asked her out. It seemed to her that all the exciting men were married.

Alex had never been married. That fact astonished the men she worked with because she was beautiful, perhaps even Hollywood beautiful. She should have had more dates than she could handle. However, most of the guys at her job were married, and outside of work, she did not know many people, except in the equestrian set. Even among the "horsey set," it was difficult to form a relationship because everything centered around caring for horses. In addition, Alex did not fit in with the traditional East Coast equestrians. Many of the members considered themselves the super elite. One, or one's daddy, had to have a bit of money to house, feed, and train a horse.

Many of the local female equestrians went to East Coast schools with stables and an equestrian program of some sort. Many rode on English saddles and wore traditional English riding apparel: hunt jackets, riding tights, and black paddock shoes and helmets. Alex's family had money, but she put on no pretenses and acted like the Montana ranch girl that she was. Alex's riding wardrobe was a variety of western outfits. She had her own western saddle and two quarter horses. She had been a champion barrel racer and champion mounted shooter during her school years and thereafter.

When she first moved to the Boston area, she believed that nobody on the East Coast had ever heard of barrel racing or mounted shooting. When she learned there were many rodeos and mounted shooting events, she was elated and asked her dad to help her pull a horse trailer with her two favorite quarter horses from Montana several thousand miles to Boston the summer before her sophomore school year.

She had formed a close relationship with her father when she was young. She felt secure around him. However, he was always too busy with his businesses. She was amazed but happy that he agreed to travel across the country, helping her move.

Alex missed Montana. She missed her parents' ranch. She missed her dogs that were still at the ranch. She missed everything about Montana. But she had chosen education over being a ranch wife, and she felt there was no going back because of the huge sum of money her father had spent on her education. She did not want to disappoint him.

Alex was as much at home at a formal dinner as she was at a rodeo. She had the elegance, grace, and manners expected in higher social circles in East Coast society. She did not care much for that scene, but she could function in it without being socially awkward. Rather than the eastern social set, she preferred the western ranch set, cowboys, country music, and swing dancing.

At work, she pretended to be oblivious to her coworkers' sexual hints and innuendos even though she secretly relished the attention. There were rumors between some of the men that, since she was not married and did not date any of them, at least so they thought, she had to be a lesbian. She also drove a pickup truck, a sure sign of a lesbian to some of them. Many of the men did not care one way or the other. "So what if she is?" most would say. "She's still eye candy."

Her boss, Phil Frane, was never more than an inch away from sexual harassment, but he knew not to cross that line. He had been accused of sexual harassment before. The company had given the victims promotions to different departments to sweep the problem under the rug. The good ole boys prevailed again and again. Alex tried never to be alone with Frane. However, he was persistent enough to find a way to invite her into his office for meetings that had little or no purpose other than his desire to look at her lustfully.

Frane was disgusting to Alex. He was about fifty with a potbelly. His face was red and his nose enlarged as if he drank too much, and he had a rash on his balding head. He was married, and Alex wondered how any woman could live with the guy.

Alex pretended that she was very innocent as a way to deflect the advances of Frane and the other married men, but she loved the attention, just wishing it was by the right guy. While she pretended to be a Miss Goody Two-Shoes, she was not. She had several sexual relationships in addition to her romance with Cal Cummings, who was ten years older than she was. It was not that he was handsome and dashing. Rather he was confident and caring. Alex felt secure when she was with him. After Alex learned that he was married, she was honest with herself and admitted that she should have suspected it from the beginning. She chose to ignore the obvious. His visits were on unusual dates and at odd times; she could never stay at his place and he would never stay overnight with her. Finally, someone at work mentioned Cal's wife. Although Alex was upset, she had known that the relationship was never going to last. In retrospect, she wondered if she was attracted to unobtainable men. Cal was both married and older, and all the other men were unobtainable for the same or similar reasons.

Maybe it was because older men made her feel secure. She quickly discarded the thought that she needed security. She loved her freedom. *Maybe I don't want a serious relationship*, she thought. *Maybe I'm exciting to men that don't want a serious relationship, and then because of their excitement toward me, I find them exciting.* The arguments battled in her head, around and around to no resolution.

She was not paying too much attention to the paperback thriller she was reading. She was preoccupied, thinking about men. "I really don't need a man," she said aloud. She fluffed up the couch pillow. *But I would not mind having one.*

Chapter 9

Alex was statistician at a division of TXA International in Southborough, Massachusetts. TXA was an international company manufacturing electronic components for the military and private corporations. The Military Division manufactured weapons for the military, primarily missiles of various sizes and capabilities. The Commercial Division manufactured electronic components for private corporations. The company was as large as many third world companies.

Alex had degrees in mathematics and statistics from Simmons College and MIT. She was a brain but did nothing to draw attention to it. Her work involved doing various types of mathematical analyses for any of the TXA divisions in the country. One of her jobs was statistical forecasting for purposes of future inventory needs and sales forecasting.

Several weeks after Cal Cummings was taken from the shopping mall, Phil Frane returned from vacation. On the Monday of his return, he called Alex into his office. It was also the Monday after her ill-fated date with Jimmy Montgomery. She sat in front of him with the most innocent face she could conjure. His office was middle-manager typical. It had a window, but the decoration was in poor taste. It had no carpet. The furniture was standard issue.

"Alex, I notice that you have been accessing some computer files recently that are only on a need-to-know basis. I realize that you have a top-secret clearance, but you have been accessing computer files regarding our Nevada manufacturing plant that should be of no help for your kind of work. You certainly have the right to run your programs on the data files, but you cannot open the text and PDF files that happen to be with the data files."

It was clear from his comment that Cal did not tell Frane that Alex had also looked at the data in the files.

Frane was leaning back in his chair, a crooked grin on his face. His dark eyes bore into her. Alex was surprised and wondered if he knew that she had looked at the forbidden information. Obviously Frane did not have her in his office to make another pass at her.

"I don't believe I overstepped my bounds. I only look at files that I need to complete my work," she responded. "Each file has data that I need. I don't remember looking at any PDF or text files."

"I am ordering you to ignore any information other than the data you need."

"Mr. Frane, I do not remember seeing anything in the files that contained information I do not need in order to successfully complete the work I am charged to do," she said with stern emphasis.

Alex knew her statement was not true and hoped that he could not detect her lie.

"Okay, let's keep it that way. Do your job and stay away from things that do not concern you."

"Yes, sir," Alex said and got up and left the office.

Phil Frane called his secretary on the intercom after Alex left.

"Call Jimmy Montgomery and tell him to come to my office."

A few moments later, a young man of about thirty years of age was escorted into Frane's office. Jimmy was over six feet tall, muscular, and handsome with a military haircut. He wore a suit with a colorful tie and highly polished shoes. He was a known ladies' man.

"Jimmy, how did the date with Alex Pipe go the other night? Did you learn anything?" Frane asked.

"Nothing," he replied. "I learned nothing. I asked her questions that were very close to giving us away, but she was evasive. I don't think she was evasive on purpose, and I am sure she was not suspicious of me. I think she genuinely did not want to talk about her work and tried to change the subject all the time. Also, I could not figure out her political persuasion, but I don't think she is a candidate for our cause. My persistence really turned her off. The date started out fine but was in the dumps when I dropped her off."

"I guess that means you didn't get in her pants." Frane laughed.

"Not hardly," Jimmy replied with a grin, "but it would have been nice."

"Keep low and I will let you know if I need you again," Frane told him.

"Yes, sir," he replied after standing. It was as if he was coming to attention and was about to salute. There was no question he was ex-military.

Alex went back to her office after her meeting with Frane. She agonized about lying to Frane. *I maybe should have told him that I was concerned about what I was seeing in the files. Perhaps he has nothing to do with Cal's abduction. Maybe I'm doing the company harm by not reporting it. But from the looks of things, military products are billed to private organizations inside this country, and that's something that's never happened while I've been with the company.*

Her worst suspicion was that someone in the company was billing and shipping products for use by terrorists. Cal had the same feeling, largely because of the foreign-sounding names of companies, all of which started with the letter Z.

She was hesitant to come forward because she might tell the wrong person. *What if Frane has something to do with Cal being abducted?* She would normally have gone to the general manager. But the new general manager, Dmitri Zakhar, was from outside the company with no technical background. He did not fit the type of person TXA normally hired. She instantly disliked him and felt he was not trustworthy. He was American born of Russian parents and thereby an American citizen, but he had spent most of his life outside the United States. He was a small man with a Napoleon complex whose aura oozed cruelty. Evil seemed to lurk in his black, piercing eyes. Even though he was a small man, everyone perceived him as quite powerful and not to be crossed. His directives received no opposition.

Since the arrival of Dmitri Zakhar, the atmosphere at the offices had changed from open and friendly to secretive and quiet. Alex thought there might be others in the plant who knew about the billing of military products to private corporations, but no one was talking about it. *They're probably as afraid of him as I am. Should I be the one to bring it up first?*

Alex stood up. She could not stand being in limbo any longer. She had to make a decision. *I am going back to Frane and telling him about my concerns.* She headed back toward Frane's office. As she went around a corner in the hallway, she saw her recent date, Jimmy Montgomery, leaving Frane's office. He did not see her and was going in the opposite direction. Startled, she stepped back around the corner.

What was he doing in there? He works in an entirely different area of the plant some distance away, and he works directly for Zakhar, not Frane.

Immediately she remembered all the questions that Jimmy Montgomery had asked her on the date. *Oh my God.* She turned around and headed back to her office. *They were spying on me.*

When she arrived back in her cube, she continued to mull over the situation. *I'll bet Frane sent Montgomery to find out what I know. I may have incriminating evidence against TXA or someone working for TXA. They want to know if I know. Perhaps Frane had something to do with Cal's disappearance. That means I may be in danger.*

Alex still had a hard time believing that the people she worked with could be involved in criminal activity. *Maybe I am imagining things, and maybe there is a logical and legal reason for what is going on. Whatever is going on, I had better be careful.*

Phil Frane sat at his desk, his right thumb nervously thumping the desktop. Jimmy Montgomery had just left his office, and Alex Pipe was still on his mind. The phone rang, and he picked it up. "Hey, Frane here."

It was Dmitri Zakhar on the other end. "I am getting impatient with your slow responses. What's the report?"

"You asked me to look into anyone else who had access to files containing information that could lead to trouble for us. There is only one other person here that works with those files on a regular basis. Her name is Alexandra Pipe, a statistician here. At this point, we don't know for sure if she has seen anything suspicious. She denies it, and we can't tell whether she is politically our friend or foe. However, we can't jump to a conclusion because it is part of her job to be in those files, totally unlike Cummings, who had no business anywhere near those files." Zakhar hung up on Frane, banging down the phone.

Zakhar called out on his secure line. "Harry, I want you to put a tail on Alexandra Pipe. She works for Frane. He'll get you the information you need. Tap her phones and do anything necessary to protect us, and I mean anything."

"I catch your drift, boss. I'll be back in touch."

Chapter 10

Alex's mind kept going back to the Jimmy Montgomery spying date. She was not in fear of being harmed; she was mad—mad at Jimmy, mad at Phil Frane, and mad that they were snooping around. Whatever was going on puzzled her, and she kept trying to figure it out.

TXA does not sell military hardware to domestic corporations. There may be nothing to it, but if there is nothing wrong with these sales, why would they be so interested in what I saw in those files? There has to be something to my suspicions. Otherwise, they would not care what I know. And Cal might be dead because of what he knew.

Alex continued to seethe. She was not faint of heart—quite the opposite. She was extraordinarily competitive and strong-willed. She was not going to let a minor threat from her boss deter her from discovering what was going on, particularly if it involved a possible terrorist threat to her country.

She decided that for the time being she would continue to look at the computer files and databases for clues and keep an eye on what was happening at the plant on a low-key level. *Maybe I can throw Frane off by flirting with him a little... God, what a horrible thought!*

She needed more time to think before she went back to work, so she decided to take the next day off and go riding. She had never called in sick before but justified it because of what had happened. She decided to practice her mounted shooting rather than barrel racing and got together her guns, holsters, and chaps, dressed in her western clothing, and headed out to her nearly new Dodge 2500 pickup that had a fifth wheel hitch and a towing package.

Alex drove to a stable/equestrian center in nearby Marlborough, where she kept her horses boarded and stored her tack and horse trailer. The horse trailer was a thirty-foot Sundowner with room for two horses and a small living area up front. Since she went to a number of rodeos and other horse events, using the living area was more convenient and less expensive than a hotel.

The Marlborough equestrian center was not set up for either barrel racing or mounted shooting, but it was close to Southborough. She would have to go elsewhere to practice.

After she stored her tack, horse blankets, and saddles in the trailer and hitched it to the pickup, she loaded her two horses and headed north toward Dunstable, where mounted shooting events were held at Goss Farm. On the way, she continued to mull over the situation at work. She became more determined to figure out what was going on. With her anger piqued, she could hardly wait to get to the farm and take out her frustrations.

In a stable on the farm, she brushed out her two horses, Duke and Hank, both registered quarter horses with good bloodlines. As she brushed them down, she talked to them in a low voice. It seemed like they knew what she was saying. They also seemed to know she was getting them ready for running, and they both were eager, snorting. Alex continued to talk in a calm manner to them. She then rode both of them for a warm up for practice on a mounted shooting course. They were ready to go. She could hardly rein them in.

Mounted shooting is a fast-growing sport. The object is to ride a designated course with ten balloons at various locations along the course and shoot to break them. Naturally, real live ammunition is not used. The cartridges are called .45-caliber Long Colts. Ten brass cartridges are loaded with black powder (like that used in the 1800s), five for each gun. This load will break a balloon up to about fifteen feet. Contestants use two single-action revolvers to shoot the balloons while negotiating the specified course on horseback. Live rounds are strictly prohibited at competitions. At each sanctioned event, another person loads the rider's guns as he or she enters the arena and unloads the guns after the rider is finished. Riders do not carry loaded guns outside of the arena or when not competing.

Alex used single-action Colt .45 revolvers. The Colt .45 is the favorite of many mounted shooters. Modern-day pistols cannot be used;

only .45 calibers designed prior to 1898 are allowed. The object is to shoot as many balloons as possible while riding as fast as possible. There is a five-second penalty for each missed balloon, a five-second penalty for dropping a gun, a ten-second penalty for not running the course correctly, and a sixty-second penalty for falling off your horse. Speed is important; however, accuracy is usually more important than speed. A typical course pattern can be run in fifteen to thirty-five seconds, so penalties can really hurt.

Alex picked Duke to run first. She saddled him, always leaving the cinch a little loose, and then put on a snaffle bit. She did not need a harsh bit for her trained horses. She was dressed in colorful western wear, including hat, boots, chaps, and holsters on a western-style leather gun belt. After she put on her gun belt and holstered the Colts, she started practicing fast draw, twirling her unloaded guns back and forth, and quickly sticking them back into the holster. She repeated this time after time. Then she would toss a gun from one hand to the other and back again. It gave her a feel for the guns. Her expression was one of intensity. Her horse Duke knew instinctively it was getting close to his time to run. The atmosphere sparked of energy.

Alex walked Duke toward the arena with long strides and a determined look on her face. When people got to know her, this expression was a sign that Alex had a goal in mind and was not to be deterred. She then handed her Colts to another rider to load the black powder. Turning back to Duke, she tightened the cinch and tightened it more. She mounted and rode into the arena. The rider who had loaded her guns handed them up to her. She turned Duke in a circle and repeated the circle several times. Duke was prancing and straining on the rains being pulled back by Alex. Approaching the starting line, she jabbed her heel into Duke's ribs at just the right amount of pressure, signaling to him to run like hell. Duke dug in his heels and lunged forward, his legs stretching out as if he were already at a gallop.

Alex looked glued to the horse as if she were part of it. Duke ran with his nose out in front and his tail waving in the breeze. Alex rode with her back and head stretched forward and her dark hair blowing behind her. They were on the first target in an instant, and the shooting began, with a blast going off about every two seconds. Five targets were shot at on the way to the turnaround barrel, and five were shot at on the way back to the start/finish line. Duke turned the barrel at high speed as only a champion barrel racing horse could. Only one target was left standing as she crossed the finish line in twenty seconds. Her score was 25 because of the missed target. It was impressive, but Alex was disgusted. She was off her normal time by at least three seconds and had missed a balloon. She rarely ever missed. Before the day was over, after three runs, she had cut her time by three and a half seconds and did not miss another target.

By her third run, word had spread about her shooting, and a crowd gathered to watch. It was her best run, and the crowd cheered and clapped. Alex was pleased but knew she was still off her championship form. Several years ago, she had been the Montana female champion in the Montana Cowboy Mounted Shooting Association. She had even gone to Houston for the national finals and come in second. Most would be pleased, but Alex was so competitive that she was upset at coming in second. There was no such thing as second place in her mind. "You either win or you don't."

A man in a sports coat and tie had watched Alex's runs. He looked out of place dressed as he was. The only other ties were bolo ties worn by some older cowboys looking on. After her last run, the man pulled out a cell phone and dialed a number. "Yeah, it's me, Harry. I followed her to a horse-shooting event up here in a place called Dunstable. Yeah, it's in Massachusetts. She has not met or talked to anyone other than chitchat with other shooters. That girl can sure as hell ride and shoot. If we were in the Old West, we'd be dead by now. Jesus, what a show… Yeah, I'll stay on her tail."

A woman in casual clothing had also watched Alex with interest. She walked to the back of a barn and got on her cell phone. She had dark hair, worn medium length, and was about 5'7" and slender. She was a pretty woman perhaps in her fifties but did not look her age. "Robinson here. I followed Pipe from Southborough to a farm in Dunstable. Pipe has just finished practicing with her horses in a sport I never heard of called mounted shooting. Nothing of interest happened, but she was followed here by a heavyset man driving a black Hummer." She listened to the man she called and responded, "Before today, I have never seen the man following her." Again, she listened. She then gave out the license number on the Hummer. "Roger that. I will stay with her and her tail, whoever he is, and keep you up to date. By the way, this girl is amazing with a pistol."

Chapter 11

FBI agent Pam Robinson watched Alex load her horses and pull out of Goss Farms, followed by the same man in the same black Hummer that had tailed Alex from Southborough. Pam had originally been assigned to follow Jimmy Montgomery, but after Alex's date with Jimmy, that changed. The FBI was hoping to find out if there was more than a casual connection between Alex and Montgomery and if Alex Pipe was involved in any suspicious activities. TXA was already under investigation. Another agent was assigned to follow Montgomery.

Pam was part of a special branch of the FBI formed to investigate various activities of multinational corporations that often violated domestic and international laws. The concentration of wealth in these mammoth giants caused their leaders to feel they were above the law. The amount of wealth was staggering, in the billions of dollars. The corporations were larger than many small countries, and in many instances the corporations ran these countries from behind the scenes. They could buy every leader at every level of government through cash donations or contributions to whomever the officials wanted the money to go.

Before Alex drove north to Goss Farm, Pam had been parked in Alex's parking lot, staking out the townhouse. Pam noticed a man pull out and follow Alex in a black Hummer. The Hummer had been parked near Pam for the duration of her stakeout, but there was nothing about it to draw it to Pam's attention. Whoever he was, he had been staking out Alex also.

After the mounted shooting practice, as soon as Alex started her journey south, the Hummer pulled out behind her. Pam pulled in behind the man and followed them both. Earlier she had called in the plate number to her office and had just found out the Hummer was registered to a company that seemed to exist only on paper, at least according to her office. Pam carefully pictured the man in her mind for the report she would fill out at the office. He was heavyset like a body builder, average height, and middle aged and had a beard, a receding hairline, and dark hair.

Pam had been planning to retire after twenty years with the FBI but was persuaded by her boss, John "Tee" Scott, to stay on for this assignment, supposedly her last. Tee Scott had been a field agent for fifteen years but was now a supervising agent in the FBI Boston field office in charge of investigating mega corporations. He preferred the supervisor job because it gave him a little more time to enjoy golf and racquetball. The only problem with the job was being awakened at all hours of the day and night with phone calls from his agents, but he could put up with the phone calls if he had more time for golf. Tee was six three and 230 pounds. Pam had heard that he was an excellent athlete with the speed and agility of a man half his size and a scratch golfer.

Tee was considered a natural leader and truly cared about his team of agents, treating them with fatherly concern even when an agent was older than his forty-five years. He felt particularly protective of Pam, who he also liked on a platonic personal level. She had sparkling, dancing eyes and a quick smile. She seemed so much younger than her fifty-four years. A stranger would guess that she had not reached forty. She was thin and athletic and had always wanted to be a dancer. In college, she had majored in French, and then she had become a French teacher. She had also spent a year in France teaching English to French children. Years ago, the FBI had had a need for an agent who could speak French. She was hired for the job, but, as is typical of the government, she never got to speak French in her job. Tee felt she made up for that by surprising him with French phrases, which he rarely understood.

Tee really did not want Pam to retire; he was short on experienced agents and needed her to stick around for the new investigation prompted by the arrival, at the same time, of two new employees at TXA in Southborough: Jimmy Montgomery and Dmitri Zakhar. Montgomery was on the international suspect terrorist list. He was not a terrorist in the traditional sense, but he seemed to show up on the scene of every terrorist hot spot on the globe. Whenever there were armed conflicts, insurrections, or assassinations, he was usually in or around the action. However, nothing could be pinned on him. No one had ever accused him of shooting a gun, exploding a bomb, or committing any direct act of terrorism. Nevertheless, due to his association with causes opposed to the interests of the United States, his activities were being closely watched.

Dimitri Zakhar was difficult to classify. He held dual citizenships with both the United States and Russia. The information on Zakhar was conflicting. Tee Scott had heard rumors that Zakhar had questionable connections with groups opposed to the United States government, including domestic right-wing radical organizations. On the other hand, Zakhar was given a clean bill of health when Scott inquired about him at the FBI headquarters in Washington. However, since both Montgomery and Zakhar showed up at TXA at the same time, Scott made a decision to watch them both, despite Washington's positive opinion of Zakhar. Something was going to go down in Southborough, he was sure, but he did not know what it was. He was determined to find out.

Jimmy Montgomery was an Englishman by birth. He was fluent in multiple languages and had extensive military training. Jimmy was a chameleon. He could be as American as apple pie with a perfect American accent, but he could also be a perfect Frenchman, a German, an Italian, or Spaniard as the need arose. He always carried second bag to someone else; he was never top dog. At TXA, Zakhar was the top-ranking corporate officer in Southborough, and Montgomery reported to him. Scott thought this threw greater suspicion on Zakhar and wondered why Washington had been so quick to quash any inquiry about him.

After Tee learned that Jimmy Montgomery and Alex Pipe went out together one Saturday night, Scott asked Pam to follow Alex. Now that she had seen Alex's ability with a pistol, Pam was somewhat suspicious that Alex might be a part of whatever Zakhar and Montgomery were doing. At the same time, Pam felt at her gut level that Alex was not a criminal.

Pam was not very careful when following the Hummer. She had given the driver the name of "Arnold" in her mind. She figured Arnold would concentrate on following Alex and not pay attention to someone following him. However, as the trio got close to Southborough, Arnold and the Hummer suddenly disappeared. *How did he do that? I'll be damned. He must be a pro to be able to vanish in midair. I should have been paying more attention.*

Pam followed Alex to her townhouse. When Alex went inside, Pam got out of her car and carefully attached a GPS locater bug to the inside of a wheel well on Alex's truck. She decided to call it a day and went home to her husband and their empty nest.

The next morning, Pam reported to her boss in the downtown Boston FBI field office. They discussed in detail what Pam had observed the day before. Tee Scott was particularly interested in the man Pam had named Arnold.

"Do you think that Arnold is with another agency?"

"That is what I thought at first. But no. He is rough around the edges and does not act like the spooks from other agencies, like the CIA. I noticed a bulge in his sport coat jacket, so he was carrying, and his disappearance act was not something the normal driver can do."

Scott thought for a moment.

"Maybe Pipe is not part of what is going on. Maybe Arnold works for TXA and they have the tail on her."

"That makes sense to me. I cannot think of anyone else who would want to follow her."

Scott stood up. "Follow me. I need to take a walk and talk to you." Pam thought this was unusual but followed him down the elevator to street level and out of the building.

"The reason I asked you to come outside with me is so we could talk where we can't be heard. I know I can trust you to keep this conversation between us."

"Thanks for the compliment. I always keep our conversations secret."

"I got a call this morning from Washington telling me to stop the TXA investigation. Something is wrong. Until recently, they were all hopped up on this investigation. Now, unexpectedly, they want to stop. Zakhar and Montgomery are major players in some kind of illegal scheme in my opinion. It is normal for the bureau to keep an eye on these types. They gave me no reason for the change, and I can't think of a good reason. My main contact in Washington seemed bewildered also. It seems that the word is coming down from very high up the ladder."

Pam took off her summer jacket and put it over her arm. It was too hot for anything but a bathing suit. "It sounds strange to me also. I don't remember anything like this in the last twenty years."

"I am inclined to continue the investigation on the sly, particularly now that Arnold has appeared in the picture. I have a gut feeling that something major is going on and this Alex Pipe is in the center of it—and probably does not know it. I am going to keep you on her tail and have Morris and Wesley follow Montgomery and Zakhar."

"I'm with you, boss. I'll keep you informed."

"Stop calling me boss, okay?"

"D'accord. Voilà pourquoi je suis là, pour régler tous les problèmes."

"Whatever the hell that means," he said with a smile.

Chapter 12

During her drive back to the Marlborough stables pulling her horses, Alex began to think about the lack of close friends in her life. She was feeling lonely. She could not remember this ever bothering her before. Perhaps it was the drive back from Dunstable with no one to talk to, or perhaps it was because there was no one to share her fun day with. Maybe it was her age. *I am not getting any younger.* Regardless of the reason, she decided to do something about it. Alex had a particular mind-set that would immediately seek a solution when a problem appeared. No use dwelling on the problem. She grasped onto the idea of a roommate.

Alex made a very good salary and did not need to have someone help her pay for the townhouse rental, but it was actually much too big for just one person, and it could be a solution to her loneliness. The next day, she put an ad in the *Villager* and began to get a few calls.

After talking to several prospective roommates and finding no one with whom she felt a fit, she received a call from a woman calling herself Renata Russo, who said she was twenty-nine years old and worked in the area. During their phone conversation, Alex could tell Renata had a quick wit and a humorous, lively voice with a distinct Boston accent. Alex invited her over to discuss the possibility in further detail.

Alex liked Renata the minute she met her. Alex usually had feelings or intuitions about people when she met them, with the notable exception of Jimmy Montgomery, who was obviously a pro at cover-up. Alex felt that Renata would be a good addition to her home, if nothing more than because she made her laugh. They made an agreement that Renata would move in immediately and pay half the rent.

"Before you move in, I should tell you something that might change your mind," Alex said to Renata. "I might be in trouble. A coworker was abducted recently by two men, and he has not been heard from in several weeks. I think he was taken by terrorists because of some information he learned from a computer data file. Unfortunately, I know that same information."

"Has someone threatened you?" asked Renata. "Are you being followed?"

"No one has threatened me. My boss told me to stay away from the data, so it is obviously important. I told him I didn't know anything about it. But to answer your question, I think that there are people following me. I keep seeing the same kinds of vehicles wherever I go. There is this black Hummer and this beige Ford. I keep seeing them here, at work, at the mall. I never see them following me, but they seem to be wherever I go."

"Does this concern you?" she asked Renata. "Because if it does, you don't have to go through with our deal."

"No," said Renata casually. "It does not bother me one bit. Maybe I can even help you out. If you find out who is following you, let me know, and it will stop."

Alex was not sure what Renata meant when she said she could make it stop and assumed that it was another one of Renata's jokes. She was pleased that her problem did not bother Renata because she really liked her and wanted her to be her roommate. Alex got Renata to tell her more about her background.

Renata was from the North End section of Boston. She had graduated from Holy Cross with above-average grades, but she had been more interested in every nonacademic aspect of college and had spent considerable time being the class comedian. She had a degree in psychology and was working in an HR job. She was a beautiful girl with all the coloring and features of women of Italian descent and had a voluptuous build. Alex, at 5'10", towered over 5'1" Renata. However, Renata did not seem or act like a small person, and after Alex got to know her, she did not seem short.

Renata had a way of talking with her whole body. She talked with her hands all the time, and with her head if she needed to make a point, and with her arms and legs if she was making a big issue of something. She was always quick to smile and looked for double meanings in everything people said around her, usually some sexual innuendo. Alex loved to watch her talk.

She had been married once for five years to a "nice Italian boy" who went to Mass every Sunday and believed sex was for procreation only, but there were no children. "I missed out on the hot Italian lovers. My strict Catholic upbringing and Saint Tony kept me on the straight and narrow for a long time. My parents didn't help. I think they wanted me to be a nun imprisoned in a convent."

"Who is Saint Tony?" Alex asked.

"Oh he is just my boring ex-husband." Renata's eyes twinkled, and her smile broadened even more. "Then I met Carlo. Wow! He made my Italian blood boil. I should feel sorry that I almost broke up his marriage, and I certainly broke up mine. I'll probably be condemned to hell by the church, but I do not feel guilty. I feel full of life and look forward to meeting the next guy that turns my crank. But to do so, I have to get away from my family. My huge family gets in the way of me dating guys. I hated the way they would stop by at all hours. Southborough is far enough away from Boston to keep my mom from walking in and finding a guy with me on the couch."

Renata looked at Alex with a guilty grin. "You think I am awful, don't you?"

"Not at all," said Alex. *Who am I to judge anyone's sex life?* "I think you are going to be a fun roommate… as long as you keep me informed on your amorous adventures." She smiled. The two broke into laughter, and Alex showed Renata around "their" place. The townhouse was a new two-story, and Alex had decorated it with western art and pictures of her with horses. There were quite a few cowboy belt buckles and trophies won by Alex. There was plenty of room for two and then some, and it was comfortable. Renata loved the townhouse.

"What a wonderful place to bring my boyfriends."

"Boyfriends? Like, more than one?" asked Alex with feigned shock.

Renata grinned. "They are only one at a time. I practice serial monogamy, except for the one-night stands."

Renata looked around at Alex's decorations. "I think our motifs are going to clash a bit. But I promise not to let anyone see the clash. I will bring guys in at night in the dark." She always ended her sexual remarks with a naughty grin and a raised eyebrow. Alex responded with a laugh or smile.

In the first few weeks after Renata moved in with Alex, Renata continued to be forthcoming about her life. It was a history of sexual adventures and her extensive family. Alex realized she had said very little about her own background. *People are willing to tell me their deepest secrets. They seem to trust me.* Others had told her that people trusted her because she had a trusting and friendly way of listening, nodding, and smiling as they talked. She would keep eye contact with the other person with her big brown eyes, would have a pleasant look on her face, and never looked judgmental about the other person.

The first thing Renata brought to the apartment was kitchenware, particularly Italian cookware. Renata claimed to be a good cook, and Alex soon learned it was true. It seemed that there was always delicious coffee and Italian ice cream and Italian bread. "My father owns an Italian restaurant in Boston. He taught me everything I know."

The two also talked about decorating the apartment. Renata's motif was Tuscan theme decor centered on rustic elegance. Warm colors and natural elements created the Old World charm of the Italian countryside.

"You have beautiful things," said Alex. "And I can tell it's expensive. How do you afford this?"

Renata smiled as if she were hiding something, and Alex dropped the subject.

Renata talked a lot about her ex, pious St. Tony, and his lack of interest in her and sex. "I used to buy expensive lingerie and dresses from Victoria's Secret, but they did not get him any more turned on then his normal let's-have-sex-so-we-can-have-a-baby. I wanted him to grab me, throw me down, rip off my clothes, and have mad, passionate, hot sex with me. That's what Carlo did," she exclaimed in an excited voice. Then with a smile and in a lowered voice, she added, "Too bad he was married." She had a way of telling her story with a gusto that made Alex laugh.

Alex noticed that Renata had a wide variety of the finest clothes money could buy, much more than a job as a human resources manager could afford. Renata also had a BMW Z4. Alex did not know anyone else with a car that nice and wondered if there had been a big divorce settlement. She didn't want to snoop, so she waited until Renata started talking about pious St. Tony again. Alex asked her what Tony did for a living.

"He is an assistant professor at Boston College, teaching the history of religion. You can probably guess the type of guy he is from the job description." She laughed.

Alex, seeing the opening, said, "He could afford the BMW on a professor's salary?"

"Oh no. That's from my daddy. He's very rich. He owns an Italian restaurant on the North End, as I told you, but he has other businesses too. He has many high-powered friends—politicians, bishops, and businessmen—but I wonder if everything he does is legal. He has some sinister-looking people working for him. Maybe 'shady-looking' would be a better description."

"Is he in the mafia?" asked Alex.

"No way! He doesn't live in New Jersey or own a garbage business." Renata laughed. "Actually, I really loved that TV show. I'll have to admit that some of the *Sopranos* characters looked like the men who follow my dad around."

Chapter 13

"Listen, Alex, your food is great, but let's go to my father's restaurant this weekend," suggested Renata as she set the kitchen table.

"Did it pass the health inspection?" quipped Alex. Alex tried to be funny, but she did not have the knack that Renata had.

"I think so. The last time I was there, the roaches were not nearly so bad," bantered Renata.

Alex grinned. "In that case, let's do it."

"I want you to meet my father, and he is usually there on Saturday nights." There was a pause as Renata pondered. "I really don't know much about you to tell him. You have told me quite a bit about your job and college experiences but not much about your past. I probably shouldn't tell Dad about you going to Simmons College. He might think you are a switch-hitter." She ducked a pair of rolled-up socks.

"You are so full of yourself today," complained Alex with a grin as she threw another pair of socks. "Those rumors are just because it is a women's college," Alex continued.

"Well I guess I can stop locking my bedroom door at night," Renata replied.

Alex opened her mouth with mock shock on her face and picked up another roll of socks. Renata ducked. They both rolled with laughter.

"I do have a boyfriend, kinda," Alex told Renata.

"What do you mean by kinda?"

"Well I met him on the Internet. His name is Pete. He seems so kind, so sweet and nice. His wife divorced him, and he still loves her. He has told me a lot about himself, and he is a gentle soul. He works for TXA but in Palo Alto."

"Tell me about him. Is he cute? How old is he? Where did he go to school?"

Alex looked at her feet. "Well, he is a little older than me, but I liked his picture. He is handsome. His words make me feel warm inside."

"How much older?" Renata asked.

"He is about twenty years older."

"My God, girlfriend, that is old enough to be your father. Are you looking for a boyfriend and a father? On the Internet? You can't make love with a guy on the Internet, unless you know a position I don't."

"I know. I know. It seems like I always want to get involved with older men I can't have. It has been the same all my life. None of the younger men ever measure up."

They sat down to eat in a more serious mood. Alex turned to Renata and said, "It is not right of me to keep you in the dark about my past, but I don't tell many people things about me. I am much more interested in hearing about other people. I have loved you telling me about yourself.

"Anyway, I am from Glasgow, Montana. I lived and went to school in town, but my father had a cattle ranch nearby in a place called Nashua, a town on the edge of the Fort Peck Indian Reservation. He made most of his money as one of the owners of a bank in Glasgow. My father is three-quarters Sioux Indian, and his ranch is half on the reservation and half on private land. We spent a lot of time on the ranch, and you might say that I grew up a cowgirl. My mother was white, and that makes me almost half Sioux."

"You do not look like an Indian or a cowgirl," said Renata. "But then what the heck is an Indian cowgirl supposed to look like?"

"Here! I'll show you," Alex said as she rushed to her bedroom. "Be back in a sec."

In a few minutes, Alex appeared in jeans, a western shirt, belt, boots, and cowboy hat. "This is what one looks like," she announced and twirled around. Renata stared at Alex, who suddenly had curves in all the right places that were not displayed by her conservative work dresses and muumuu dresses at home.

"Sei molto bella! Which were the toughest to fight off?" Renata asked. "The Indian braves or the cowboys?"

"What did that mean?" asked Alex, referring to the Italian words. Renata smiled and waved her hand, fanning her face, and blew through her lips slightly as if she were trying to cool off.

"Maybe I'll switch-hit after all," she said laughing. "You are very, very sexy without those frumpy work clothes and muumuus. I better take you shopping and bring your wardrobe up to date."

Alex had an exceptional figure. Her waist was very thin, which made her breasts and hips seem even larger. She was also very fit. "But I am not interested in attracting any guys at work. I made that mistake once and never again. Work is the worst place to meet men."

"There are other places to meet men besides work. When we go to my father's restaurant, maybe you will meet a sexy *ragazzo* Italiano, but then again, I might meet several. Wouldn't that be fun?"

They finished dinner and stacked the dishes. "Why don't we go for a walk? It is a beautiful night." They walked across the parking lot toward a nearby park.

"How come our conversations always end up revolving around men?" Alex smiled. "One minute we were talking about the ranch in Montana, and now you have me thinking about hot Italian men in Boston. I like speed, but you have me thinking of men all the time now. Speaking of speed, I was a barrel racing champion and love to ride and even drive fast, but I'm not speedy with men, at least not now. You talked about wanting to have a man throw you down and make mad, passionate love to you. I want that also, but I'm reluctant, and I always pick guys I can't keep anyway. Maybe you could help me get over that."

Alex paused and looked at Renata with a naughty grin. "Maybe you can be a consultant on men for me."

Suddenly Alex stopped. "There is that black Hummer in the parking lot." They both ducked down behind a car and peered out toward the Hummer but could not see anything inside.

"Let's sneak up on the Hummer and see who is in there," said Alex.

"Okay, but let's be careful," responded Renata.

They moved from car to car, stooped over and on their tiptoes. They were within thirty feet of the Hummer when it burned rubber and fishtailed its way across the parking lot.

"It looks like we weren't as stealthy as we thought," said Renata.

"Yeah, I better practice up if I am ever going to be a detective," said Alex. They watched the Hummer speed away, its taillights getting dimmer and dimmer.

Chapter 14

On Saturday morning, Renata took Alex clothes shopping in preparation for their night out in Boston. The women's stores Renata picked were very fashionable, high-priced stores, much more in line with Renata's budget than with Alex's. Alex kept telling Renata she could not afford to buy anything at those prices.

"I'll buy you an outfit then," Renata told Alex.

"No you won't. I won't wear it if you buy it. I can look nice in something costing much less," argued Alex.

"Well, it's not my money anyway. Consider it as a gift from my father and let me help you pick out something. I know the kind of clothes you need," Renata retorted. She was insistent.

Alex was losing the fight. She nodded her head, as if to say she was okay with it but did not like the idea. Renata headed toward a sales lady and told her that her friend needed to buy an outfit. "What is this outfit for?" asked the young sales woman.

"A night on the town," replied Renata.

"Is there a particular style you would like?"

"Anything sexy!" replied Renata.

"How sexy?" asked the sales clerk.

Renata was tired of the questions and looked at the clerk. "How about the fuck-me look? Do you have anything like that?" Renata smiled at the clerk.

The clerk looked startled momentarily and then started to laugh. She turned around and asked the girls to follow her toward the back of the store. After an hour of trying on outfits, including commentaries on each outfit, Alex and Renata finally decided on one.

"Boy, are we gonna have fun tonight," said Renata as they left the store.

That evening at about seven thirty, Alex and Renata went into her father's restaurant. Two finer-looking women would be hard to find outside of Hollywood, and eager eyes stared at them everywhere they went. All the employees knew Renata, and several went out of their way to escort the two beauties to the back room. It was dark in the room. They approached a table with a group of men around it.

Renata yelled, "Papa!"

A large man, obviously of Italian descent, rose to greet them.

"My beautiful daughter," he said as he threw his arms around her. She disappeared into his giant bear hug. "I love you, Papa."

She turned toward Alex and said, "Papa, I want you to meet my friend and new roommate, Alexandra. Call her Alex."

Alex looked up at him. Even though she could judge someone upon meeting them, it was difficult to assess this man. On one hand, he looked capable of violence, and on the other, he looked capable of great love.

"Glad to meet you, Mr. Russo," Alex said, holding out her hand.

His huge hand grabbed hers. "Any friend of my daughter is a friend of mine," he said with a large smile. Alex was surprised. *He really means it.*

"Call me Dominick," he ordered. *Powerful*, Alex thought. *That is the word that fits him.*

Everyone sat down, and there were introductions all around. Alex immediately disliked the other men around the table. Not one of them had the light of the soul in his eyes. A few looked like businessmen. The others looked like the mafia guys on TV. Normally Alex would have wanted to get away from them, but she felt secure with Mr. Russo at the table. He dominated everyone and everything without having to say a word. Alex felt protected by Russo, but she still did not like the other men around the table.

A waiter handed Alex and Renata menus.

"No," said Dominick. "I will order for them. Take the menus away. Bring them an Italian-cut pan-seared pork loin with sweet fig jam and a braised veal shank over saffron arborio risotto and a bottle of Giacomo Conterno's Barolo... and bring me the check."

Turning toward Alex, Dominick said with triumph and a big smile, "You are about to have the best meal of your life."

Shortly after Alex and Renata were served, Dominick told them he had to speak alone with the men at the table and they would go to another room. Alex was relieved to be away from those men and alone with Renata. The meal was excellent. It was great fun for them both. They laughed until they cried and then laughed some more. Afterward, they went to the bar.

It was an upscale bar designed for the professional twenty to thirty-five party set. Both sexes were decked out in expensive, provocative attire, hairstyles, cologne, and perfume. They were there for one reason only; they wanted to meet attractive members of the opposite sex for love, whether overnight or long term. The girls inched their way through the crowded room trying to find a place to sit. Finally, they gave up and stood near the bar with what seemed like hundreds of others.

Renata pushed her way to the bar.

"Tony," she yelled at a bartender.

Tony knew Renata and quickly appeared in front of her.

"What'll you have?" he asked.

"Sex on the beach! Make it two," said Renata.

Pushing back through the crowd with the drinks, Renata found two men practically on top of Alex. As Renata handed Alex her drink, Alex started to introduce the men but could not remember their names. They introduced themselves. The one named Phillip took an immediate liking to Renata. The other man's name was Robert. Phillip and Renata were immediately immersed in each other. Alex stood there with Robert (do not call me Bob) feeling out of place. Robert was attempting to impress her with his degrees from Harvard, his father's law firm, which was started by his grandfather, his watch, and his job as a mortgage broker that, he told her, paid very, very well. Alex was not impressed. *What a jerk.* She told him that she had to find Renata. Renata was in a booth flirting with Phillip and getting drunk. Alex got Renata aside and told her that she had a headache and needed to go home but that Renata should stay; Alex would take a cab. On the way home, Alex's thought about her bad luck with men.

Renata did not return home until the next morning. Alex was having breakfast. Renata's hair was a mess, and she ran upstairs to her room. She changed her clothes, brushed her hair and teeth, and put on a little makeup. She ran downstairs and headed for the front door.

"Renata, where are you going? Don't you want some breakfast? You just got here."

"I have to go to confession and Mass. You know how it is with us Catholic girls. We raise hell on Saturday night and then get our sins taken away in the Sunday morning confessional. Bye."

Alex thought about Renata going to confession. *I have never confessed my sins to anyone, let alone a minister. Would the guilt I feel about Cal Cummings go away if I did? Having an affair with a married man was wrong, but I really loved him. By now the terrorists have probably killed him. It all really hurts.*

Chapter 15

After the Jimmy Montgomery date and her meeting with her boss, Phil Frane, Alex no longer felt secure at work. With each task, she wondered if she was being monitored or recorded. She wondered if someone could trace each file she accessed on her computer and whether her phone was tapped. She also noticed that Phil Frane treated her differently. *Am I being paranoid?* she wondered. *It feels like eyes are watching me wherever I go in the offices.*

She hated the fearful, paranoid atmosphere and wondered whether she had created it herself. *Cut it out,* she told herself over and over whenever the cloud of paranoia would envelop her. By force of will power alone she began to think more rationally, but it took her more than a week to regain this sanity. She became more observant of those around her rather than the imagined persons lurking in the shadows. She also paid attention to which computer files she worked with, making sure that no one could argue whether or not it was within her job description to access the files. On the phone, she made sure that she discussed nothing more than her immediate project and never any personal matters.

When driving to and from work or shopping, Alex watched carefully to see if she was being followed. She noticed a black Hummer while she parked her car at the mall. *I think I saw that same Hummer the other day when I left work.* She was unsure if she was being paranoid again until she noticed it behind her on the way home from the mall. Adrenalin rushed through her. Her immediate thought was to attack. But she remembered she did not have her guns, and reality prevailed. *I wonder if I can lose him,* she thought. *But he already knows where I live. I'll just see what happens.*

She immediately took a hard right into an alley and accelerated rapidly. The Hummer driver was caught off-guard, and Alex watched as it passed the alley behind her. She was approaching a one-way going to her left. It was little traveled. She turned right against the traffic, hoping that police were not in the area, went a block, and turned into an alley heading back in the direction she had come from. Back on her original street, she watched her rearview mirror for the Hummer. It did not reappear. She smiled but realized it was a shallow victory.

At home, Alex continued to talk to Renata about her problems. "I hate to burden you with my problems, but the more I think about it, the more I think I am in trouble. I can't think of anyone else to talk to. I can't talk to anyone at work because it will get back to management, I am sure. I can't tell my online Facebook friend Pete Oxwood. He works for TXA also."

"Oh, Alex," Renata said. "What is it?"

"I am being followed by someone and being watched at work. It is all because of those computer files I told you about."

"Was looking at those files illegal?"

"I don't think so, but Phil Frane and who knows who else do not want me to view them. The data files are classified Top Secret, but I have a top-secret clearance. The files have to do with TXA's sale of missiles and missile components and parts, which in itself is not unusual. That's their business. But missiles are normally sold to the Defense Department. The information I saw shows that some of the missile sales are being made to corporations, not the Department of Defense. My boss warned me. He even went so far as to set up a guy who works at the company to ask me out on a date so he could interrogate me. Now I am being followed by someone in a black Hummer, probably a terrorist."

Renata tried to make light of it. "I didn't realize I was signing up with such an exciting roommate."

"Thanks for making me laugh, but it is actually a bit scary. And I don't scare very easily. I started carrying a gun in my car."

Renata's expression turned serious. "I might be able to help. My daddy has lots of connections. Also, my roommate at Holy Cross is a famous investigative reporter in DC. She can uncover anything. Her name is Clancy McCleary. Oh you know, we talked about her before."

"Yes, you talked about Clancy before, but thanks, Renata. I don't want you or your family or friends to go to any trouble for me, at least not yet. But I do have an idea of something you can do to help."

"What's that?"

"I think they may be tapping my phone at work and maybe at home. Let's have a phone conversation, and you give out some misleading information about where I will be at a particular time and place. I know I can give the Hummer the slip just before I am to be at this place, wherever it is. But I won't go there. You will be waiting at this place to see if the Hummer shows up."

"Wow. A real intrigue. Like a detective movie. If he shows up, I will talk to my dad, and Mr. Black Hummer will never follow you again."

Alex laughed. "Renata, you are kidding, right?"

"No, Alex. I'm not.

Chapter 16

The older man Alex Pipe talked to on Facebook was Peter Oxwood who worked for the marketing department of TXA International, Commercial Division, in Palo Alto, California. TXA was a global company with fingers in electronics and military weapons in many locations in the United States and in most industrial countries. It was said that the value of TXA was larger than the gross national product of some small countries around the globe. He had been with the company and its predecessors for over twenty years.

For many years, Pete was TXA's top salesman of commercial parts to business and industry out of the Chicago regional office. He was a natural born salesman, but he had started losing his top position over the last two- to three-year period. He had been transferred to the West Coast to the marketing department. They said it was a promotion, but it did not feel that way to him. A desk job was not his cup of tea. He felt like he was being put out to pasture—the top racehorse being retired.

He felt he was stuck in his new job, working with a bunch of electrical engineering majors from Stanford. He did not have a degree from Stanford. And worse yet, he was not an engineer. "I fit in like a cat at a dog convention," he would say. He had nothing in common with most of the technical employees.

Pete was a likable guy. He was unassuming and normally made everyone around him feel comfortable, except the engineers at TXA. Women thought he was very handsome. He was always polite to everyone but particularly to women. He was not pushy or overly talkative; rather, he was attentive. He looked ten to fifteen years younger than his actual age of fifty-one. If you talked to him, you would come away with a positive impression, but watching the girls flirt with him would make any man jealous. He was never aggressive with women, but he did not need to be; whether he made the initial contact, they made all the advances thereafter. He was six two, slender with sandy blond hair cut short on the sides but long on top. It looked good on him.

Even though he was in the marketing department of the Commercial Division in Palo Alto, he was given a job with technical expertise written all over it: statistical forecasting for commercial component sales.

"Hell, when I started, I did not know anything about the basic components of statistical forecasting like regression analysis, seasonal adjustment, or beta weighting," he would say. "Stupidly, I tried learning as I went. It took me six months to figure out seasonal adjustment and another six to figure out beta weighting. The engineers barely tolerated my existence. Management should fire me, but I've been with the company too long and have allies within the company. So they tolerate my blundering and incompetence."

Pete was born in Radford, Virginia, and was in the Corp of Cadets at Virginia Tech, reaching the lofty rank of regimental commander. He majored in history, with a minor in political science, unusual at this well-known technical school. He was terrible at math and science and stayed away from any subject that was technical in nature. By carefully selecting his courses and staying away from all math and science, he graduated magna cum laude. He felt that it was ironic he had ended up in a job as a statistician. It was no wonder that he despised the job. It was no wonder the engineers disliked him.

Pete was commissioned a lieutenant in the US Army after graduation. He spent the next eight years with the Army Intelligence Agency, primarily out of Arlington Hall Station in Arlington, Virginia. The desk job he was given was a cover for his actual job with a special ops unit for the agency. The unit was similar to the Navy Seals and other commando units except their missions were to gather intelligence information that was very hard to get otherwise. He had to stay in shape, practice parachuting, and go through weapons training and obstacle courses, among other activities, to train for his job.

His unit would parachute into hostile territory and capture or destroy equipment for encryption, communications, missile guidance systems, and other equipment that the enemy did not want our side to know about. He became an expert at breaking and entering, a questionable talent except in the military.

After eight years, he rose to the rank of major but was tired of not having much of a life outside the unit. The camaraderie with his troops was something he enjoyed, and he would often sneak into the NCO club to drink beer with his men. Pete wanted to get married, have children, and settle down in a house in the suburbs, so he quit the army. He found a job as a sales representative for TXA in Chicago, met a woman, Eve Evans, bought a house in the suburbs, and together they raised two children, a boy and a girl.

Pete thought a great deal about how much he disliked his job and the possibility of retiring. He could retire at any time, but he felt he was too young for that; he wanted to increase his pension by working a few more years. It seemed perhaps he was given the terrible job because they wanted him to quit. He had been a great employee for many years and probably wouldn't get fired unless he punched a vice president.

He wondered why they did not fire him when his drinking had gotten so bad. The TXA national sales manager, Jim Arthur, probably had been protecting him. They were close friends, and Jim could match him drink for drink, but he did not seem to have a problem with alcohol. Jim had saved him from being fired; Pete was sure of it.

Pete's marriage had broken up because of his drinking. He missed Eve, his ex-wife. In his eyes, the women he dated since his divorce could not compare to her. Pete was always on the lookout for another soul mate, but no one ever lived up to his expectations. All the women he dated seemed to fall in love or lust with him immediately. However, he never turned down a good-looking woman, and there seemed to be a never-ending supply of them, particularly in California. He figured that one day he would find the right woman, but he could not get Eve off his mind.

Pete rarely went to sleep before midnight, usually spending several hours on his home computer. He signed up with Facebook and other social media and was able to track down some of his high school and college friends. He was hoping to meet and talk to women online, even though in Palo Alto there were more women than he could handle.

One night while he was on Facebook, he noticed that there was a page for TXA employees, like there was for his high school and college classes. He looked through the members in the TXA group. There were quite a few. TXA was a large international company.

One picture of a TXA employee drew his attention. The picture was of a beautiful woman. He could not stop looking at it. He was stunned that a picture could have that much impact on him. He studied it again and again, thinking how beautiful she was. She had a stocking cap and coat on. It was obviously taken during the winter with snow piled up in the background. She had a big, beautiful smile on her face, and her eyes sparkled. Her name was Alexandra Pipe, and she worked for one of the TXA divisions in Southborough. *Wow*, he thought. *I sure would like to get to know her.* Her other Facebook pictures were just as spectacular. It occurred to him that she looked much younger than him, and she probably would have no interest in him. Intrigued as he was, he did not send her a message or ask her to be a Facebook friend.

Several days later, Pete decided he had nothing to lose, so he sent a message to Alexandra on Facebook, telling her that he was an employee of TXA in Palo Alto in the marketing department, where he did statistical forecasting on component sales. Several days went by, and he did not get a reply. *Oh well, it was long shot.*

One evening, he noticed that she had accepted him as a friend and had sent him a short message. "Hi there, California," it said. "Alex in Southborough." That was the entire message. He typed back that he was happy to get her note and wondered what she did in her job. The next day, he got another message from her saying that she had degrees in mathematics and was a statistician in the TXA plant in Southborough. He typed back that he was in statistical forecasting but that he was not a mathematician by training and felt like a blundering idiot. She seemed to warm up to that. The messages went back and forth until finally she said it would be a lot easier if they could e-mail or chat than waiting for Facebook messages. They sent each other their work and home e-mail addresses.

As the weeks went by, Pete began to think more and more about Alex. She was so intriguing, so far away, so unobtainable. At night, he could hardly wait to get home to read her e-mails. They wrote back and forth about everything, particularly about their feelings on various issues. They began to talk about their inner feelings. Pete really liked the way she expressed herself about her feelings, about men, work, and a host of other issues. Pete expressed his feelings for his ex-wife in considerable detail but never told her about his drinking problem.

One night he was overwhelmed with the desire to talk to her. He sent her an e-mail and gave her his home phone number. He wondered if he was being too bold and whether she would be offended. He got an e-mail back almost immediately. "I'll call you tomorrow night." Pete wondered if she was as eager to talk as he was with her. The next evening, they talked for an hour. That resulted in lengthy long-distance phone calls every day. She was easy to talk to, and he told her everything about himself, including admitting that he was still in love with Eve, his ex-wife, and that he missed her. Afterward, he regretted doing that.

Have I fallen in love with a picture and a voice? Stupid! She is young. I am old. I am setting myself up for a big fall. She is just being nice to me. Why did I talk to her about my ex-wife? Stupid! Stupid! Maybe I'm attracted to her because she is unobtainable. It must be. I have all these obtainable women throwing themselves at me. And look at me; I'm goofy about a girl who is thousands of miles away. Am I so afraid of a new commitment that I chase a girl I can never get?

Weeks passed, and Pete and Alex continued their almost daily talks. Pete stopped beating himself up about his age and other concerns, and the discussions moved in a positive direction for both of them. They even talked about taking a few days off and meeting in Chicago. Alex was not detailed about her love life. She did not mention her former married lover. She did not mention the Jimmy Montgomery matter or the files she had read. Alex's conversations with Pete were actually superficial; she was not forthcoming on personal matters.

One weekend Alex told Pete that she had had a good week and mentioned the day she spent riding and shooting. She had to explain what mounted shooting was all about. Pete had never heard of the sport. "You mean to tell me that you are that good with a gun? Have you ever shot real bullets with it?" Alex told him that she had often been to a firing range with live rounds and was considered a marksman with both a pistol and a rifle and that she had been in fast-draw contests. She was quick to point out with a laugh that the quick-draw contests did not use live ammunition.

Pete was taken aback. "I never would have guessed that the pretty statistician in the picture would be a gunslinger." Pete laughed.

One night Pete asked her about how things were going at her job. She was hesitant. "Well, I would rather not talk about my job," said Alex.

"Why not? What's wrong?"

"Pete, I have to go."

"No, you don't have to go. Something is wrong about your job, and I want you to tell me about it."

Alex was silent for a few seconds. She had not told anyone other than Renata about Jimmy Montgomery, Cal Cummings, and her fears about what might be happening at her job. She brushed off his question: "It's that a close coworker was abducted recently, and everyone is uptight at work." That answer seemed to satisfy Pete because he did not ask any more questions. Pete, however, did not think that she was being truthful and wondered what was really going on.

Alex hung up the phone wondering if she was ever going to reach out for help. But she believed that her phone was bugged and could not ask for help over the phone. For a woman so confident about herself in everything she did, her confusion about what was happening at work was almost debilitating. *I must solve this problem. No, I will solve this problem. But how?*

Chapter 17

Weeks passed, and Pete and Alex continued their almost daily talks. The relationship had evolved to the point that they were discussing, with considerable enthusiasm, the prospect of flying to some city in the Midwest to spend the weekend together.

Pete's job was drudgery tolerated by thoughts of Alex. It was a Friday, and Pete was in his cube at work. He was struggling with statistics and trying to stay awake. He noticed a file named "Zaad" on the network disk drive that he did not remember ever seeing before. He turned to his cellmate.

"Sam, old buddy, have you ever heard of a file around here named Zaad?" Sam was not his buddy. Pete always called him that in a sarcastic tone.

"Never heard of it," answered Sam from across the cube.

Turning back to the computer, he pondered how it ended up in the files he could access from his workstation. Pete, being curious, opened the file, which was full of PDF documents as well as data, and began to read the documents.

The first thing he noticed was that they were stamped Top Secret. Immediately he knew he should not be looking at this information without a current top-secret clearance. Before he retired from the army, he had a top-secret clearance. While in the service, he had worked for Army Security Agency at Arlington Hall Station in Arlington, Virginia, and had had a top-secret crypto clearance. However, his clearance expired when he left the army.

TXA was a subcontractor for the Department of Defense. The personnel in its Military Division needed to have secret or top-secret clearances to work on military projects just as if they worked for the government. However, since he worked for the Commercial Division, he was not one of them.

The information in the Zaad file did not seem particularly unusual because it consisted of TXA Military Division invoices to buyers. But then he noticed that the billing was to nonmilitary private organizations. His Commercial division billed and shipped to nonmilitary, industrial customers, but the Military Division never billed products to companies in private industry. If a shipment went to a commercial company, it should be a Commercial Division shipment of Commercial Division products. However, the part numbers being billed were not Commercial Division part numbers. They were Military Division part numbers.

It also bothered him that he had never heard of the corporations being billed. The billing addresses for all the companies were in northern Virginia. It was also strange that all the company names started with the letter Z, names such as Zafir Co., Zabar, Inc., and Zabeeb, LLC.

In another part of the file, he found shipping information. He tried matching up the billing information with the shipping information, but it became too complicated, and he decided to wait. "Ship to" and "bill to" normally appeared on the same invoice. In this case, they were separate and confusing. He wondered if there was an intent to confuse.

Pete felt he could figure it out if he could do it at home, and even though the information was classified, Pete forwarded the Zaad file to his home e-mail address. He knew he should not forward the information, but his curiosity, emboldened by his background in military intelligence, took over his normal caution.

On Saturday morning, he took another look at the file. There were a considerable number of bills to the Virginia corporations in the last thirty days that had no ship-to addresses. In another part of the file, there were shipping documents, but they were all shipments to US military bases. Pete figured they could not be connected to the billing invoices. But on the other hand, what were they doing in the same file? *What's going on here?* He felt like a kid who had his hand in the cookie jar.

Pete knew that Alex worked in the Military Division in Southborough; maybe she could shed some light on this. Pete attached the file to an e-mail he was going to send her anyway and clicked on the "send" button.

That night in his apartment, Pete tried to relax, but he could not put his ex-wife out of his head. His sordid marital history repeatedly ran through his mind. Often this would keep him awake at night. Tonight was no exception. She had wanted the divorce. He did not want it. The kids were grown, so there were no small children affected by the divorce. Pete had spent too much time with the guys, playing poker, going to see the Cubs, the Bears, the Bulls and the Black Hawks. On the weekends, it was golf or fishing. And there was the beer. She was neither a sports fan nor a drinker.

His drinking had increased as time went on. There was always beer at the games, the poker table, everywhere he went. Was beer everywhere or did he only go to places there was beer? He was not at home very much, and his wife was lonely and felt unloved. *I was too much into myself and into the booze to notice. I was stupid.* Pete regretted what he had become. He was a far cry from his younger self, having doted over his wife and children for years. He had even been named Father of the Year in the Chicago suburb of Elk Grove once. Despite women being attracted to him, in the beginning he had resisted going to bed with them. This changed as the drinking increased, and he had many affairs.

After the divorce, his wife remarried within a few months. Her new husband seemed like a good man. Pete would tell people, "I was jealous of her new husband, but whenever I felt jealous, I always remembered that it was my own damn fault."

After the separation, Pete moved to the near north side in Chicago in order to be near the Rush Street bars. He felt lonely without Eve. Being alone was not what he wanted, and he spent a lot of time in all the wrong places looking for someone. Was he looking for a replacement for Eve or just someone for company? Pete was the target for any woman in the bar. He thought about how far down his life has gone. He needed something to happen that would pull him out of the hole he had created.

He woke one morning with a horrible hangover and could not remember the night before. Nothing. He had gone to Rush Street after work and remembered stopping at Gibson's and ordering a drink. That was the last thing he remembered other than a vague memory of being thrown out of a singles bar. His apartment was on Roscoe Street off Belmont Harbor. He was not sure how he had gotten home.

He went through his pockets and found a note from "Sheri" saying, "Thanks for the good time. Call me," followed by her phone number.

He racked his brain and tried to remember her and where he had met her. He wondered for a second if he should call the number. *What if she looks like a linebacker?* he thought. The note went into the trash.

Early that Saturday afternoon, he went outside looking for his auto, still feeling horribly sick. It was nowhere to be found. He went up and down the long blocks coming off Belmont Harbor. It was cold, and as usual, it was colder near the lake. Walking toward the lake in winter with the wall-to-wall buildings on both sides acting like a wind tunnel only made him feel worse.

"Damn it's cold," he muttered. This was not the first time he had lost his car. Parking was a problem around Belmont Harbor, and it was much worse if you were a drunk.

Giving up his car search, he looked in the phone book for towing companies and called the closest one. Bingo. He ended up at a towing company in a rough area on the near west side and learned quickly that an attitude does not help get your automobile back. The entrance was dingy and dirty. It matched the cloudy, cold Chicago day. The guy was behind bulletproof glass; he was huge with a shaved head and tattoos all over, the kind that guys get in prison. Pete started to complain. He gave Pete an "I am an ax-murderer" glare. Two ill-tempered German shepherds snarled and lunged at him. Chains prevented them from getting to him. Quickly, he got the idea to shut up and pay the huge bill.

"This place has mob written all over it," he muttered to himself and left as quickly as he could. The huge guy gave him a crooked, evil grin.

Pete spent the rest of the weekend in isolation. His mind matched the gloom outside. The only light in the apartment was the gray, weak light from the window and the changing colors on the TV screen. He did not call any of his old buddies. They had drifted away from him anyway. All of them were married; he was single and just didn't fit in with the married crowd anymore. He did not know it, but his old crowd had simply tired of his drinking. He watched football on TV but mostly thought about how far down his drinking had taken him. He did not even drink a beer while watching the games, as he was fearful of its probable Jekyll/Hyde effect.

He spent a lot of time thinking about his marriage. More and more he began to realize his drinking had to be the main reason for the divorce. *Did I go to those games because I loved sports or did I love the booze? Could I go to a game and not drink?* He began to think it was the drink that attracted him more than the sports. His mood was black, depressed. He thought vaguely about AA and pictures of the Salvation Army; food lines and homeless shelters came to his mind. He quickly shoved the AA idea from his mind, thinking *I have not gone* that *far down.*

On Monday, Pete went to lunch with George Funk, a fellow salesman. George noticed that Pete looked like he had a hangover. They chose a favorite Italian eatery on Cicero Avenue, Roma's Italian Beef and Sausage. Roma's had one of the best combo Italian beef and sausage sandwiches, and they both ordered one. Pete asked if they served beer but was told that they served only soft drinks. George had told Pete in the past that he needed to watch his drinking, and this seemed like the opportune time to remind him.

"I have worried about your drinking for a long time," George said. "I think you look hung over and tired. You just can't seem to handle your booze. It's affecting your job too. A few years back, you were far ahead of all of us sales representatives. But you wanted to drink. I told you it was a bad idea taking clients to lunch and drinking every day of the week. People began to tell me they smelled alcohol on your breath almost every afternoon. In my opinion, you need to go to AA, my friend."

For at least a week after that lunch, a fight raged inside Pete about calling AA. His mind would immediately rationalize his drinking. *I've never had a DUI. I don't sleep under a bridge or at the mission. I don't stand on street corners begging for money to get something to eat.*

Then Pete would remember the blackouts and the hangovers. He knew it affected his work except with those clients who liked to drink like he did. He remembered the times he told himself not to go into a bar because he knew that if he did he would get drunk. Bars were like magnets. Every time he got near a bar, he would end up in it; he never turned away. He had no control over it. The booze seemed unstoppable.

Pete finally gave in and called the AA number in the phone book. They gave him the time of a meeting on the near north side. He waited until the last minute, slipped in the door, and sat in the back, avoiding the greeters. The room was large, and there were maybe a hundred people in the room. Every time someone new said anything, the crowd would yell, "Hi, Bill," or whatever their name was. There was talk of the "Big Book." He thought they were talking about the Bible. There were twelve different steps, "first step," "fifth step," "twelfth step," and others. Pete thought these steps were like masonic degrees or some rank within AA.

One day, after sitting in the back of meetings for weeks, he stood up in a meeting and said, "Hi, I'm Pete, and I'm an alcoholic."

"Hi, Pete," everyone roared. He felt a burden was lifted from his shoulders.

When he transferred to Palo Alto, he began to attend AA meetings in the area. There was a meeting near his apartment in Mountain View that he attended on a regular basis. He was feeling physically and mentally healthier every day. California AA was a bit livelier than Chicago AA. Everyone seemed to yell, "Hi, Pete," with more enthusiasm.

Pete started going out for coffee with some of the AA members after the meetings. He particularly enjoyed talking to a man named Ted. He was probably in his fifties, divorced, and a member of AA for twelve years. Ted and he talked endless hours about their drinking stories and Ted's belief in AA to help him stay sober. Pete talked to Ted more than once about his feelings toward his ex-wife. Ted told him that guilt and remorse about his ex-wife could cause him to drink again. "Live in the present. That's all we have," Ted had said.

One of the things that Ted warned Pete about was "thirteenth stepping," a term used by AA members to describe dating among the members, particularly new members. It was obvious to Ted and everyone else that Pete was the center of attention for every eligible female in the AA group, and there were lots of them. Pete had no resistance to their charms, all the while missing Eve. The disconnect kept Pete in a mental turmoil, feeling guilty and missing Eve all that much more. During one of these moods, he had first connected with Alex on Facebook.

When Pete sent the e-mail to Alex with the Zaad file attached, he shook his head. He had spent too much time running over and over his drinking history in his mind. *I need to get outside of my head. I am driving myself crazy. I need to do something different. Ted told me my mind is a dangerous place to go alone. Maybe I will drive up to San Francisco.*

He thought about Alex and wondered what she was doing. He called but got her answering machine. "Hi. It's me. I just wanted to chat. I will call again later." He wondered what she would think about the file he had sent her, and then his thoughts shifted to all the things to do in San Francisco.

Chapter 18

Pete drove to San Francisco late Saturday morning. He had never done the tourist thing there and felt it was time. It was warm out, and he decided to dress like a tourist and be comfortable. He put on a sleeveless shirt, shorts, white socks, and tennis shoes. He looked the part. He put a camera around his neck for an added touch.

He drove to Interstate 280 and headed north. He drove straight to Fisherman's Wharf, parked in a parking garage near Pier 39, and walked east on Beach Street to Embarcadero and then to Pier 33 where he bought tickets for the cruise to Alcatraz later in the afternoon. He then went back to Pier 39 and spent several hours seeing the sea lions, marina, and other attractions.

As the day progressed, he began to feel colder and colder, to the point that his teeth were chattering. He decided to buy a sweatshirt in one of the shops. Later he found on the Alcatraz cruise that the sweatshirt was not enough; he was still cold. He went inside the old prison with a tour group listening to the tour guide and taking pictures. He happened to look down at his legs and swore they were blue. He decided to buy some slacks back in the city. *"The coldest winter I ever spent was a summer in San Francisco," or something like that. Was that Mark Twain? This is damn near as bad as Belmont Harbor in the winter.*

On the cruise back across the bay, Pete tried to find the warmest spot he could on the boat. He was huddled in a corner when a woman in her thirties came over and tried to squeeze in next to him. She brushed against him and excused herself. *Was that an accident or intentional?* he wondered. Pete noticed that she was not dressed in warm clothing. She wore a yellow sundress and sandals without socks. Her bare arms were wrapped around her and had a blue tint. He could not help but notice that she was quite pretty, despite her state of misery. She was about five eight, brunette, and thin. She had a long torso and long legs, and everything fit together in a nice package.

"You wouldn't be a little cold, would you?" he asked her. She was standing close but turned slightly away from him. When he spoke, she turned and looked at him. One corner of her mouth turned up a bit.

"Oh no," she replied with as much sarcasm as was possible in her situation. "This is normal weather for us girls from Fargo." She put her arms at her side and pretended she was not cold.

"Fargo? I heard that place blew away years ago in a blizzard."

"You betcha, but I took out my North Decoder Ring, and its back in place."

Pete grinned at the sudden accent. "You sound like you are imitating Frances McDormand in the movie *Fargo*."

The slender woman grinned back. "That's because they hired me as her accent coach. She was imitating me."

Pete could tell that if he continued, she was going to get the best of him no matter what he said, so he changed the subject.

"I moved to Palo Alto from Chicago not very long ago. This is the first time I've been in San Francisco, and I was not prepared for this cool weather."

"At least you have a Giants sweatshirt."

"I brought it before we left. There are no warm pants to buy on this ferry." He paused. "I would be happy to share my sweatshirt if you like."

"Okay," she said. "Put your arm around me and pull me close."

Pete had meant he would let her use the sweatshirt, but he did not mind pulling her close. Her body felt good. She had a pretty smile. He could not resist pretty women.

"Here I am holding you in my arms, and we don't even know each other's names. I am Pete Oxwood. What's yours?"

"Susan Swanson," she replied. "I'm in the city for a convention of high school guidance counselors at the Convention Center. Most of us are staying at the Hilton nearby."

Pete and Susan engaged in small talk the rest of the trip across the water. He bought her a sweatshirt in one of the shops on the piers. They decided to walk to see the trolley cars, shops, and other sights. They talked and laughed as they walked, and when they were walking across a grassy area, Susan started to laugh and twirl around.

"I was bored today, so I am playing hooky." She laughed as she twirled around like Mary Tyler Moore.

"A guidance counselor playing hooky? You don't look a bit guilty." Pete laughed, grabbing her hands and twirling her around some more.

Later, another tourist told them of a good Italian restaurant. They took a cab to California Street and went into the Perbacco Ristorante and Bar. Pete was feeling very upbeat, and he liked Susan as company. The eatery had a romantic atmosphere and décor, and he felt like they had made a good choice. He was hoping he and Susan would have a little romance later.

Susan was overjoyed with Perbacco. She studied the wine menu with particular interest. When the waiter came around, she ordered a glass of Caymus Napa Valley cabernet sauvignon 2007. The waiter asked if she would like a bottle instead. She immediately said yes before Pete could say anything. Pete turned his wine glass over. Susan did not notice.

When the wine came, Pete said he did not feel like any wine right then but might have some later. Susan liked the wine and soon started on a campaign to get Pete to taste it. *I should not have any, but it's only wine. I won't get drunk. I'll be careful. No harm, no foul. She thinks I am great. I don't want to disappoint her.*

Pete had a glass of wine before the entrée arrived. To his great delight, he noticed that it had no effect on him. *This means I can have a few more glasses.* Halfway through the Italian dishes, Pete ordered another bottle of wine. Susan was having great fun, and her flirting was even more intense.

They took a cab to the Hilton after dinner. She snuggled up to him in the backseat.

"You feel fabulous," she told him.

"You feel even better than that," he replied, turning his head to kiss her. The kisses and the embrace lasted most of the trip to the Hilton. They clung on each other, staggering slightly as they entered the front doors.

"Let's go to the bar for a nightcap," she said, pushing him in the direction of the bar.

"A girl after my own heart."

Pete knew he was drunk by now but could not stop and did not want to. They sat down at the table in the back and ordered several more rounds of drinks. Pete started to have lapses of memory. Several times when he went to the men's room, he thought he had just been there moments before. When he returned to the bar, the hands on the clock behind the bar had moved mysteriously forward. *Where had the time gone?*

Pete woke up slowly. He was in an unfamiliar place in an unfamiliar bed. He looked around. It was a motel or hotel room and the curtains were closed. It was daytime. He had a headache and felt sick. He lay there a few moments trying to get his bearings. He looked on the other side of bed. There was a woman in bed with him. He then remembered Susan and the night before. She was still asleep. He could not remember going to the room. The last thing he remembered was drinking in the bar. He looked down at the floor and shook his head. *No, no. I slipped. I got drunk again. Damn it.*

Pete staggered to his feet and stumbled into the bathroom. He splashed water on his face. His skin was oily and his hair in a mess. His mouth tasted like shit. He smelled like sour wine. He thought about taking a shower. He looked into the room and stared at Susan sleeping. She did not look nearly as good as she looked yesterday. He got into his clothes and left without saying good-bye.

Chapter 19

After leaving the hotel in downtown San Francisco, Pete caught a cab to the parking garage near Fisherman's Wharf where he had parked his car yesterday. He was too sick to walk from the hotel.

The trip back to Palo Alto was a blur. Pete's physical condition had taken over his emotional and intellectual capabilities, leaving him in an almost catatonic state. When he arrived at his apartment, he threw himself on his bed, clothes and all, and slept.

At five o'clock Monday morning, Pete woke up. He felt like he had the flu. *I must have mixed wine, beer, and whiskey to feel like this.* He slumped over a cup of coffee and felt the warmth rise to his face. He tried remembering what had happened on Saturday. It had started out as a good time and turned into a disaster. This was the worst hangover in his life. *I wonder how Susan feels. She must be back in Fargo by now.* He got a whiff of his own breath and went to the bathroom to brush his teeth and shower.

It was getting late, and he needed something to eat. He had not eaten anything Sunday. There was a Hobees' Restaurant on El Camino Real that served a good breakfast, and he pulled into their parking lot. He ordered a large breakfast. The place was busy, and Pete was late to work by the time he gulped down the last of his coffee and threw a tip on the table.

Sam was leaving their cube as Pete raced in. "You are just in the nick of time. Dunning has called everyone to an important meeting," said Sam. Pete hated the general meetings. He considered them boring and a waste of time. *Good ole Sam just eats these things up.* Pete followed Sam up to the large conference room. It was filling up fast, but some seats were still available. Instead of taking a seat, Pete stood in the back with a group of other men. He had never sat up front when he was in school either. He always wanted it to appear that he was one of the guys and tried to draw no attention to himself.

Pete noticed a number of burly men in suits standing around the walls of the room watching the crowd. The suits did not hide the fact that they looked like thugs, like men in a movie Pete had seen about the Russian mafia. Their eyes scanned every person in the room. Pete became concerned and wondered if this had anything to do with the top-secret information he had found. He moved farther back into the group of men as Jim Dunning, vice president and general manager of the Commercial Division, went to the podium at the front of the room.

"Gentlemen and ladies," he began. "I received word this morning from the head of our Military Division that some top-secret data on their servers has been compromised. This is a very serious situation. All of our computers, Commercial and Military Divisions, went through their nightly backup and restore. One file that was supposed to be restored to the military computer system was put on our commercial system by mistake. That file contains information vital to our national defense. This was not discovered until last night, and it was determined that someone had accessed that file during the day on Friday, someone in our Commercial Division. It is important that we talk to whoever opened that file. If any of you saw or opened an unfamiliar file or knew of anyone else who did, we must talk to you immediately."

Pete felt his eyes grow wide and his jaw drop. Then he stared at the floor, hoping that no one noticed his reaction. When he finally looked up, one of the suits was staring a hole in him. The thug did not look happy. *He must have noticed my reaction. Damn.*

The meeting ended with Pete close to a panic attack. He fought hard to look nonchalant. He walked slowly to the door and he felt like every eye in the room was watching him. He dared not glance back.

When Pete got back to the cube, good ole Sam was sitting at his desk. They did not greet each other. Sam looked sheepish and said nothing about the Zaad file.

Pete sat down at his desk. His mind kept going over the sequence of events that had happened since Friday. He found the file on Friday; it was top secret. He opened it; the information he found was very unusual. He e-mailed the file home, and on Saturday morning he e-mailed it to Alex. Early Monday morning, there was a general meeting of the entire Commercial Division in Palo Alto, and there were some sinister-looking suits watching him. *How could they have known about it so quickly? The file is obviously very important to someone.* Pete knew he was in trouble, but he did not know how bad the trouble might be. *I am probably going to be fired over this.*

The secretary for the marketing group came into the cube and told Sam and Pete that Dunning was going to meet with each employee that afternoon. Pete knew that even if he denied reading the Zaad file, Sam would damn sure tell them. Pete's mind was in a whirlwind of thought wondering what he should do. He knew one thing for certain; he needed to get out of there so he could think. He stood up and looked at his cube mate.

"Sam, I am not feeling very good. As a matter of fact, I feel rotten."

"I'll bet you do," sneered Sam.

"I am going to a walk-in clinic. I think I am having a flare up of an old problem."

"Yeah, sure."

Pete knew that Sam did not believe a word he said. It was only 10:00 a.m. Pete figured he would have at least a three-hour jump on anyone looking for him. He still did not know what he was going to do or where he was going to go. He headed out the door and walked toward his car. It popped into his mind that he ought to warn Alex about the file. It would be about 1:00 p.m. back east at her office, and she might just be getting back to work from lunch. He dialed her cell phone number. The call went directly to voicemail. He left a message for Alex to call him.

Pete was standing in the parking lot not knowing what to do next. His mind was still foggy from his bout with the booze. *I can't think. Am I having a panic attack? What's wrong with me?* He went to his car, sat in the driver's seat, and continued to try to think.

Pete continued to ponder and slowly began to calm down. *What am I so upset about? I don't need to put up with this crap. To hell with this job. I hate it anyway. I have enough years in to retire.* He got out of his car and headed back to the TXA building. He went directly to HR.

A young woman with short red hair and an ample build sat behind a counter.

"I am here to quit my job."

"Have you seen your supervisor about this?" she asked.

"No, I just want to sign whatever forms are necessary and leave."

"Well, we have procedures, sir. You have to see your supervisor, and he has to fill out some of our forms. And then we have to set up an appointment for your interview and signing of the forms."

"What if I just quit and didn't show up for work at all?"

"Well, we have a form for that also. If you don't show up for work for five days, your supervisor fills out a report for us. After two weeks, you are fired for not showing up to work."

"Does that mean I don't get my final paycheck and pension?"

"No, you still get them. But your record will show that you were fired."

"So if I tell you I quit and don't show up for work for five days, then I am fired even though I quit."

"Yes, sir, that's correct."

"Can I give you an address to send the checks?"

"You have to fill out a change of address form that goes into your permanent file."

"Okay, give me your form. Do you have a form for everything?"

"Yes, sir. Pretty much everything."

Pete filled out the form and put down his parents' address in Virginia. He was not sure where he would be living in two weeks.

"Thank you, sir. Good luck."

Pete walked out of HR with a big packet of retirement brochures and went back to the parking lot. It was eleven thirty Monday morning. He thought he should look through his desk before he left and went back into the building. Sam was not in the cube as Pete looked through his desk and picked up a few personal items. As Pete was starting to leave, Sam came into the cube.

"Feeling better already? Listen, Pete, while we have never gotten along, I think I need to warn you. Those tough guys that were in the meeting this morning came by looking for you. I don't think they are playing games. And they spoke Russian to each other."

Chapter 20

Sunday afternoon, Alex was reading an e-mail from Pete and looking at an attached file labeled Zaad. She was perplexed by the information in the file and was staring at it with her head cocked to one side and a frown on her face. *This file seems like the same kind of files I have been noticing at work. Why would Pete have this file?*

The telephone rang. Renata answered it. There was a pause followed by Renata screaming. "Oh my God. Oh my God. I don't believe it. It can't be true. Murdered? Oh my God."

Alex raced from her room to Renata. She was still screaming into the phone.

"I'm coming right down, Mr. McCleary. I will fly in tonight. I'll call you and let you know when and on what airline."

"What's happened? What's wrong?" asked Alex urgently.

"My college roommate and best friend at Holy Cross has been murdered. Oh my God! Her name is—was—Clancy McCleary. She lived in DC. She was a reporter. I need to pack a few things. I can't believe it. I need to see her parents who are in D.C. right away. I'm going to catch the shuttle to DC."

"I want to go with you. I can take the rest of the week off," exclaimed Alex. "I don't want you to go down there by yourself into a murder scene."

"Thank you so much. You are very kind. I am so glad you can go with me," responded Renata. "Let's get going then. Should we take a cab or drive to the airport?"

"The cab costs a hundred dollars each way. Parking is no more than twenty dollars a day. The parking will be cheaper unless you are gone for more than 10 days," Alex said.

"Let's take the cab anyway," Renata decided. "I'll pay for it. I just don't feel like driving, and I won't let you drive me in this weather."

Renata began packing a carry-on bag while Alex called a cab. Alex started stuffing things into a backpack, not spending any time thinking about what to take or how long they might be in DC.

The cab pulled up in front of the townhouse in a steady downpour. Renata and Alex raced to the cab but still got wet. The cab drove south toward the Mass Turnpike, its windshield wipers at full speed. The driver was obviously not in a hurry due to the weather.

"US Airways. Shuttle. Terminal D. Step on it," barked Renata. She then slumped back into the seat and started to cry quietly. Alex put her arms around her and let her sob.

No one noticed a car pull in behind the cab as it left the girls' apartment. It followed the cab at a safe distance to the airport and pulled into a parking area reserved for police. A policeman approached the car, and the driver flashed a badge. The policeman turned away, no longer interested.

In the terminal, the girls ran to gate 19 at the end of the terminal, but they arrived in plenty of time. They looked disheveled. They had not put on makeup. They were still in their lounging clothes, jeans and tank tops. Their hair was wet, and they were sweating from the run. They looked at themselves in the mirror in the women's room. "Jesus, Mary, and Joseph," muttered Renata.

They boarded the plane, put their carry-on bags under the seats in front of them, and strapped in. They both breathed a sigh of relief.

In the terminal, Pam Robinson talked into her cell phone while watching the girls go through security. "She is on US Air flight 2651 into Reagan leaving in fifteen minutes. I'll catch the next flight down. Have someone follow her and let me know where she is staying."

"It's only a forty-five-minute trip to Washington National," said Renata.

"Renata, they changed the name to Reagan Airport a long time ago," replied Alex.

"It's still National to me," she said in an irritated tone. "I have my reasons."

They immediately turned their attention to where they might stay in DC. Finally, it occurred to them they should stay wherever Clancy's parents were staying or close by if it was booked.

They arrived at Reagan Airport at 10:00 p.m. At the exit, Renata recognized Clancy's parents. She raced up to them and threw her arms around each, crying. Renata, wiping away tears, introduced Alex to the McClearys as her good friend. Alex felt a deep sorrow for them all and hugged Mrs. McCleary, who starting crying again. A dark aura hung over the group. The rain outside dampened everyone's spirits even more.

The McClearys were booked at the Holiday Inn at the airport. The girls decided to book a room together to keep each other company. Mrs. McCleary asked them to meet at the coffee shop after putting their bags in the room.

After check-in, Alex and Renata crossed the lobby to the elevators and waited for an elevator to return to the first floor. Alex was restless and kept looking around.

"Renata, I felt like someone was watching me at the airport. It is a most peculiar feeling. Maybe I am getting paranoid."

Renata smiled. "I saw a couple of cute guys at the airport."

They went to their room, freshened up, and returned to the lobby. The whole time, Renata told about her college days with Clancy and all the things they had done together. At times, the stories were funny, and Renata would laugh, and at times Renata would get a tear in her eye. It sounded to Alex like they were party girls having a lot more than a little bit of fun while they were at Holy Cross. Alex felt sorry for Renata's loss and her tears and gave her kind words and several hugs in support. They soon arrived at the coffee shop and sat down with Clancy's parents.

"Tell us what you know about what happened to Clancy," said Renata.

"We don't know very much yet. She was shot and killed this morning around two o'clock. She was an investigative reporter, as you know. I don't know if it had anything to do with her work. It was in a rough part of town. That is about all we know."

No one noticed the young, well-dressed man sitting across the room at another table, sipping coffee and reading a copy of the *Washington Post*. If anyone were to watch him carefully, he was more interested in the group across the room than he was in the newspaper, but he was very good at hiding that.

Chapter 21

On Monday morning, Alex, Renata, and Mr. and Mrs. McCleary went to the crime scene. There were police cars everywhere. The first thing Mrs. McCleary noticed was the neighborhood. "Why would Clancy have an office in such a nasty place?" she asked. Whether the question was rhetorical or not, no one answered.

Alex noticed a bearded man standing in the crowd who was dressed in a suit and tie and looked familiar. She had seen him before but could not place him. *How can I ever be a good detective if I can't remember details?*

Alex did not realize it, but the young man from the lobby of the hotel was also in the crowd. Next to him was Pam Robinson. Their entire attention was directed toward Alex. Pam knew that Renata was Alex's roommate but was still attempting to work out the connection between them and the death of the reporter.

The McClearys, followed by Alex and Renata, approached the yellow tape and told one of the uniformed officers that they were family. The officer pointed toward a group of policemen and told them to see Detective Lt. Mitchell. "He is the one not in uniform."

They spotted the man in plain clothes. From a distance, he looked rather sloppily dressed. His tie was already at half-mast, and his pants had avoided the ironing board for months. Alex was particularly interested. *He looks like Lt. Colombo.*

Mrs. McCleary approached him first. "Lt. Mitchell?"

"Yes, what can I do for you?" he responded.

"We are Clancy's family. I am Jennifer McCleary, and this is my husband, Herb. We are her parents." Mrs. McCleary said nothing about

Alex and Renata. Lt. Mitchell probably assumed they were relatives also. "Could you tell us what happened?"

"First my condolences to you both for the loss of your daughter. That is a terrible tragedy," he replied.

"To answer your question," he continued, "the body was discovered Sunday about four o'clock. She was shot twice from close range. The time of death is estimated to be Sunday morning about three o'clock. We don't know what the motive was, but it was not a robbery. She still had her purse and a large amount of money in it. We were able to call you quickly because of her black book of numbers in the purse. Her calling card says she is a freelance investigator, so we are assuming that she was working on some type of investigation."

"What kind of an investigation?" asked Alex. "Who was she working for?"

"We are not 100 percent sure at this point. We found Senator Jennings Randolph's card in her purse. That is a possibility. We also found a calling card for a Jim Darling of Technical Professionals Recruiting. We have sent out officers to investigate both of these leads."

"Why was her body in this nasty area of the city?" asked Mrs. McCleary.

"We are trying to find out who owns this building. We should find that out before the end of the day. By the way, there was probably at least one other person here at or near the time of death."

"Why do you believe that?" asked Alex.

"There are two different areas with coffee cups and fast-food wrappers. The coffee cups in one work area had lipstick on them. The ones in the other area did not. That leads us to believe a man was working here also. In addition, there are two sets of man-sized footprints coming in and going out to the alley. That could mean that there were two killers, or it could mean that there was one killer and the person who was already in the building with Clancy. We don't know who the other person is or what happened to him or her. The only thing in this office was some computer equipment. We did not find any computers, but we did find two printers, printer paper, and computer cables. We believe that there was at least one computer here or perhaps a laptop and that it was taken."

"Is it possible that she was killed by the people that she was investigating?"

"We think that's a possibility," answered Mitchell. Just then, Mitchell's cell phone rang. "Excuse me while I take this," he said. It became obvious that he was talking to someone about the employment agency. Mitchell finished the conversation and turned back to the group.

"That was the officer we sent to look into the employment agency. It seems that Clancy hired a computer hacker by the name of Carl Jones. He is not responding to our phone calls. I have dispatched officers to his address. They are on their way as we speak. Jones may be more than merely a person of interest."

#

From the edge of the crime scene, a man watched intently. He could see Alex with the small group talking to the detective, but he could not hear what they were saying. He walked to the back of the group watching from the yellow tape and pulled out his cell phone.

"Boss, it's me. I followed our girl to DC last night. You should have seen this old, fat guy running to get on that plane. Anyway, this morning she is visiting a crime scene where a reporter was killed. She is with three other people, two women and a man. I don't know who the older man and woman are; they act like relatives of the victim. The younger woman flew down here from Boston with Pipe."

The man on the other end of the line listened and then responded. "From our bug of Alex's home phone, we learned that the younger woman is Pipe's roommate. The older man and woman are the reporter's parents. The parents called Alex's roommate yesterday at her apartment. Keep an eye on the group and let me know anything that seems suspicious but don't lose track of Pipe."

Lt. Mitchell continued to talk about the evidence at the scene to Alex, Renata, and the McClearys. "The only other thing we found were trace marks on a piece of paper that was underneath a piece of paper someone wrote on. It looked like some kind of organization chart. Some of the lines and boxes were clearer, depending on how hard the writer was pressing down. Each box had a word in it, but none of them could be read other than the word Zafir. I don't have a clue what that means. Since you folks knew Clancy well, that might mean something to you. If anything about it has meaning, let me know."

Mitchell's cell phone rang again. He talked for several minutes with someone about Senator Randolph. When he got off the phone, he turned to the McClearys.

"That was Senator Randolph's assistant, Butch something or-the-other. He acknowledged that Clancy was working for the senator but would not tell us what she was doing for him. He said it involves national security. I'll have a personal talk with him. Too many things get buried in this town in the name of 'national security,' things that shouldn't be buried."

The McClearys, Alex, and Renata continued to ask questions of Lt. Mitchell. It was getting close to lunch, and he gave them his card, telling them if they had any more issues to call him. He jotted down the name of the motel where they were staying and everyone's cell numbers, saying he would let them know of any new developments.

They left the crime scene and headed for the McClearys' rental car. "The name Zafir seems familiar for some reason," Alex told the others. "But I don't know why. Maybe I should go back to the motel and think about that while you all go to the morgue and arrange to transport Clancy's body home. I feel like I would be in the way."

"Oh no, Alex, you are never in the way," said Mrs. McCleary. "You have been so supportive of us in this horrible time. But we would be happy to take you back to the motel. We will be back later before dinner."

At the motel, Alex bid them good-bye and started to walk into the lobby. She noticed a man in the parking lot out of the corner of her eye. *That guy with the beard. It's the same guy that was at the crime scene this morning. I've also seen him before back home. He's following me. It has to be about those files at work. Cal is probably dead because of those files. I could be next. I have to get my hands on a gun.*

After removing her coat, she flung herself on the bed and looked up at the ceiling, wondering about being followed. Her cell phone rang. She ran to her purse and answered. It was Pete.

"Thank goodness you're there," exclaimed Pete in breathless relief.

"Something awful has happened," said Alex. I am in DC right now because Renata's college roommate was murdered here yesterday morning. I am trying to help her and the roommate's parents. Her name was Clancy McCleary."

"I am sorry to hear that, Alex. And please tell them I am sorry to hear of their loss," he replied. "I have big news also. I just quit my job. It all started because of that Zaad file I e-mailed you. TXA is very serious about finding the person who looked at the file, namely me."

Pete told her the whole story about the meeting. "There were some serious-looking Russian thugs scanning the crowd and looking at me. I just got fed up. I don't need that. Life is too short. I hated the job anyway."

"Pete, I'm being followed also, and I am now sure it is for the same reason."

"Alex, I'm sorry I got you mixed up in this mess. Here I am worrying about myself, and you are in the same situation. It's my fault."

"No, Pete, it isn't your fault. In fact, I was looking at the content of similar files at work before I received your e-mail. Although I have authority to look at the files, I was not supposed to open the top-secret PDF sister documents, at least according to my boss. TXA is spying on me because of it. Yesterday, before we knew about the murder, I looked at the file you sent me. It is quite similar to the top-secret files I discovered at work. I think we both are in trouble because of those files."

Then she remembered something. "Zafir. That is the name of one of the companies I saw in the Zaad file you sent me."

"What?" Pete asked. "What are you talking about?"

"Clancy McCleary was an investigative reporter who was murdered, and there's a piece of paper that shows she had been investigating a company named Zafir. A company with that same name shows up in the Zaad file you sent me as a company purchasing military products from TXA."

"Do you think there is a connection between Clancy's murder and the files we have been looking at?" asked Pete.

"Let's look at this logically," said Alex. "There is a connection between the company named Zafir and TXA as shown on the invoices in the Zaad file. Clancy was investigating something to do with Zafir. We don't know for sure if she was also investigating TXA. But both of us are being followed by TXA because of the files that contain an invoice to the company named Zafir. If Clancy died while investigating Zafir and we are being followed by TXA because we have seen the files with the Zafir name in it, the probabilities of a correlation between the two are high."

Alex then told Pete about Cal Cumming's abduction and disappearance. "I have a feeling that Cal is dead. Clancy McCleary is certainly dead. We are probably in serious trouble. We may be next on the murder list."

Alex heard someone at the motel room door trying to open the door. "Pete, I'll call you back."

She ran toward the bathroom, not knowing where to hide. She had not brought a firearm with her. The door opened.

Chapter 22

Pete pushed the *off* button on his Blackberry. He wondered why Alex had hung up so quickly. She was almost whispering when she cut off her cell. After thinking about what Alex had told him, he was certain he was in more trouble than he previously had believed. *Quitting my job is not going to make this situation disappear.* Pete was still in the parking lot, and it suddenly dawned on him the Russian thugs were probably hot on his tail. *I had better get out of here.*

On the way to his apartment, Pete thought over the situation. *They are going to learn soon that I'm not returning to work. Then they'll come by the apartment looking for me. Perhaps I had better leave Palo Alto. I have no reason to stay here. I don't even own anything here.* Pete's furniture had come with the apartment. The apartment rental included pots, pans, and utensils. All he owned were clothes and personal items. He could load up his Suburban and be gone in less than an hour.

While loading his clothes into his vehicle, his Blackberry rang.

"Hi. This is Alex again. I had a minor scare and had to hang up. Someone was coming into the motel room, but it turned out to be Renata. Renata and Clancy's parents couldn't go to the morgue. They have to do it tomorrow, so Renata came back early. Renata and I are going to go back to the crime scene and see if we can figure anything out."

"Don't you think that the police should handle that? I mean, you are not experienced in solving crimes."

"I have read so many mystery and detective novels. I believe I know enough to solve murders." She laughed. "Actually, I am too curious to sit here and do nothing."

"I don't like the idea. Be careful!"

"I will call you when we get back and bring you up to date," said Alex.

Pete decided to finish packing, get a quick bite to eat, and come back to do a walk-through with the apartment complex manager. When he finished packing, the Suburban was filled up with only a little more than when he arrived in California. He drove to the same place he had had breakfast. After eating, he sat drinking coffee and thinking about what direction he should drive. Perhaps he should drive back to Virginia to see his parents. On the other hand, he really wanted to talk to his ex-wife in Chicago. His children lived in Pennsylvania and New Jersey. He could get a chance to see them also. He spread a map on the table.

When he had first arrived in California, he had made plans for places he would tour. One of them had been to drive up the Pacific Coast Highway into Oregon and then Washington. He had heard people rave about the Oregon coast and a small town named Newport. One of the places he had heard about was a French restaurant in Newport that had a unique breakfast menu. He realized that direction was not the best route to Chicago and Virginia, but he reasoned he could cross Washington state, see Coeur d' Arlene, Montana, Yellowstone Park, and Jackson Hole and then head to Denver. He did not have a timetable, and that fact alone heightened his sense of freedom.

Pete stopped by his bank, pulled out all his money, and then drove back to his apartment where he went through a satisfactory walk-through with the manager of the complex. They returned to the office where Pete turned in his keys.

"Oh, by the way," the manager said. Pete stopped in the doorway and turned back. "While you were gone, a couple of big guys were looking for you. They looked like a couple of hoods. I didn't tell them anything about you or where you were."

"Thank you for doing that."

Pete kicked himself for taking so long to get out of town. He drove north on Highway 101 and stopped at a motel north of San Francisco for the night. It was a ma and pa motel but looked clean. Out of habit, he paid with his credit card. The owners were a nice older couple, and they highly recommended the restaurant next door. He walked across the parking lot to a local eatery that was obviously not a franchise. It looked like they served comfort food. He ordered ham, mashed potatoes with gravy, turnip greens, green beans with bacon, grits, cornbread, and sweet tea. Pete thought his Virginia stomach had gone to heaven. Engorged with food, he headed back to the motel to think about all the events that had taken place in the last few days. He also mulled over what he wanted to say to Eve, his ex.

His thoughts turned to his flabby body. In the army, he had been in top shape, all muscle, no fat. *I can't believe I let my body deteriorate to this point.* He immediately dropped to the motel floor and started doing push-ups. Then he did sit-ups and a variety of stretching exercises. He was tired and sweating when he finished.

Pete suddenly realized that he had taken no evasive maneuvers to throw the goons off track if they followed him. *I used my real name when I checked in and my credit card. That's stupid of me.* He smacked his forehead with the heel of his hand in disgust. *I have been using my cell phone. They can track that right to this motel. Shit. I need to leave here and go to another motel, pay cash, and use landlines.* He sat on the edge of the bed thinking that he did not want to move to another motel, that he wanted to go to sleep, and that the goons probably didn't have any high-tech equipment.

He lay back and went to sleep.

The phone rang. Pete woke up. He had been asleep about fifteen minutes. He picked up the phone and grunted a greeting.

There was momentary silence on the other end. "Oh. I dialed the wrong number. Sorry."

The phone call put Pete's mind back into perspective. He packed his clothes and carried out his plan to find another motel, call himself George Smith, and pay cash for his room.

Back in her DC motel room, Alex put down her cell phone and looked at Renata. "Pete quit his job at TXA," she said. "There was a big meeting trying to get the employees to admit they had seen the Zaad file or that they knew someone else who had looked at it. Pete's cellmate knew he was looking at it. Further, Pete said some thugs looked at him in the crowd at the meeting as if he might be the one. He had just quit his job when he called. I don't know what he is going to do next."

"This situation is too weird to fathom," replied Renata. "The world is crumbling for all of us—you and me and even your Internet boyfriend. I am scared to death. When I came in the door, you were freaked out. Both of us are jumpy and looking over our shoulders. You keep seeing people following you. This is weird, weird, weird. Maybe I better call my dad."

"What are you going to tell your father? That things are weird? What could he do to help us right now?" asked Alex.

"I guess you're right. We don't know for sure that we are in trouble. I better save my calls for a real problem," replied Renata.

Alex's face suddenly changed to one of determination. "I am not going to sit around here anymore and do nothing. Let's stick to our plan to go back to the crime scene. Maybe we can find something. Maybe the piece of paper with Zaad on it means something. Maybe Carl Jones, the hacker, killed her. Maybe we can find something about him."

"The last I heard, the police hadn't found him yet," Renata replied. "Lt. Mitchell called the McClearys when I was with them and told them that they still could not find Jones. The lieutenant said he is going to go see Senator Randolph tomorrow."

Renata and Alex left the room, got into the McClearys' rental car, and headed toward the crime scene. Both of the women were on edge, watching to see if they were being followed. Alex was driving and watching the traffic behind her. It was getting dark, and the headlights of the vehicles behind her made it difficult for Alex to see if they were being followed. She made a series of evasive maneuvers even though she was unsure if anyone was actually following.

At the crime scene, Alex got out of the car, and Renata followed closely behind. The neighborhood, which did not look too safe that morning in daylight, gave the girls shivers at dusk. They both wondered what had possessed them to put themselves in this situation. There were no streetlights in front of Clancy's old office. The yellow police tape was prominent, but there were no police watching the place, at least not at that minute. The women looked around with wide eyes and hustled under the tape. The front door was locked. They went back to the street and then down the alley. The alley was very dark.

"Are you sure you want to do this?" asked Renata in a whisper. "Clancy was *my* friend. Why risk your life for someone you didn't know?"

"Because *you* are my friend, and it seems like all this is related to the Zaad file, which involves me directly. Let's go."

Alex led the way down the dark alley, stopping now and then to listen. They got behind the building that Alex thought would be

Clancy's old office. There were no signs, numbers, or anything to identify the back of the storefronts. She tried a door. Locked. She went to the next door. Also locked.

Renata whispered. "Let's get out of here."

"Not yet." Alex went back the other direction and tried a door. It was unlocked. The two women stared at each other. Alex slowly pushed the door open. Listening, she heard nothing. *No flashlight. Damn. How could I forget that?* She put her hand inside the door and felt for a light switch. Fumbling for what seemed like an eternity, her hand finally found a switch box, and she pushed down on what felt like several switches. The lights inside and in the alley went on. It blinded them temporarily. Alex looked into the alley and noticed that there was yellow tape partially across the back of the building where she had not been able to open the doors. She turned off the switch for the outside light and closed the door. They were in the store next door to the crime scene. The room was empty and dusty.

"We are in the store next door. Maybe there is a way through this wall into Clancy's old office."

The girls searched the walls, pushing as if there might be a hidden door. They came to a closet and opened the door. It was a large closet, flush with the wall but set back so that it had to protrude into the room next door. The closet was almost the size of a small room. It was empty. One wall had numerous plug-ins for power, video, and telephone, as if the room were designed for audio/visual equipment. There were video camera plugs hanging down from the ceiling to a shelf on the wall. Alex began to push on the walls going toward Clancy's old office. Renata held back at the entrance. Alex suddenly discovered part of a wall that gave way. A small door opened. She was in the room where Clancy had died. Enough light came through the door to allow Alex to see light switches on the back wall. She crossed the room and turned them on.

When the lights came on, Alex jumped. Renata screamed. A man was sitting at one of the tables in the room.

Alex looked at him sternly. "You are lucky I did not have my guns with me. You would be dead. Who the hell are you?"

"My name is Carl Jones. I have been following you ever since this morning."

"You are the computer hacker. The police are looking for you."

"They won't find me, and I won't talk to them. I don't like cops."

"Did you kill Clancy?"

"No. I wasn't here when it happened. I was helping her in her investigation of UPA."

"Who is UPA?" asked Alex.

"United Patriots of America. A super PAC supporting corporations and conservative causes."

"Were you here before it happened?"

"Yes, I was working with her that night and into the morning. I got sick because I had not taken my medications that day and went to my apartment to take them. When I returned, she was dead. The only thing I can figure out is that the killer or killers were in the room next door and came in through the secret door you found. The back door to this office was still locked. There was no sign of forced entry when I returned. I looked for places they might have entered the room. I found the office you came through and saw electronic listening and video surveillance equipment. They were watching and listening to Clancy and me while we worked."

"Who owns this building?" asked Alex.

"A company named Zafir Corporation owns this entire building," replied Carl.

"That's a name in the Zaad file," gasped Alex.

Renata interrupted. "Who killed Clancy?" she asked Jones.

"I know who did it, but I do not want any further involvement, and I am not going to tell you. I want to give you the opportunity to walk away from this without knowing anything. This situation is too dangerous. It's too dangerous for me or you or anyone else. I have a disk for you containing data from my investigation. No one else has this information, not the FBI, the CIA, or any other person. The FBI and CIA are not even capable of putting together this information. I am the only one good enough to have found the information that is on this disk. The people you are looking for are technology-wise and as capable as the FBI but they are not at my level of technical sophistication. Nevertheless, it's only a matter of time until they find me and kill me. That is unless I get out of town. After I give you this disk, I am going to disappear. And if I were you, I would throw it away and disappear also."

Before either Renata or Alex could respond, he walked up to Alex, gave her a disk, and left by the back door. Astonished, the two women stared at each other, incapable of saying anything. He was gone. Alex yelled, "Who owns Zafir Corporation?"

A voice yelled from the alley, "It's on the disk."

Chapter 23

Alex and Renata turned off the lights in the Zafir building and scurried back to the rental car. At every turn and stop, they looked furtively in every direction. As they drove, Alex kept a close lookout for autos following her. She soon realized one was following her. Alex tried to lose the car behind her, but another car picked up her tail. "Ever since we left the building, I have spotted several cars after us, and I can't seem to shake them," she told Renata, her voice filled with excitement.

Alex drove straight for the motel. "I'll let you out at the front and watch to see who is following us," Alex told Renata.

They pulled into the motel parking lot. Alex let Renata out at the front door, making sure she took the disk in with her. Renata ran into the lobby. Alex parked the car and sat for a while, looking to see who might pull in behind them. Alex slumped down into her seat to keep from being noticed.

It was dark in the parking lot. Without the engine and street noises, it seemed too quiet. After a few moments, a car pulled in and parked about ten cars away. Another pulled in and parked in a different part of the lot. She waited for someone to get out of either car. Time went by, but no one got out.

Finally, one of the car's front doors opened. Straining to see who it was, Alex was surprised to see that it looked like a woman. The woman walked across the parking lot toward the front door of the motel. As she approached the lights in front, it was clear to Alex that her stalker was a female. She looked to be slightly over medium height and slender. She had a bag or a laptop computer slung over her shoulder.

Alex thought about the other man who she had seen following her earlier, the one with the beard. It seemed too much of a stretch that this woman was also following her. *It has to be the other car, not her. Was the bearded man in the other car?* She drove around the lot looking for the second car. When she passed it, two men she had never seen were sitting in the front seat. They tried to duck down when they saw her.

Alex drove toward the front door looking for the closest spot to park near it. The only available spots were too far from the front door for comfort. She got out of her auto and ran into the lobby. Out of the corner of her eye, she saw the woman from the parking lot sitting in a lounge chair in the lobby. *If she is staying here, why is she sitting in the lobby? I am sure she is following us. That means I am being followed by a woman, a bearded guy, and two unknown men.*

When she got to the room, Alex called Pete. It was still only nine o'clock in California. "Pete. Where are you?" asked Alex. Pete told her about the two thugs that had come looking for him when he had vacated his apartment and about leaving Palo Alto before finally telling her his location.

Pete said to Alex, "The more I think about this, the more I think I'm in real danger. I drove north today thinking that I was escaping, but if the people after me are sophisticated, they can easily track me. I'm going to stop using my credit cards. In fact, they probably know where I am right now. Maybe I ought to move to a different motel."

"A number of people seem to be following me," said Alex. "I'm going to have to find a way to get them off my back. Everywhere I go, I'm being followed. I definitely think you need to move to a new motel. Renata and I are getting out of this place tonight, as a matter of fact, as soon as possible."

"How did your investigation go at the murder scene?" asked Pete.

"I have eliminated Carl Jones, the hacker, as a suspect in the murder. He was sitting in the dark at Clancy's office tonight. He is one creepy, arrogant guy, but he gave us a disk and said that we should be able to figure out who hired the hit men who killed Clancy. I haven't had an opportunity to look at the disk yet. What's really bothering me is the warning Jones gave us. He said if we were smart, we would throw away the disk and disappear. He thinks that we're in grave danger for getting involved in this."

"Did he give you any clues about who killed Clancy or who is after us?" asked Pete.

"No, but he told us that a company named Zafir Corporation owns the building. Also, the Zafir building has a secret surveillance room. The killers were watching Clancy from that room. On top of that, Clancy or Jones wrote Zafir Corporation's name on a piece of paper that was found at the scene. It was an organization chart showing it was connected to a number of other corporations."

"But what would be the motive for a building owner to kill a tenant?" asked Pete.

"I didn't say that Zafir was behind the killings," responded Alex. "Carl Jones said Clancy was investigating UPA. There has to be a connection between Zafir and UPA. Perhaps UPA and Zafir were involved in something illegal. I'll bet Clancy found out what they were doing, and they murdered her to keep her quiet."

"So if the UPA/Zebra organization finds out you have the disk, they will be after you also," said Pete.

"It could be that they are already following me," responded Alex. "Another thing that bothers me is the Zafir Corporation name is in the Zaad file as one of the companies billed by TXA for TXA products shipped to an unknown location. That means that TXA might be mixed in with this UPA/Zebra group."

"TXA is upset enough that they are sending thugs after me because I looked at that Zaad file," Pete replied. "So TXA has to be mixed up with UPA and Zafir. Not only that, but I think the Russians are involved too. The thugs following me are Russian. Also, aren't the names starting with Z Russian names?"

"I agree. All of them are mixed up in some kind of criminal activity and are willing to kill people to keep it quiet."

"This is bizarre. No wonder Jones told you to throw away the disk and disappear. I am going to pack up and move to a new motel right now and will call you later," said Pete.

When Alex turned off her cell phone, she headed for her laptop to take a look at Jones's disk. Renata had been listening to her phone conversation and stepped between Alex and her laptop. "Hold on a minute, Alex. I think we better move on right now. Those people know we are here. We are in danger. Let's forget about the disk for a while until we are safe.

"What you need," continued Renata, "is a change of identity and to disappear just like Jones suggested. I don't think they care about me. I think Pete needs a new identity also. My dad owns places that give people new identities. I am going to call him now. While I talk to Dad, please pack up all our things and get ready to go."

"Getting my identity changed will take forever. My present identity will be dead long before my new identity is born."

"I don't think so. Go pack!"

Renata called her father. Alex could hear his cheerful, booming voice across the room. "Papa, my roommate has a real problem, and I think we need your help."

"I will call you back on the secure line. Hang up, sweetheart."

Renata's second cell rang a few minutes later. She explained in detail all the problems to her dad, including Pete's situation. Renata began to write down information from her dad on the motel notepad. Suddenly she stopped writing and said, "The one I practiced with the most was the Beretta M9." She then turned to Alex. "Did you tell me your two guns were .45 Colts?" Alex nodded yes, and Renata told her father about Alex's weapons of choice. Finally, she said good-bye and cut off her cell. Renata turned to Alex. "We need to get out of here now. My dad was adamant about it. He told me about a safe place we can go, and you can get an identity change there. And I also got an address for Pete to get his identity changed."

"Okay. Everything is packed. We don't need to check out. Let's go." Alex threw open the door, and they ran to the elevators with their bags and laptop. "When we get to the lobby, Renata, you run to the front doors first, and I will hang back a few seconds to see if anyone follows. I'll tackle anyone who tries to follow you. Don't stop; just keep running to the car. Here are the keys."

Renata ran across the lobby as fast as she could go. Alex stuck her head out of the elevator and watched the lobby as Renata crossed it. No one was in the lobby, so Alex stretched out her long legs and took off for the car. Renata reached the car first and put the keys in the door as Alex was running toward the car. Just as Renata started to get into the driver's side door, a shot rang out, and Renata fell to the pavement. Alex was there in two seconds; she grabbed up Renata and pushed her in the car.

Another shot rang out. It missed Alex, hitting the door just as Alex was pushing Renata across the driver's seat into the passenger seat. Alex slammed the door, put the car in reverse to get out of the parking space, and pealed out, burning rubber, backward all the way toward the back of the motel. The shots had come from the front of the motel. There were several ways out of the parking lot, but all of them exited toward the front of the building. Alex chose the exit that was the farthest from the motel and gunned it. The car tires made so much noise Alex did not hear any more shots, but a bullet came through the back window and hit the dashboard, destroying the radio.

Alex kept the gas pedal all the way to the floor and ran several stoplights. There was a car coming up fast on her tail. It was gaining ground. Suddenly another car came alongside the one following her and swerved into it. Repeatedly, the car bashed into Alex's pursuer. Suddenly, both cars went off the road into the ditch. Alex saw one car roll over and was quickly out of view. *My God! What was that? Whoever you are, thanks.*

She turned her attention to Renata, who was groaning. *Thank God she is alive.* "Where are you hit? Where are you hit?" Alex yelled excitedly. Renata's voice was weak, and Alex had to pull over and put her ear closer to her wounded friend. "Tell me again, Renata."

"It's my arm. I am bleeding. It hurts horribly. I don't want to die."

"If you are hit in the arm, you probably won't die. We need to get you to a hospital." Alex drove on with the intent of finding a hospital.

"No. No hospital. They will know who I am… too many questions… go to address in purse… Dad's place." Alex thought she had to stop the bleeding. However, both of their bags and the laptop never made it into the car and were in the motel parking lot. At least she had the disk. There was nothing to use as a tourniquet. She thought for a moment, took off her blouse, and tied it as tightly as she could on Renata's arm above the wound. Renata still had her purse over her good shoulder. Alex struggled to get the purse off. She was leaning over Renata, and blood was all over her remaining clothes and bra. Renata groaned.

Finally, Alex got the purse and opened it. The notes were easy to find. Her hands were causing blood to get on the notes, and she had trouble reading them. The address was in the 2000 block of Fairview Avenue, NE. She put the address in the car GPS. Alex knew she did not have any time to waste and drove at higher than normal speeds. However, she did not want to get pulled over wearing only a bloody bra with a bleeding woman with a gunshot wound in the front seat. *It'd be hard to explain to a cop, but I can't let Renata bleed to death.*

Alex pulled up to the address on Fairview. Renata told her to turn off her lights in front of a chain-link gate and then flash the headlights twice. Alex positioned the car in front of the gate, turned off the lights, waited fifteen seconds, and then flashed the headlights twice. They waited. Nothing seemed to happen. Renata was groaning. Then like magic two men were opening the gate and waving them forward toward the building. A large overhead door opened into a warehouse, and another man waved her in.

Once inside, Alex started yelling. "Renata's been shot. Renata's been shot. She needs help. She needs a doctor."

At the sound of Renata's name, several men ran to the car and threw open the door. Immediately a stream of swear words came from the men. One of them yelled, "Get Doc over here." Soon an older man started running toward the car and took charge of the scene.

"Get her into my office now," the man told the younger men. The biggest one picked up Renata in his arms as if she were a doll and carried her across the warehouse toward offices in the front. The door shut.

Alex looked around. At least six men around the warehouse were staring at her. She wondered if it was the blood on her but soon realized that she was standing in front of the men with only a bra and shorts on, both covered with blood. She blushed with the realization. "Does anyone have a shirt they can lend me? And how about a bathroom?" Three men rushed forward, pulling off their shirts; after all, Alex was very well built.

Chapter 24

Alex looked in the bathroom mirror. There was blood on her face, arms, hands, and seemingly everywhere. Her bra was soaked with blood. She tossed it in the trash. She had carried in a shirt from one of the men, and it hung behind the bathroom door. She found a towel and started wiping the blood off, then put on the shirt and buttoned it up. There was a knock on the door, and a woman entered the room. She was short and blond with a ponytail, and she had tattoos on her arms. She was about twenty-five, well built, and dressed in black. Alex figured there were probably tattoos elsewhere on her body and she probably had a biker wrapped around her finger.

"If you are finished cleaning up, please follow me. My name is Sandy."

The woman led Alex out of the bathroom and down a hall to an office. "Someone will be in shortly to talk to you." Sandy left. Alex could hear noises from the warehouse and wondered what went on at this location. She figured it must be one of the many businesses that Renata's father owned. She looked around the office; it was plain but neat. It had no personality, and Alex figured that more than one person, maybe many, used the office.

A man walked in and closed the door. He was a little older than Alex with average build and dark hair, and his face was covered with a two-day stubble. He sat slightly sideways to her but tilted his head toward her. It seemed like he talked out of the side of his mouth.

"I understand you are a friend of Renata's. You probably already know she is the boss's daughter. Mr. Russo is going to want to know what happened. I want you to give me all the details, but first I need to tell you that Renata is going to be okay. She lost a lot of blood, but Doc says she will recover. Doc has lots of experience with gunshot wounds, so he should know. Mr. Russo has already talked to Renata but just long enough to comfort her. Tell me what happened. My name is Anthony."

Alex told him the whole story about TXA, Clancy, the investigation, Carl Jones, the crime scene, and people following her. It took almost half an hour. The man listened carefully, his head tilted sideways toward her. He did not interrupt but seemed to hear every detail.

"Is there anything you want me to go over again or repeat?"

"No. That is not necessary. I have an unusual memory. I can repeat what you said verbatim back to you. You did a very good job of detailing the facts. Mr. Russo will get a full report. I do have one question. Who do *you* believe shot Renata?"

"Through the process of elimination, I would say that someone who works for TXA, UPA, or Zafir Corporation ordered it done. I also think that there is some connection to Senator Randolph. He put Clancy in an office full of electronic surveillance that was monitored from next door. On the other hand, the building is owned by Zafir Corporation, whatever that is, so it might be the culprit. However, my pick now is TXA. They have been following me and are the most logical one to be shooting at me, thereby mistakenly hitting Renata."

After Anthony left, Alex wondered if she had done the right thing in leaving the disk out of the story. It was in the car. She had managed to throw it into the car when the shots were fired and Renata went down. She was determined to be the first one to look at that disk.

Sandy walked back into the room with clothing in her arms. "Here is an outfit to wear. I guessed at your size. I am good at guessing sizes. Of course, if you guess sizes all the time like I do, you would get good at it also."

Alex took the clothes and examined them. They were quality material and in her sizes but definitely not her style. A bra and underwear were included. "What kind of job has you guessing at clothing sizes? And why would you just happen to have nice clothing in my size here in this warehouse in the middle of the night?"

Sandy paused for a second. "Let's just say that we are professional outfitters for newly created people. Get dressed and yell when you are finished. We have lots more to do."

Alex finished dressing. She was amazed at how well the clothes fit her. "I'm done," she yelled.

The blond lady waved Alex out of the office and down the hall to another room. The room looked like a hair salon. There was a male hairdresser waiting for her. *Gay? Probably. But why do you even care if he is gay? We are all God's people.*

"I think we should make her into a blond with short hair and put glasses on her to give her a scholarly look," said the hairdresser. "What do you think, Sandy?"

"That sounds good, but I think we should put black, thick-rimmed glasses so they can be seen from a distance," replied Sandy.

"Shouldn't I have a say in this?" asked Alex." Why don't you just give me a wig?"

"They come off too easily when things get physical, as they often do," replied Sandy.

Alex did not like the idea of changing the way she looked. On the other hand, she reasoned that there were people who wanted to kill her, and the tradeoff between a new look and death was not really a contest.

Alex sat in the salon chair, and the hairdresser began cutting her hair. An hour later, she looked like a different person, particularly when she put on her glasses.

"We have a few more stops. Follow me," said Sandy.

They went into another room that was equipped with lighting fixtures and cameras; it looked like a photography studio. Alex did a double take. The man behind the camera was the hairdresser. "How did you get over here so quickly?" asked Alex.

"That was my twin brother that did your hair. We are almost identical, except for one body part, which can't be mentioned in mixed company," he said laughing. "Sit down on that stool," he said, still laughing at his inside joke. He proceeded to snap numerous pictures.

Sandy led Alex back to the office. Tony came back in and sat down. "We are changing your identity to Patricia Sanchez from Flagstaff, Arizona. You will get an Arizona driver's license, an Arizona birth certificate and passport with your pictures and an address in Flagstaff. You will also get a voter registration card for voting at an elementary school in Flagstaff. Remember the name. That is where you went to school. Memorize the data on your birth certificate in case someone starts asking questions. You will get a Visa card, a debit card to a bank in Arizona, and a Kohl's credit card. There will be a health insurance card in case something happens to you. All of these cards are real and are good for six weeks. You will also get an automobile with Arizona tags and the registration in your name. After six weeks, call this number and tell us where the vehicle is. We will pick it up. We can give you a start on your new identity, but we can't finance you forever. The boss sends us many customers, but they aren't all taken care of as well as you are. Good luck. By the way, we will take care of your rental car and get it back to the motel."

"Won't they figure out that the address in Flagstaff is fake?" asked Alex.

"It isn't fake. It's an empty house. Someone would have to drive by and look in the house to figure out there is a problem. If that is brought up, just say you forgot to change the address on your license."

The hairdresser or photographer came in and handed her a woman's purse with a credit card wallet inside. Alex examined all the documents and was astonished at how real they looked. Tony then handed her $1,000 in cash, car keys, and a cell phone. "Get out of town, don't call your parents, don't go see your parents, and don't go back to your apartment, just get lost. The cell phone has the number in it to call if you are in trouble and the number for Mr. Russo. Calls to both numbers are encrypted. And here is the address for your friend Pete in Reno to go through the same process. Everything is in place. He just has to get there."

Tony handed Alex a new Colt .45 and a shoulder holster. Alex put on the holster, and Tony helped her adjust it. The pistol was larger than the usual pistols put in shoulder holsters. It was uncomfortable, and the bulge in her clothing would be noticeable.

Tony left the room, and Sandy told Alex to follow her again. This time they went into a room that looked like a hospital room. Renata was in a hospital bed across the room. Alex dashed over to her, and Renata opened her eyes, looking very sleepy. "How are you, Renata? How do you feel?"

"They say I am going to live and should be up and around in no time. Right now, it hurts even with the pain pills. What happened to your hair?"

"Say hello to Patricia Sanchez from Arizona. Your father is changing my identity, and I understand that Pete is having his changed also. Do I look different?"

"If they had changed your voice also, I would have a tough time recognizing you. You look pretty good as a blond."

The phone beside the bed rang. Renata answered it. "Hi, Daddy… I am feeling better but am still tired and need to sleep quite a bit more. Okay I'll put her on. Alex, my father wants to talk to you."

Alex took the phone with trepidation. *Renata would not be in this hospital bed if it had not been for me.* "Hello, Mr. Russo."

His voice boomed over the phone. "Hi, Alex. I hope my people are taking good care of you. I want to thank you for your efforts to get my daughter to safety after she was shot. She could have bled to death."

"But, Mr. Russo, they were trying to shoot me. I had been the driver, and they aimed at the person who was getting in the driver's side. I wish it had been me rather than Renata. I feel so bad for her. If it had not been for me, she would be okay."

"Alex. Don't fret. I am not mad at you. People can be in the wrong place at the wrong time, and that is what happened here. You did not fire the shot. I want to find out who did it. From what Anthony said, you have narrowed the suspects but are still working on it."

"Yes, sir, and I will call you when I know who it is."

"Thank you. Good luck." The line went dead.

Alex and Renata hugged and said their good-byes. They promised to stay in touch through Renata's dad. Alex went to the car she had driven to the warehouse and got the disk. She then headed over to where her new car was parked and drove away from the warehouse.

#

At Reagan Airport, a stocky, bearded man was standing in line to catch the shuttle to Boston. "Hey, boss. It's me, Harry. I lost her. I'm sorry, but DC traffic is difficult, and she is pretty good at evasive driving. She lost me one other time."

"Lost her? You shot at her. What do you mean you lost her? You missed and hit Renata Russo. And do you know who Renata Russo's old man is?"

"What are you talking about? I never shot at anybody. I lost Pipe in traffic and never caught up with her again."

"Well who the hell shot at her?"

Chapter 25

Alex stopped at a truck stop north of DC on I-95. The sun was fully above the horizon, and it was 6:30 a.m. She was hungry and needed to call Pete. She walked into the eatery and sat in a booth in the back. Her new clothing allowed her to wear a shoulder holster with her new Colt .45 in it. Russo's identity change company had thought of everything, including a pair of sunglasses over the visor. She kept the glasses on in the booth. A heavyset waitress walked up to her. "What'll you have?"

Alex ordered the biggest breakfast on the menu with three pancakes, five strips of bacon, three eggs, grits, and toast. "Bring me coffee right away." Alex was a big eater. Her mother used to ask her where she put all that food and then answered her own question by saying, "You must stuff it down those long legs."

Alex thought about the problem of calling Pete. *If they are listening to his cell phone, I can't give him the address of where to go to get his identity changed. It is easy to find out a person's cell number. Maybe if I asked him to call me back on the motel landline, I can give him the address. He probably changed motels, and they don't know where he is presently. If they don't know which motel he's at, they would not be able to hear our conversation about the address he has to go for the identity change.*

Since it was only 3:30 a.m. in California, she thought she would eat before calling him.

By the time breakfast got to her table, she was very hungry and gulped it down. It was 7:30 a.m. on the East Coast and 4:30 a.m. in California. She was weary. She had been awake over twenty-four hours and needed a nap, but she had to call Pete first. She dialed Pete's cell number on her new encrypted cell phone. She had his number memorized. A sleepy voice answered the phone.

"Pete. This is Alex. This is very important. Wake up and listen to me."

"Okay. Okay. I'm awake."

"Give me the telephone number of the motel where you are staying. Don't tell me the name of the motel or town."

Pete fumbled around and looked for the phone number of the motel, gave it to her, and hung up. A few minutes later, the motel phone rang. "Alex?"

"Get a pad of paper and write down this address." She gave him an address in State Line, Nevada. "Go directly to that address immediately. You will be able to get a change of identity there. Don't call me on your cell. They will give you a new cell that has encrypted communications. Also they will give you my new cell number. Call me when you are through. Don't ask any questions. They now have the phone number of your motel so leave immediately!"

When Alex cut off her cell phone, she drove to the back of the truck stop parking area. She closed her eyes and fell asleep sitting up.

Pete jumped out of bed and threw on some clothes. He did not bother to shower or even brush his teeth. He stuffed his clothes in a bag and ran out to his Suburban. He looked at a road map and located State Line. He left the motel and drove back toward San Francisco. The quickest way to Lake Tahoe/State Line was to take state Route 37 east toward Sacramento and then US Highway 50 to Lake Tahoe. He drove south from Novato, California, and picked up Highway 37 heading east.

He was concerned about Alex's brief phone calls. *There is more going on than I know about.* He drove too fast and weaved in and out of traffic. He finally decided it would be better if he slowed down. Ending up in a wreck or delayed by a cop was not an option.

It occurred to Pete that if the thugs now knew the number of his latest motel and knew his vehicle, they might be following him. He decided that stopping for breakfast or even coffee would not be a good idea. It looked to be about a four-hour drive from San Francisco to State Line.

Pete kept a watchful eye on vehicles behind him. After Pete left the interstate and got to Placerville, California, the scenery changed to a winding road lined with pine trees. The drive became much more relaxing, particularly since it was now obvious that no one was following him. He stopped in Camino, California, and had breakfast and coffee. It was 9:30 a.m. when he walked back to his Suburban in the parking lot. It was not that much farther to Tahoe. He felt relaxed and confident. He leaned back against his Suburban and soaked in the sun. The cozy feeling didn't last very long.

A black car with tinted windows pulled into the parking lot. Pete gazed at the car with the passenger-side window rolled down. He immediately recognized one of the men from the meeting at TXA and ducked down behind the dashboard. They had not seen him, but there was no question that they would soon see the Suburban. He turned on the ignition and drove quickly onto Highway 50. The road was only two lanes and narrow with curves. He could see the black car turn in the parking lot and quickly head back onto the highway. Pete drove as fast as he could for the road conditions, which were treacherous. Large logging trucks were coming and going in both directions. Visibility was terrible because of the ever turning, twisting road. The black car pulled up beside Pete and tried to bump him off the road. A large logging truck coming from the other direction forced the black car back into its own lane. Pete had been in tight situations in some of his black op missions in the army, and his adrenalin was just as high as he ever remembered.

Whenever the black car sped up and tried to come alongside Pete, he veered out in front of it, forcing it back in the driving lane behind him. More often than not, traffic, particularly truck traffic, kept the black car from attempting to move up beside Pete. The veering autos continued their dangerous trek toward Tahoe.

The wild chase continued down the winding road into South Lake Tahoe. The TXA goons were only two cars behind Pete when they stopped at the first stoplight. As they proceeded into Lake Tahoe, the stop-and-go traffic continued with the distance between the cars not changing. Pete wondered how he was going to get them off his tail. His hands were slick with sweat, and they slipped on the steering wheel. As the next light began to turn yellow, Pete accelerated into the intersection and ran the yellow light, which changed quickly to red. The car behind Pete came to a stop, blocking the TXA black vehicle. Without much hesitation, the black car pulled around the car in front of it and ran the red light. Unfortunately for them, a Tahoe policewoman was sitting at the intersection and promptly pulled them over.

Pete laughed with relief and kept driving. As he drove over the California/Nevada line, casinos hugged the state line, rising vertically toward the heavens. It looked like the casino builders had put the buildings as close to the state line as legally possible. Pete continued on Highway 50, looking for Kingsbury Grade Road. It was the second major intersection. After turning right at the intersection, he took the first right possible, drove into the parking lot of a warehouse, and stopped near the building. Pete did not know what do next. *Am I supposed to knock on a door? How will they know I am here?*

Pete waited for a few minutes and decided to knock on some doors. He got out of the Suburban and closed the door. He turned toward the building, and a man walked up to him, seemingly from nowhere.

"Are you Pete?" he asked.

"That's me."

The man pointed toward the warehouse. "Drive your car up to that overhead door and honk once. When it opens, drive inside until your car trunk clears the door and then stop."

Once inside, the overhead door closed. Pete's eyes took awhile to adjust to the dark. A large black man opened the driver's side door and told Pete to follow him. Pete was led to an office where he sat down in front of a woman in her forties who looked like a former showgirl. It was obvious that she had once been beautiful. Time had taken its toll on her beauty, which she fought with too much eyeliner and makeup. But it was hard to cover up for what he suspected were too many years of late nights, drinking, and drugs, and the makeup did little to cover her hardened look of a life filled with hard knocks.

She looked at him without smiling. "When you leave here, you will be a different person. You will have a new name, new automobile, new clothes, and a new look. All the paperwork will be in order. You will have a driver's license, passport, birth and certificate, and your car will have new tags and registration. We will keep your auto, your clothes, and your old papers. We will give you a handgun, but you will be on your own. Do you have any questions?"

Pete was deeply concerned about his appearance and whether he would still be considered attractive to the opposite sex. He did not want a radical change in his looks, and he was concerned that he would spend his life on the run, away from family and friends. On the other hand, if a new identity and a new look kept him from being chased by Russian thugs, he could accept it without too many complaints.

The former showgirl seemed to be getting impatient for a response from Pete. Despite that, she gave Pete the impression that she really did not want to hear any questions. "I can't think of any right now."

Pete watched her as she got up and moved to the doorway. *Pretty good figure for a tough old broad. Maybe I can ask her out for a drink.*

Chapter 26

Alex woke with a start. In her dream, she was attempting to get away from a vague, indeterminable evil force she could not describe, except that she could feel that it was evil and was about to catch her. In her dream, she tried to scream but could not. She was sweating. Relieved that it was only a dream, Alex could not tell if her sweat was from the dream or from the sun outside baking the car. She looked at her watch. It was new, just like everything else she wore. She had been asleep for three hours but did not feel rested.

She got out of the car and walked back into the truck stop. The air-conditioning felt wonderful. As she ordered a cup of coffee, she wondered if she had ever been in a hotter place than the DC area.

The coffee cleared her head. She wondered how she looked after sleeping in the car. Alex went to the ladies' room and got refreshed, splashing cold water on her face and patting it dry. Things began to come back to her. She wondered how Pete was doing. He was supposed to call her when he finished. *Either he's not finished or they caught him before he got to State Line. I hope he'll call soon.*

Alex bought a map and came back to her coffee. She figured it would take her about eight hours to get to Boston. She sighed. *That's a long drive, but it's quicker than driving across Montana.* Alex gauged all distances by driving time in Montana. She did not want to waste time; she had things to do in Boston. She had to see Renata and get her pickup truck, trailer, and horses. Then she figured she would escape back to Montana. *They will be watching my townhouse. How am I going to get my pickup? Get going, girl.* She paid for her coffee and headed back into the heat.

Alex drove back onto the interstate and headed north. She drove about three hours and was feeling tired and hungry. The next truck stop was in New Jersey close to Philadelphia. She got gas, parked, and went in the truckers' eatery. When she ordered coffee, she noticed a great-looking steak being served to a trucker. She ordered steak and steak fries with her coffee. It was delicious. She thought about Pete and wondered why he had not called. She looked at her watch. It was lunchtime in Nevada. *He could still be going through his identification change. I need to stop worrying.*

Alex passed the exits for New York City. She had been driving for about three hours when her cell phone rang. *It has to be Pete.*

"Hello, Pete?"

"No. This is not Pete. This is Harold."

"How did you get this number?" Alex was startled.

"I got it the same place you did, Alex. I used to be Pete. Now I am Harold Bushman."

"You rat. You scared me half to death."

"So how are you, Alex? It is really great to hear your voice."

"I am sorry, but you have the wrong person. This is not Alex." She paused. "This is Patricia Sanchez. You can call me Pat."

Pete laughed. "Seriously, do you think that we should call each other Pat and Harold?"

"Both of our cell phones are encrypted, so I don't think it matters if we are on the phone. However, we might want to get used to our new names so we don't slip up when we are together with other people. Listen, I am headed back to Boston to pick up some of my things, and then I am heading to Montana to hide. Maybe you should think about going with me. You also need a place to hide out."

"Yeah. I was wondering which direction I should go. They told me not to go to my parents or ex-wife or any friends. I am just supposed to disappear. Isn't Montana home for you? Maybe that is not such a good idea for you."

"They told me the same thing, but Montana is a big place, and I know my way around a very large ranch and a nearby Indian reservation. I could be home for years, and neither my parents nor anyone else would see me if I do things right."

"Where are you going to spend the night?" Pete asked her.

"Boston, but I am not going to sleep at my apartment. What about you?"

"I could go north to Reno or south to Las Vegas, but I think I'll go to Reno since it's on the way to Montana."

"I have some bad news for you," said Alex. "Renata was shot. Someone thought it was me and shot her while we were running to our car. She was hit in the arm. There was a lot of blood. It was scary, but she is fine and will recover completely."

"I'm very sorry for Renata, but I'm glad it wasn't you! This whole thing has turned into something very serious. I'm glad they gave me this .38 Smith and Wesson. For the life of me, I can't figure out what TXA is doing that needs to be covered up by killing people."

"I'm going to figure it out. I have a disk with information that could tell us everything. I haven't had time to look at it, and right now I don't have a computer. I'll let you know as soon as I get a chance to review the disk."

Pete thought for a moment. "What color hair do you have, Pat?"

"I am a blond. What about you?"

"I bet you look great as a blond. I'm no longer a blond. It is brown, and I have a spiky type of hairstyle. I look like a middle-aged guy trying to look young so he can pick up chicks."

"Don't pick up too many chicks. You better be alone when I call you later," she laughed.

Alex continued her journey toward Boston and Vincent Russo's restaurant. She figured that she would arrive at the restaurant while it was still busy, and Mr. Russo would probably be there. The first thing she did upon entering the restaurant was to go to the ladies' room and apply new lipstick and makeup. She wanted to look presentable to Mr. Russo. She walked out of the ladies' room and told a waitress she wanted to see Russo. The waitress asked her name and told her to wait a minute. She came back and escorted Alex into the back dining area.

"Alex! It is so good to see you again," Russo said in his loud voice. He dominated the room. Russo's huge arms engulfed Alex in a hug that Alex could only describe as a bear hug.

"How did you like my people in Washington? Did they take good care of you? I see they turned you into an attractive blond."

"They were very helpful. Thank you, Mr. Russo, for everything you are doing to protect me. My biggest concern is Renata and how she is doing."

"She is doing great. After you have something to eat, we'll visit her. Okay?"

Alex thought it was a good idea. Even if she had not, she was concerned about disagreeing with the dynamic man. He was very persuasive. "That sounds fine, Mr. Russo, and I am hungry."

After Alex devoured another Italian dinner, she and Russo left to see Renata. They drove to a strip mall and parked near a walk-in clinic. "This isn't a hospital," Alex said.

"The doctor who runs this clinic is a friend of mine. He has a back room that is a small three-bed hospital, off the record, including a surgery room. We send people to him often. He is well paid for his work."

Russo walked around back and knocked on the door with three rapid beats and then two slow ones. A man who was obviously a guard opened the door. Alex followed Russo into a room that looked like a nursing station at a hospital, including a nurse. "Hello, Gina. How are you tonight?" Russo asked of the nurse.

"I'm fine, Mr. Russo," replied Gina. "Your daughter is doing well. You can go ahead to her room."

Passing another guard in front of Renata's room, Russo and Alex entered to a joyous Renata. Her smile was radiant. She had makeup on and was reading a copy of *People* magazine. "Dad, Alex! What a wonderful surprise."

Her arm was in a sling. Otherwise, she looked great. "Oops, oops. You are not Alex anymore. Pat? Right? Give me a hug, Pat."

"Call me whatever you like. I am just happy to see you looking so well. When do you get out of here?"

"There haven't been any complications, but I am on pain meds. I should be out in a couple of days. But I'm in no hurry to get out; the doctor is so cute. I just love being around him."

"Renata, do you ever stop thinking of men? You will probably be thinking about men on your deathbed," Alex replied with a big smile.

Renata put a sleepy smile on her face. "Sounds like it would be a lovely way to die."

Alex changed the subject, telling Russo and Renata that she was going to figure out who had shot Renata and who was following her and Pete. "I really need to get on a computer with a disk reader to figure out what's going on. I understand that everything is on this disk." She pulled a disk from her purse and held it up for them to see. "After I figure out what is going on, I will need to hide somewhere, and Montana is the logical place for me."

Mr. Russo turned to Alex. "Don't worry about going to Montana now. You are safe here in Boston. This is my territory, and I can and will protect you. But the most important thing at this time is for you to get some sleep, right? So, I'm going to put you up in a hotel at my expense for however long it takes for some resolution on these matters. Tomorrow I'll get you a computer."

Chapter 27

Alex's room was at the Boston Harbor Hotel. One of Russo's men drove her there. She left the car at the restaurant. The room was elegant, but she was too tired to explore it. She threw herself on the bed and went to sleep without changing her clothes.

She woke up with a start, initially confused about where she was and how she got there. The message light on her phone was flashing. She picked up the phone and talked to the front desk. She was told there was a bag and a package for her to pick up. She immediately recognized the bag as one she left in her car.

She waited until she was in the room to open the package and was happily surprised to find it contained a new laptop computer.

The bag had been given to her in DC as a part of the identity change. It was stressed to her that she must leave with nothing from her past. Everything she took with her had to be new. But they did not know about the disk that she retrieved just prior to her trip north.

The clothes in the bag consisted of a pair of jeans, a summer blouse, and a change of underwear. It also contained such necessary items as a toothbrush, toothpaste, hairbrush, and other travel items. She unpacked the bag and immediately took a shower.

Alex loved to wear jeans. She had grown up wearing jeans everywhere. Virtually everyone wore jeans in rural Montana, even bankers and lawyers, unless they were in court. The only problem was the jeans they had packed for Alex were designer jeans. Even though they fit, she preferred cowboy-cut jeans and without a design on the back pocket.

She changed into her new clothes and took the elevator down to the restaurant on the main floor. She ordered coffee and a large breakfast.

She had brought with her the new laptop computer. She had asked at the front desk the password to the hotel's secure WIFI. She signed onto the Internet to check it out. Everything worked perfectly. She soon realized that the computer was probably the latest in technology, and the price had to have been more than most could afford.

After breakfast, Alex went back to her room, started the computer, and loaded the disk.

The first thing that appeared on the screen was an index. She picked "Organization" and clicked on the icon. The file contained an organization chart. UPA was in a block at the top. Underneath UPA were names of a number of corporations with names that began with Z: Zafir, Corporation, Zabar, Inc., Zaad Company, Inc., Zabeeb Corporation, and many others, some bearing the designation of LLC. When she highlighted and double-clicked on a company name, information about that company would be displayed. Each corporation had the same street address in Arlington, Virginia, but with a different suite number except for one registered in Moscoe. And each one had the same lawyer as its incorporator and registered agent. Many corporation was a solely owned subsidiary of another one of the Z corporations. The organization chart was a quagmire, and Alex realized eventually that the chart was leading her in circles; there appeared to be no real owners of the companies.

There was a picture of the building at the street address in Arlington that was listed for each company. It came from Goggle Maps. It looked like a rundown, empty building.

The information on each corporation allowed Alex to review bank accounts and bank account activities. The bank accounts were all offshore accounts. There was a considerable amount of activity in each account with many millions of dollars flowing in and out of each account. Most of the inflow was from UPA. Some of the inflow was from other Z corporations. Most of the outflows were to large corporations in the defense contracting business. Some of the outflows were to other Z corporations and to conservative super PACs. The outflows from the Z companies to the defense contractors referenced invoice numbers. Alex could highlight any transaction and see a copy of the invoice. These were the same as the invoices she had seen on her computer workstation.

There were quantities and part numbers on each invoice. *Carl Jones must be one hell of a good hacker. He had to have hacked into TXA computer files and other huge defense contractor computers to get all this information. TXA has sophisticated anti-hacking software. He's good.*

Alex recognized the part numbers on the TXA invoices as missile parts and components. *Weapons. TXA is selling missiles to the Z companies. Oh my God! Who are these Z companies? Are the names Russian names?*

Alex did a Goggle search on the name Zafir. It was an Arabic word meaning "victorious." *Is TXA selling to terrorists? Oh my God, that is even worse! But where is the shipping information? There is nothing that shows where these parts are shipped.*

It became apparent to Alex that the Z corporations and their unusual names were intentional efforts to confuse anyone looking into the flow of funds. The key to what was going on had to be the location where the missile parts were shipped.

Alex began to look through the volumes of shipping orders from various defense contractors on the disk. All of them showed the destination of the goods to be US military bases, including all of TXA shipments. *There must be a way to connect an invoice to a shipping order.* Alex saw a TXA shipping order with Malstrom Air Force base, Great Falls, Montana, as the destination and decided to try to find a connection between one of the invoices and that shipping order. After hours of searching, Alex noticed that if she read the number on an invoice backward, it matched a shipping order with the same goods listed as those listed on the invoice.

An invoice from TXA to Zafir Corporation for a long list of part numbers with invoice number 357951 matched a shipping order for those same parts being shipped to Malstrom Air Force Base with the number 159753. Alex noticed that the shipment was to be made in just over a week.

"Let's get this straight, Alex," she said to herself. "Shell corporations are ordering missile parts from TXA, and TXA is shipping them to US military bases around the country, including Malstrom. That doesn't make any sense. Further, the shell corporations are getting the money to pay for the missiles from UPA, and part of that money is coming from TXA contributions to the super PAC UPA. That also does not make any sense."

Alex sat back from the computer to summarize what she was seeing. *UPA is a super PAC, dedicated to corporations and conservative causes, and gets contributions from large corporations, both here and abroad, including TXA. UPA does not have to disclose where the money comes from or how much is received, so no one knows that TXA is giving money to UPA. Everyone knows UPA funds conservative causes, but a majority of the money goes to the Z corporations. Probably billions of dollars. The Z corporations buy military goods and hardware from the defense industry with the money sent in by the donors. One of the donors is TXA, and they are getting part of it back by selling its military hardware to the Z corporations. But what are the Z corporations doing with the military goods? From the records on the Jones disk, they are shipped to our own military bases. Why would UPA have this elaborate scheme to supply military goods to our own military? Something must be happening to the goods once they arrive at the military bases. Are they being given to terrorists? That doesn't make sense. UPA is for big oil and against unrest in the Middle East. They wouldn't be shipping arms to the terrorists. Something is happening to those missile parts once they get to Malstrom and the other military bases. What is it?*

Alex had to take a break. She had been staring at the laptop screen for six hours without anything more than a bathroom break. She decided to take a walk outside and get something to eat.

The Boston Harbor Hotel overlooked Boston Harbor. Alex walked down to the docks and viewed the boats. It was early September; the temperature had cooled off, and the breeze off the ocean felt cool on her skin, and the sun felt warm on her face. It was a perfect combination of temperatures. The day was a harbinger of fall, and the view was thrilling. The sun was bouncing off the choppy water in the harbor; everything was sparkling, colorful, and warm. She wanted someone to share this scene with and then realized that she had not talked to Pete last night. It was 2:00 p.m. Boston time and noon Reno time. She used her encrypted phone and dialed Pete's new cell number. A groggy Pete answered his cell.

"Get up, sleepyhead."

"You are always waking me up. I was sleeping soundly, and you startled me back into this cruel world."

"Run and get some coffee and call me back. I've got lots to tell you."

Pete was staying at the Sands Regency in downtown Reno. He had gambled late into the night, winning at first but ultimately losing.

He was proud of himself for only having had one drink, considering the atmosphere in the casino. He thought about how much additional money he would have lost if he had been drunk. He felt he had his drinking problem under control. He made coffee in his room, drank a cup, and showered before returning Alex's call.

Alex told Pete about the trips to Russo's restaurant, to the clinic, and to the Boston Harbor Hotel.

"I finally had a chance this morning to review the disk Carl Jones gave me. It tells me that TXA and UPA are in some type of scheme involving the shipment of military hardware, paid for under the table by PAC contributions. I think that both UPA and TXA are responsible for what has happened to us and to Renata. Unfortunately, more parts of the puzzle need to be put together."

Pete asked her some questions that caused her to go into more detail about what she had found on the disk. She finished by saying, "And so two of the missing pieces of the puzzle are why do the shipments go to our military bases and what happened happens to them after arrival? We can find out the answers to those questions by going to one of the military bases receiving shipments. That means we are going to have to break into Malmstrom Air Force Base."

"What?" yelled Pete. "Break into a military base? You are out of your mind. They will put us both in Leavenworth and throw away the key, assuming they don't kill us first. No, no, no. I want no part of that."

"Ah, come on, Pete. Don't you have a sense of adventure? Don't you want to find out what's going on?" Alex's voice was sweet and pleading.

"Alex, we could get our asses in a bigger sling than they are already. Aren't you the least bit concerned after being shot at? You told me about Carl Jones telling you about the danger and how he said to throw the disk away and get lost. We need to take that advice."

"Well, we might not have to break in to accomplish our goal. I have some ideas."

Alex finished her conversation with Pete but didn't feel she had convinced him to break into Malstrom Air Force Base. At least she had brought him up to date on her findings about TXA and UPA. Next she needed to tell Dominic Russo what she had learned and tell him who she believed had shot at her and hit Renata instead. She planned to meet Dominic Russo that evening at his restaurant.

The thought of meeting with Russo concerned Alex. He was, as best she could tell, a leader in organized crime. *Is he mafia? Does the mafia even exist anymore? He can be so kind and loving. I don't feel threatened, yet he is such a powerful person. Alex, girl, put aside all your preconceptions and concerns and just go talk to him.*

At 7:00 p.m., Alex walked from the hotel to Russo's Italian restaurant, told the doorman her name, and said that she wanted to see Mr. Russo. She was escorted to the back room where Russo sat with a table full of men, all drinking. When he saw her, he motioned for her to come with him to his office nearby. He closed the door behind her.

"How are you, Alex? Did you sleep well?"

"Thank you for putting me in such a beautiful, comfortable place."

"There is no need to thank me. A friend of my daughter is a friend of mine."

"I spent some time studying the disk and thinking about what has happened to all of us. I know who shot Renata."

"And?"

"It had to have been done by hired guns for UPA. UPA is a super PAC."

"I know who they are. I read a considerable amount."

"UPA is involved in some kind of criminal scheme that also involves my former employer, TXA. It has to be criminal; otherwise they would not be killing or trying to kill those who learn about it."

"How do you know that it was UPA people that shot her?"

"You remember I told you that Renata and I went to the office where Clancy was murdered? When we left, we were followed by two cars. One was driven by a woman, and the other had two men in it that I had never seen. The TXA person who was following me was a heavyset man with a beard. I have seen him following me quite a few times. So it was not TXA who did it."

"How do you know it was UPA then?"

"The building where Clancy was killed is owned by a corporation that is controlled by UPA. The lawyer for UPA is also the lawyer for the corporation. All of the money that goes to the corporation comes from UPA. Clancy was told to use that office by Butch Butler, the assistant to the senator who hired Clancy to investigate UPA. Butler is on UPA's payroll. The office had a surveillance room that they used to spy on her. When she was getting close to the truth, they killed her."

"How do you know this Butch Butler is on UPA's payroll?"

"Clancy took pictures of the pages in a book that was in General Preston White's desk. The book contained lists of government officials and others who are being paid by UPA. White is the CEO of UPA."

"Yeah. I know who he is. I also know that UPA group."

Dominic stood up and walked around the room. Alex could feel his powerful presence across the room. She didn't know whether to fear or admire him. Perhaps both.

"Alex, let me tell you a few things," he said. "I am a businessman. I read a great deal. I know a lot of rich and powerful people. And this I do know: UPA promotes the idea that corporations should control this country. Nothing could be more harmful. Nothing could be worse for us."

Alex was surprised. She didn't expect that Russo would have a passion for political ideals. "Why do you say that, Mr. Russo?" she asked, somewhat intimidated.

"Corporations have no heart, no soul. People who call themselves businessmen hide behind them, use them to protect themselves," said Russo. His tone of voice was emphatic and strong. "Corporations have two purposes, to make money and to hide those for whom they make money. They are not for the good of the people."

Alex could hardly believe what she was hearing. *He is a criminal. Why would he care for the good of the people?*

"I know what you're thinking, Alex, and I cannot criticize you for thinking it. I know you think of me as a criminal, a member of the mob, organized crime, mafia, and all the other terms for it. But I tell you, Alex, many of those who run the big corporations, particularly in the financial sector, should have been put in prison for the harm they have done to the American people. They take, take, take money away from the everyday Joe and put it in their pockets."

Russo paused for a moment, paced to the other side of the room and back, and leveled his eyes directly into Alex's.

"I don't do anything to hurt people anymore. Maybe at one time… but even then I made money off of people's vices. I did not take homes or jobs away from the poor. Corporations, and banks are corporations also, can and have done so."

"But isn't it the same thing if you take a man's money from his family when he gambles it away?" asked Alex.

"No. The banks intentionally lured families who were not credit worthy with subprime loans into borrowing money for a home that was overvalued. They knew their house of cards would tumble. When it did, it almost broke the back of this country, let alone the families who lost their homes."

Alex wanted to change the subject back to UPA. "The thing that bothers me is that donations by corporations to UPA and other super PACs are not disclosed," Alex said. "And UPA is hiding what it is really doing with the money. As I said before, whatever it is they are doing, it is criminal; otherwise they would not be trying to kill people who look into it."

"We can thank the Supreme Court for this mess," replied Russo. "They ruled that corporations have the right of free speech, even though they cannot think, and that corporations have the right to give, without disclosure, unlimited amounts of money for political purposes, even though they cannot vote. Should it surprise anyone that their rulings have been the wellspring of the criminal activity you have uncovered?"

He continued, his voice raised. "This is fascism, the merger of corporations and government. My father, God bless his soul, saw this under Mussolini in the old country. It did not work there, and it will not work here."

"Mr. Russo, I agree with all that you say. I think I can help uncover their activity. I know of a way I can find out what exactly UPA and TXA are doing. All I have to do is go to Malstrom Air Force Base in Montana and find out what the TXA missiles are being used for."

"How can you do that?"

"The disk I was reviewing showed that a shipment of missile parts is due there in eight days. I can show up at the same time as the shipment and follow its progress to see where it goes. I want to meet my friend Pete Oxwood there, and we can check it out together."

"Oh yes, Mr. Oxwood. He visited us in our State Line office. Even without him, I believe you can do it. You have heart. That's important. And if you get in a pinch, you can always call me."

"After all you have done, I hate to ask another favor."

"No problem. What is it?"

"I need to get my truck back from in front of my apartment, but I feel sure the place is being watched, and I don't think it is safe for me to go there. The keys to the truck are inside the apartment."

"I can take care of that. You have a good dinner here and get some sleep in your room. The pickup will be here tomorrow morning."

Later that night in Southborough, two men drove up to the front of Alex's apartment and stopped. Because the apartment's parking lot was poorly lit, it was impossible to get a good look at them. The man on the passenger side got out and quickly walked up to Alex's truck. He pulled something from his jacket and moved in close to the driver's side door. In a few seconds, the door opened, and the man jumped in. He disappeared under the steering wheel. A few seconds more, and the truck started. He backed up and followed his partner's car out of the parking lot.

Two other men were in a car nearby facing Alex's truck. One was asleep, and the other was in a relaxed stupor. He was jolted out of his reverie by the man who jumped in Alex's truck.

"Wake up. Wake up. Someone is stealing her truck."

Before he could start the car, the thieves had already disappeared.

The next morning, there was a message for Alex at the front desk stating that her truck would be available at noon at the restaurant and that keys were being made for it. Alex decided to have breakfast at the hotel and think about her plans. Alex ordered a big breakfast as usual. She had a high metabolism and burned up the excess food quickly.

She decided that she would drive to her bank and withdraw cash. From her extensive reading of detective stories, she surmised that UPA or TXA would have her account monitored and would be alerted when she withdrew the money. But they would not know which of the many branch banks she would visit, and they did not know about her change in appearance. So she felt safe that the only thing they would learn was that she was in Boston.

She decided on a plan, left the restaurant, and went back to her room to pack for her trip. She called Pete, and they agreed to meet in Chicago at a yet to be determined place. She also called Renata to tell her good-bye, but she did not tell her about her potentially dangerous plans. At noon, she picked up her Dodge pickup at the restaurant. There was a new license plate on the truck with her old plates in the backseat. The truck was freshly painted a bland color so it wouldn't stand out or command attention.

Alex parked the truck near the main office of her bank. She figured that even if TXA goons were at the main office, they would have difficulty picking her out of a crowd, particularly with her short blond hair. She stood outside the bank, watching people walk in. She wanted to enter the bank at a time when it was crowded and the teller lines were long. She also wanted to make sure there were at least two women who were as tall or taller than her in the bank when she entered.

At a few minutes after 3:45 p.m., a large group of women entered the bank at about the same time. They looked like they might be from the secretarial pool at a large law firm. Several of the women were tall, three to be exact, each one with a different style and color of hair and color. Alex followed them into the lobby and joined a teller line as if she were with them. They were all talking to each another. She did not want to look out of place, so she started talking to the girl in front of her about how beautiful the day was, whether or not she had kids, where she worked, and what her husband did. When she reached the head of the line, Alex had planned to draw out all her money, but she realized it would cause certain extra bank procedures to kick in if she took out over $10,000. If there was a delay, TXA could start looking at the cameras before she got out of the bank. To be safe, she asked for $9,500, which would be more than enough to get her to Montana; she would get the rest of the money in the future. Once she had the $9,500, she had an urge to run out of the bank, but she knew that would draw attention, so she decided to blend with the other secretaries going home after work.

Alex got in her truck and drove toward Marlborough where she boarded her horses. The drive was about an hour in the four o'clock traffic, and she had time to think. It occurred to her that she should call ahead in case she got there after five. She would need to pay her last month's boarding charges. She didn't want to leave a forwarding address to Montana.

After calling the stables on her cell, she wondered if TXA had the stables staked out. If so, she felt she was ready. One of her Colt pistols was in the glove compartment and the other under her seat, both loaded with live ammunition. Despite her confidence, she was still concerned. *I've never shot a person before. If they try to stop me, I'll have no choice but to shoot to kill. Dead men tell no tales.* The last thought dwelt in her head. It frightened her somewhat that she was the kind of person who could harbor such thoughts, but she quickly put things into perspective. *They tried to kill me. They missed, but I won't.*

Chapter 28

The TXA facilities at Palo Alto looked more like a college campus than a corporate office. The trees, shrubs, and landscaping had all been professionally planned. It created an image of quiet sophistication and culture. The buildings had been designed to create a serene, peaceful ambiance similar to the La Jolla based Neurosciences Institute. Undoubtedly beautiful, it was nonetheless a deception. The apparent temple to knowledge and science was actually dedicated to the God of greed and power.

One of the buildings was not beautiful. It was block-like, made entirely of concrete and without windows. Antennas of various sizes and shapes adorned its roof along with communication satellite dishes pointing in various directions and a structure resembling a small cell phone tower in the middle of the roof.

The concrete block building was connected to a building located in the least conspicuous part of the campus.

The entrance to the concrete building, which was located in the back, looked like a window-less service door. Two men entered the door.

"This way, General White," said Ron Fenton. "You are about to see some of the great things the private sector of this country can accomplish without government assistance."

Ron Fenton was the TXA director of security. He had been an officer in the Army Military Police and had then joined the CIA thereafter. He had mysteriously disappeared while on assignment with the CIA in Russia. He had been seen from time to time around Europe, but it was unknown whom he worked for. In November 2008, he had been hired to his present post with TXA. The concrete building was erected after he took the job. Rumors had it that Fenton was a confidant of Dmitri Zakhar, former KGB agent and the new general manager of the TXA plant in Southborough. They were allegedly involved in espionage activity together in Europe.

Fenton continued, "As a matter of fact, private industry is close to surpassing the US government in surveillance sophistication, and we are in the forefront of that cutting-edge technology."

"Accomplishment through free enterprise: that's what I like to hear!" the general replied. "I've been waiting a long time to see this facility."

They took an elevator to the top floor. A massive room full of flat-screen monitors greeted them. The monitors covered the walls from desk height to the ceiling. Workstations were located around the room, each with multiple monitors. The monitors on the walls were streaming videos. In front of each workstation sat a male or female operator looking at their monitors. Their ages ranged from teens to seniors. Every now and then, they would glance up at the video monitors on the wall. Each station had what appeared to be game controllers that the operators would use to zoom in or out on a video or move it from side to side.

"This is a rather eclectic group of people," General White commented as he looked around the room. "What are their backgrounds?"

"Virtually all of them are computer hackers," replied Fenton. "Their jobs are to hack into every database, surveillance system, and control system in this country to allow us to potentially control the country. They are indeed an odd lot. They come from the best technical schools, prisons, basements, and anywhere there are talented hackers who are willing to work for the highest bidder. Many of them have been in prison for computer hacking crimes. Those are the easiest to recruit. You can identify a lot of them by their prison tattoos. They are a sharp contrast with the college geeks."

"Tell me more about your control systems," said White.

"We can hack into any video surveillance system that is digitally controlled. We can take over any kind of power plant, even nuclear, railroad control systems, or air traffic control systems; we can bring the country to a complete halt. If there is a digital control box and digital communications to and from that box located anywhere in this country, we can control it."

"Impressive. You will be playing an important role for us. You did a good job for me in the army, Col. Fenton, and I expect the same now."

General White walked to a workstation and looked over the shoulder of a female operator. "Have her show me what she can do."

"Okay, General. We can pick any person in this country to spy on, but who is your most hated political rival? Maybe we have some dirt on him."

"How about Senator W. Jennings Randolph?"

"Trixie. Pull up Senator Randolph for us."

A picture of the senator flashed up on the screen along with basic information about his address, wife, children, education, work history, and a variety of other areas. There were numerous hyperlinks to choose from. The general pointed at the screen. "Click on Present Location."

Trixie did as directed, and a map of Arlington, Virginia, popped up on the screen with an arrow pointing to an intersection with the address displayed next to the arrow. General White was amazed. "How do you do that?"

"Cell phones are easily tracked. Most have GPS location devices in them. Even without them, we have the capability of determining the location of any cell phone. A person can turn off the location services on his or her phone, but that doesn't prevent us from measuring the signal from any tower and triangulating the location. That is how the E911 works. Not only that, but we can use a spy satellite to zoom in on the triangulated location. We obtain the signal from commercial satellites that now rival the quality of the government's spy satellites. In this case, the senator has his GPS locator on, so it makes it easier. Trixie, zoom in on that cell location."

The picture on the screen showed Arlington, then zoomed to the intersection and then to the senator's limo.

"That means that anyone could locate where I am right now and take a picture," said General White.

"The answer is yes, but not just anyone can do it. Technical sophistication is necessary. A motivated hacker who has access to a telephone network's switching equipment for mobile communications, access to a spy satellite, and an encryption algorithm can locate you and take your picture. This kind of technical capability narrows the field as to who can accomplish these kinds of surveillance to governments and very large corporations. And we at TXA are at the top of the capable corporations. Further, I think we are ahead of the FBI and CIA."

"In other words, if they have enough money, someone can track me by my cell phone," replied the general.

"It means that the only way to prevent someone from tracking you is to turn off your cell phone and take out the battery. Trixie, listen in to what Senator Randolph is saying."

Trixie clicked on several links on the screen. "His voice communication is encrypted."

"Try some of our new encryption buster algorithms."

Trixie clicked on several links on the screen. Suddenly the senator's voice came in over the speakers. The group listened to his conversation for a few minutes.

"He is talking to his staff. Nothing juicy."

"What other information can you give me about the senator?"

Over the next fifteen minutes, the group learned the location of the senator's new young wife, who was shopping in a mall, and where his two children were, who were college age and goofing off. They also learned that the senator had used his influence to get his son off of a drug charge at *the* University. They even learned the senator's bank balances in the United States and those accounts in the Cayman Islands.

Each of the family members had a hyperlink to Sexual History. "What have you got on that old coot Randolph and his pretty young wife?" asked White.

It was clear that Randolph liked younger women and was famous for his dalliances. His young wife was a power groupie, one of those women who liked to attach to older men in high government positions in Washington. She apparently had had several affairs with Washington elite before she snagged the senator.

General White looked concerned. "There is nothing I can hide from you, is there?"

"That is true, sir, but we have no reason to be snooping at your background. You're on our side. We don't have enough manpower or time to snoop in on everyone, just those who cause us concern."

"That's good to know," replied General White. "Keep up the good work."

"Thank you for the kind words, General."

"You would make J. Edgar proud, Col. Fenton."

Chapter 29

The Sebastian, Vail, was one of those resort-meeting hotels catering to the money class. It was designed with luxury in mind to please those who had plenty to spend. During the last week of August, there was a group meeting at the Sebastian that had no name. Everyone referred to it as "the business meeting." No one at the Sebastian knew anything about the meeting other than the attendees would consist of about fifty business executives. Only the head of marketing for the Sebastian knew the name of the person who made the arrangements for this meeting, and she was told to keep it a secret. The Sebastian staff was told they could not discuss the meeting with anyone, under penalty of being fired.

Lt. General Prescott White was the first person who walked into the meeting room. He made sure that the coffee and morning snacks were in place and then stood by the door greeting people as they entered. Those attending were not any ordinary group of executives. These were the top executives of some of America's biggest corporations, particularly those in the defense contracting business and the petroleum industry but also executives from the banks that were too large to fail, executives from Wall Street and insurance companies. Of particular note was the fact that there were no women executives in the group. Another was that there was no literature distributed and no notepaper allowed. General White seemed to know each of their names.

There were guards posted around the room. Everyone was frisked when they came through the door. Electronic sensors were in place to make sure no one was recording the meeting.

As everyone began to sit down, White went to the podium in front. In the peculiar lighting for the podium, White looked more sinister than usual. The scar on his face was more visible. His facial expressions showed hatred.

"Greetings, gentlemen. As you know, this meeting is secret, and you are not to take notes or record any part of this meeting. We do not want any information to fall into the wrong hands. Also, as you know, this is our last meeting before the big event. Each of you knows what is expected of you. This weekend, through a series of committee meetings, we will go through the details one more time to make sure we are ready when you go back home and meet with your subgroups. Before we go into our meetings, it's important for me to remind you why we have dedicated ourselves to this monumental task."

General White paused for dramatic effect, straightened his back, leaned forward, and continued. "This country has the most regulated, overtaxed businesses in the world. The money that should be going to our shareholders is being spent on the poor, the sick, the illegal immigrants, Planned Parenthood, abortion, medical attention to keep poor old people alive, and a host of other ideas dreamed up by the antibusiness community in this country. To make matters worse, the government that spends the money is managed by people who have no business management experience, and the result is monumental inefficiency and waste. This county needs you, even if it does not know it yet.

"What we are doing shows pure patriotism on our part. The country needs to return to its roots. We have tried very hard over the last several years to form a political coalition to take back control. We have spent millions upon millions of dollars. We formed a coalition of unlikely allies including the Catholic clergy, the KKK, the Tea Party, bikers and truckers, John Birchers, the Christian Identity movement, the NRA, and many others. Despite this, we have failed politically. Washington is in gridlock, and the minority population is growing at such a rapid rate as to soon dominate whites. Gentlemen, we need you. You are the best and the brightest. Together we can lead America back to greatness. That is all for now, gentlemen. God bless you all and God bless the United States of America."

White went from committee to committee, visiting with the groups and some of the individuals. He began a dialog with the members of the committee he called Foreign Relations. "How are things going with the Saudis?" White asked the head of the committee. The chairman of the committee was heavy, like a person who sat behind a desk and never got exercise. He was round—his face was round; his stomach was round. He was bald on top with a ring of white hair around the sides.

"The Saudis are in line. They believe in us; after all, they are really like us in many ways. At least that's the way we see it in the oil business. In fact, all the Middle East is behind us except the Muslim religious terrorists and Iran. Let them battle things out with Israel."

"How about Canada?"

"The Canadians are so mad about the pipeline being stopped that they are willing to help also. It is ironic that the place where the pipeline would have crossed the Montana border is very near the place we have picked for bringing in our hired help."

"Yes. I know. It is not ironic. I planned it that way," replied White.

"General, may I interrupt?" A man came up behind White. It was the chairman of TXA. "I need to talk to you for a minute." They walked far enough away that no one could overhear their conversation.

"Okay. What's up?"

"We have a problem with the two TXA employees that have looked into our data files."

"Why are they a problem? Just kill them!" the general responded.

"It's not that easy. They have disappeared. Vanished into thin air."

"How can that be? TXA has the most sophisticated electronic tracking and communication search capability in the world. It rivals, if not exceeds, the government's capability."

"I understand, General. Even though the two people involved are smart, they could not vanish without someone's help, someone who also has capabilities."

"Well, we know it's not the government who helped them. Key government personnel have been on our side from the start. The rest we have bought off, including the FBI, Homeland Security, and the border guards, as well as communications security agencies everywhere. They redirect or eliminate anyone who tries to investigate or snoop into our business."

"If it's not the government, who is it?"

"We'll find out. What you need to do is post some of our assets near the two TXA employee's homes, as well as their friends and relatives' homes. Find out everything about them. Post people everywhere you think they might go. If they have disappeared, they will surface somewhere familiar to them. Once we find those two, we will find out if there is an organized group against us. We will force it out of them. Water boarding will be like a picnic compared with the techniques they are in for. Now get moving!"

Chapter 30

A large U-Haul type moving van pulled out of Malmstrom Air Force Base. It wound through the streets of Great Falls and turned onto US Highway 87, heading east and southeast. It was not a military vehicle, nor colored like one. It had a dark grayish, greenish hue. There was no writing on the truck, no logos, no advertising. It was as inconspicuous as possible for a large truck.

It was only 5:00 p.m., and the sun was edging toward the horizon; it was a typical Montana September afternoon. The truck was heading eastward with the setting sun behind it. Lacking humidity, smog, or dust, the air was as clear as a sparkling crystal glass, making the sun too bright to look at. Driving west would be difficult even with sunglasses. However, this truck was pointing east, and visibility was as good as anywhere in the world.

The driver had made this run many times and was getting tired of the repetition. However, when he considered the cause, the tedious drive was worth it. He pulled a can of Copenhagen from his shirt pocket and stuffed a large chew into his lip. On the seat next to him was a red coffee can he used as a spittoon. He wore old military fatigues without badges or identification. In his belt holster was a .38-caliber Smith and Wesson.

The highway was narrow. Driving this road required his complete attention. He knew deer would be crossing the road soon, which always posed the threat of a dangerous accident. But that was the purpose of the large front grill guard. It was unwise to try to evade deer that wandered onto the road. Evading them was a good way to end up in the ditch. The deer could still move in front of the vehicle whichever direction you swerved. Further east, the road would be flat and straight, but the deer would still be everywhere. It was best to stay in your lane and not to hit the brake hard.

His name was Frank Smith. He was short, age fifty-three, had a beer paunch, and was balding. His complexion was pasty white. Frank looked like thousands of other guys his age. There was nothing about him to make him stand out in a crowd. When he talked, however, it was clear that he was very opinionated and had little education. He had been a long-haul truck driver for twenty-five years and had saved some money. He had bought twenty acres and a mobile home with cash. He had no debt. His wife worked as a waitress and provided them with all the cash he wanted or needed. He was very proud of what he had accomplished. He felt if he could do it all by himself, everyone could do it and those on unemployment were weak and lazy.

As the driving became easier the further east he drove, Frank had plenty of time to think about what was happening to America. He believed Mexicans and blacks were taking over the country with the help of liberal communists. Ultraliberal atheists, except one news channel and a few radio commentators, ran most of the news media. He despised the government. It kept passing policies to take away his family's freedom. He felt that measures needed to be taken to get the county back into the hands of true Christian Americans. The attempted political solution had not worked. Despite the influence of the Tea Party and the election of patriots at the state and federal level, the government had not changed. Drastic measures were necessary.

It was getting dark when he reached Lewistown, Montana, home to six thousand people and the Yogo Sapphire. The sapphire mine was fifty miles from Lewistown, but fifty miles was a close distance to Montanans, so the mine was considered to be in Lewistown. At that time of the evening, there was little activity in the small city, and he slowed down to the speed limit. The very last thing he or the organization could afford was for the truck to be pulled over and have a law enforcement officer ask what he was hauling. The driver put another chew of Copenhagen in his mouth and continued east.

He drove through the town of Grass Range, population 150, where Highway 87 turned south toward Billings. However, he did not turn south; he continued east on Montana Highway 200. He saw neither cars nor people. Typical. Farther up the road, he reached Winnett, which had a population of 160 souls. Still no cars, no people. He had once heard that Winnett was not the end of the world but it could be seen from there.

Ahead, Highway 200 crossed the Musselshell River and continued toward Jordan, Montana. In Jordan, Highway 200 made a sharp right turn. However, Smith continued straight on a country road headed north toward the Missouri Breaks and the Charles Russell Wildlife Refuge, very rough country.

He began to slowly bounce north on the rough road. It had no gravel; it was just dirt. The truck lights revealed only the empty road and barbed-wire fences. It was dark and silent. There was nothing out there but animals, and Frank could not see them. He felt tired. He didn't need to be at the compound until dawn and decided to pull off the road and sleep for a couple of hours. It would be safer than proceeding in the dark.

He stepped out of the cab to relieve himself. It was so dark he couldn't see his hand in front of his face. The only sound was the wind blowing, which whistled around the truck. He locked the cab and put his .38 within easy reach.

Miles ahead of Frank's truck, at the top of a high hill, a man lay on the ground near the road. A dark horse was standing over him, reins loose and hanging down, saddle still on. A cowboy hat lay on the ground ten yards away. The horse snorted, and the man slowly opened his eyes. The sky was turning pink off to the east. He was still a little drunk as he staggered to his feet and looked around. After getting a bearing on where he was, he talked to the horse. "Good boy, Midnight. You are a good Indian pony. You will get many apples when we get back to the rez."

His name was Max Iron Cloud, a Sioux Indian from Fort Peck Indian reservation. He was a poacher. He had killed an elk the day before near the point where the Musselshell River flows into Fort Peck Reservoir, a reservoir that had been created by damming the Missouri River. He knew killing the elk at this time of year was a crime in the Charles Russell Wildlife Refuge and that the penalty was harsh. However, this was not the first time he had poached here. He had a great deal of experience.

He had gutted and quartered the elk and put it in a cool location. He would later come by boat across Fort Peck Reservoir to the entry point of the Musselshell. The boat had a false bottom. He would store the elk below deck and head downriver and across the reservoir to the "rez." People in Montana shortened the word "reservation" to simply rez. Even if Montana Fish and Game got on the boat, they could not find the elk.

Max couldn't ride his horse and pack out the elk at the same time, so he had devised the false-bottom boat. It was more dangerous to pack the elk out than to float it across the reservoir. The US Fish and Wildlife had jurisdiction on the land while Montana Fish and Game had jurisdiction on the water. There were considerable more federal agents, and he was more fearful of them than he was of Montana Fish and Game agents.

Max looked Indian but dressed like a cowboy, which was very common on the Montana Indian reservations. He was about six feet tall and in excellent shape. He had few problems in his life except alcohol, and that was only from time to time. After killing the Elk yesterday, he had decided to celebrate and had drunk Jim Beam from a pint bottle he carried in his coat pocket. He had sung and talked to Midnight as he rode back toward his rig, a 1988 Ford F150 and an old single horse trailer. He could not remember falling off his horse the night before. Midnight was getting used to it.

As Max looked around, trying to clear his head, he reached for the bottle that was not there. "Damn," he said.

Then he noticed a vehicle miles away heading north toward him, its headlights rising and falling as it went over the rough road. Max retrieved a canteen of water from his gear on Midnight.

"Good pony," he said again as he turned to watch the vehicle come closer. When it got closer, Max saw that it was a truck, a big one.

"What would a big truck be doing out here?" Max asked, as if the horse could answer him.

Thinking it might be a government truck, he decided to move where he and the horse could not be seen. As it passed him, Max noticed there was nothing on the truck to identify it and decided he and Midnight would follow it at a distance.

Ahead of Max and Midnight, the truck went up one of many hills, passed over the rise in the road, and went out of sight. When Max came over the rise, the truck had disappeared. He urged Midnight forward. He only had to raise his heel and touch the horse's side, and it would break into a gallop. After some distance, he still could not see the truck.

It had really disappeared. He knew that the truck could not have gotten so far ahead of him that Midnight could not catch it. The truck must have turned off somewhere. He turned Midnight around and headed back up the road. It was now light enough to track, and Max looked for tire marks.

As he neared the spot where he had lost sight of the truck, he noticed tire marks heading into a rough area. He followed the tracks and came upon what looked like a huge boulder in the road. He touched the rock and realized it was not a rock but some lightweight material made to look like a boulder. He pushed it. It was so light it easily went to the side of the road. The tire tracks went through the boulder so the driver must have gotten out, moved the boulder, driven ten yards, and then moved the boulder back. Max followed the tracks past the rock. The tracks went into the side of the mountain.

Max knew that God did not make fake rocks and allow trucks to drive through the sides of mountains. He reasoned there was a hidden entrance into the mountain and wondered if it was a secret government site. He yanked the reins, turning Midnight in a fast circle. They circled twice. Taking one last glance, he urged Midnight into a gallop back toward his rig. When he reached his hidden rig, he put Midnight in the trailer, leaving the saddle on, and drove off toward the Fred Robinson Bridge to cross the Missouri River and return to the reservation.

Chapter 31

In the control center in Palo Alto, Trixie was busy working on several jobs, one of which was to determine the location of Alex Pipe. A message flashed up on her monitor. She said into her intercom, "We've got a bank withdrawal by Alex Pipe in progress."

Ron Fenton rushed over to Trixie's station. "Where?"

"Sovereign Bank, Boston financial district."

"Switch on the surveillance cams."

The technician typed codes into her computer, directing the video surveillance system at the bank to be displayed on one of the monitors. From her keyboard, she could control the system.

"Zoom in on the teller lines."

The screen showed eight teller lines. In four of the lines, people were finishing transactions, and in the other four, the tellers were still working with the customers. Of the four that were finishing, three were women, and of those, two were above average in height. Both were blonds, one with short hair and one with average-length hair.

"She used to be a brunette with long hair. She must have dyed and cut it. But which one of those two is her?"

"I'll bet it's the one in the jeans. The other woman is dressed like she's been working in an office."

The technician tried various views of both women as they left the lobby. They then switched to the outdoor cameras to follow the girls.

"Let's try to see what kind of vehicles they get into."

The women had gone in almost opposite directions, but neither one was parked close enough to the bank for the camera to determine their vehicles.

"Damn! Well, at least we know she is back in the Boston area, is now a blond, and is probably wearing jeans. But we don't know what she is driving or where she is going next."

The man who had done none of the talking said, "Maybe she is driving her truck. Her truck was stolen while several of our men were watching her home. Maybe she had someone steal it for her."

"Okay. Let's assume she is driving her truck. Where would she be going? Put yourself in her shoes. Where would she want to go first?"

"Wait, wait, wait. Remember Harry calling in and telling us she was at some horse event somewhere in Massachusetts a week or so back? Maybe she owns horses and is going to get them. That could be the reason she owns a pickup to start with."

"Possibly. But where are the horses?"

"Harry might know. He was following her that day."

"Get Harry on the line."

Trixie pushed a button on her console.

"Harry, what's your location?"

"I am about an hour and a half south of Boston headed north. Whatcha need?"

"Did Alex Pipe own a horse?"

"Yeah. Two actually."

"Do you know where she keeps them?"

"In a stable near Marlborough."

"How far away are you from the stable?"

"A couple of hours, maybe a little more."

"She is back in Massachusetts, and we think she is driving to the stable to pick up her horses as we speak. Check it out, and if you find her, take her out."

"I'm on my way."

#

It was after five when Alex pulled in front of the office at the stables in Marlborough. She paid the owner for the rent and for hay and grain to take on the trip and went into the barn where her horses, Duke and Hank, were kept. She talked to them; they were obviously happy to see her. Afterward, she hitched up her horse trailer to the pickup and loaded hay and grain into the trailer. It was now 6:30, and she knew it would be getting dark soon. Before she left, she wanted to give her horses some exercise. It would be a long trip. She jumped on Hank's back and rode bareback into the arena, using her knees to guide the horse. She rode them both long enough for the horses to break a sweat.

By the time she finished riding, it was after seven. It was getting dark, and everyone else who had been riding had left. While she was loading her saddles and other tack into the trailer, she found one of her gun belts with two holsters among the bridles and blankets. She buckled on the belt and walked to the cab of the pickup and put her new Colts in the two holsters. *I might have some unwelcome visitors. Better safe than sorry.*

She tied up both horses to the side of the trailer, but before she put the horses in the trailer, she decided to walk back to the tack area in the barn to make sure she had gotten everything.

After Alex checked the tack room, she closed and locked the door. Outlined against the dusky light coming through the barn door she saw a figure. The figure moved into the darker shadows inside the barn. The outline was of a man, no question. She stepped into a vacant horse stall and drew a Colt from one holster. She listened. It was silent other than the movement of some of the horses in the barn. *If this man belonged here, he would not silently duck into the shadows.*

She peeked around the corner of the stall toward the front of the barn but couldn't see anything. *He's on the same side of the barn as I am. To get a better look, I need to be on the other side in that stall across from me. I need to get over there. If I go to the back of this stall and start running toward the other side, I will gather more speed and cross the open space more quickly.*

Without giving it more thought, she went to the back of the stall and ran as fast as she could to the stall on the other side. Alex felt the wind of a bullet missing her head and saw a flash out of the corner of her eye followed by the gun report. *Close! He won't expect me to immediately turn around and run back. He will lower his gun for second, probably blinded a little from the flash.*

She immediately turned around and ran back toward the stall she had just left with both guns drawn. She twisted her body slightly to the right and aimed at the spot where the flash had come from, about three feet off the ground and four feet from the edge of the barn door. She jumped toward the opposite side of the barn. Her feet left the ground, and she fired both Colts in midair. A fraction of a second after she pulled the triggers, she heard another shot coming from the opposite direction. No bullet whizzed by this time. She scrambled to one knee, covered with hay and dirt, and turned toward the open stall door. She listened. *I might have hit him. If he is wounded, wouldn't I hear a groan or heavy breathing?*

Alex waited. There was still no noise from the front of the barn. She pulled a small section of hay from a bail and threw it into the middle of the barn. Nothing. She decided to run back across to the other stall. She arrived safely in the stall. No shot was fired. *I must have hit him.* She slowly walked toward the front of the barn, both guns drawn.

The man was dead, his eyes in a death stare. There were two bullet holes in his chest with one through the heart. Alex knelt on one knee beside him and stared down at the body. His pistol was still in his hand, flung off to his right side. He must have been pulling the trigger of his gun when the two bullets hit his chest.

Alex had killed wild game but never a human. Her heart was beating fast, and she gasped for breath as if she had just finished a foot race. As she calmed down, she wondered if the man had a wife and children. She did not rejoice in what she had done. *He was going to kill me. I had no choice.*

Alex reached to open the jacket of the dead man to find some kind of ID. She hesitated, thinking about leaving fingerprints, and pulled her hand back. *The police will investigate this. I had better not touch him. They will probably want to question me anyway since the manager will tell them who was here when she left at five o'clock.* Alex stood up, brushing off the dust and hay from her clothes, and walked toward her pickup. Untying her horses one by one, she put them in the horse trailer and drove off, heading west.

Chapter 32

Alex was aware of an overnight horse-boarding farm near Albany, New York, and called ahead, asking if the facilities were available if she arrived about ten thirty that night. She received an affirmative reply and called Pete on the encrypted cell phone. Pete was pulling into a motel in Salt Lake City. Alex told him she would be staying in Albany.

"It's getting close to eight o'clock there," said Pete. "It will be late when you get into Albany. Why don't you just stay there and start out early tomorrow?"

"I can't, Pete; I need to get out of here tonight."

"You sound tired and anxious and like you could use a good night's sleep."

"All that is true, Pete, but I just shot and killed a man."

"What? Alex, I can't tell when you are being serious and when you aren't."

"I'm serious. I made a mistake and withdrew some money from my bank. I didn't think they would be so sophisticated to track me from there, but they did. A man slipped into the barn at my stables and shot at me. He came very close to killing me, but I shot him, and he's dead. When they find out, they will be after me again. Maybe the police also."

There was silence on Pete's end for a long moment. "I don't know what to say exactly, Alex, but I'm glad you are alive. I can see why you want to leave immediately."

"Pete, have you called any relatives or taken money out of your bank?"

"No. I got my money out of my bank before I left Palo Alto and had the identity change. I haven't called my folks. I'm sure their home is bugged and being watched. So I am staying completely away from them. Same with my two brothers."

"Good," replied Alex. "I wish I had been more careful. I won't make any more mistakes. I should be in Albany about ten thirty."

"Be careful. I'll be awake if you want to call me when you get there."

Alex drove to Albany and put up her horses. She slept in her section of the horse trailer for the night. She woke as the sun was peeking over the horizon. She used the tiny bathroom in the horse trailer, brushed her teeth, and put on a change of clothes.

Traveling across country with horses was not easy. It wasn't like the old days where every town had a livery stable with a hotel virtually across the street. Places for overnight horse boarding were hard to find. Plus, you had to show all the papers on each horse, showing proof of a negative Coggins test and vaccinations and brand inspection certificates, at each stop. In addition, it was best for the horses if you stopped every four to five hours and walked them. It was difficult to find places to do that. A comfortable three-day trip without horses could turn into a long four days. She thought briefly about leaving the horses at a stable for a month and coming back to get them, but she had a motherly instinct toward her horses and didn't want to leave them in a strange place without her being near. In addition, she thought it would take TXA at least a day to find out their hit man was dead. She had forgotten to call Pete before bed last night, so she punched his number into her cell. A sleepy voice answered.

"I keep forgetting you are three hours behind me. I'm sorry for always waking you up early. It's only 5:00 a.m. in Salt Lake."

"Yeah," Pete replied sleepily. "I'll be glad when we're in the same time zone."

Alex told Pete that she wanted to make it to South Bend, Indiana, or even closer to Chicago. He told her that his objective was Omaha, Nebraska, but that it was a fourteen-hour trip and he might end up short of his objective. Both told the other that they were eager to meet in person for the first time.

#

While Alex and Pete were talking, Agent Pam Robinson was entering the downtown Boston offices of the FBI. Pam had been back only a few days from her trip to DC where she had followed Alex. After Pam had run the car off the road that had been chasing Alex, she lost Alex's trail and had to return to Boston. She walked by her boss's office. "Bonjour, patron," she said to her boss, Tee Scott.

Tee always pretended to scold her when she spoke French. "Pam! You have to start speaking English around here. What if a bigwig was here from DC and we're dancing around speaking French?"

"Cela me rendrait encore plus heureuse."

"And a very good morning to you too." He bowed slightly at her and smiled. She had a way about her that perked him up.

"C'est une bonne matinee. Okay, what's on the agenda today, boss?"

"Stop calling me boss. There is nothing new on any of your existing cases. But there was a murder of a man last night out in Marlborough that could have federal jurisdiction, and I would like you to take a look at it. The murder took place at a horse stable."

"Wait a minute, Tee. Alex Pipe kept her horses in a Marlborough stable. Remember, I followed her up to Dunstable and back to Marlborough. Maybe the same group that was after her in DC caught up with her again. She is such a good shot I'll bet she got them first."

"Okay. Get going."

"Au revoir, patron, et bonne journée."

"Yeah, yeah, whatever, and same to you."

#

The body at the horse stable was not found until 7:00 a.m. by one of the stable workers. Pam arrived only about an hour behind the police and sheriff deputies. The investigation was under way when she pulled up. She walked up to the captain in charge and pulled her badge.

"Pam Robinson, FBI."

"What are you guys doing out here?" he sneered.

"Glad to meet you too. We think this has something to do with one of our cases. I will look around and be out of your hair."

"Just stay out of the way, and we will get along just perfect."

"Can I see the body?"

"Yeah. Don't touch anything."

Pam walked around the body and pulled up the shroud enough to look at the dead man's face. She noticed that the man was the same one who had been tailing Alex from Dunstable to Marlborough. *Très intéressant.* Pam sometimes thought in French. *This is the same man I called Arnold.*

Pam turned to one of the policemen. "Have you determined the type of bullet that killed him?"

"Yes, ma'am. Right now we are thinking that it was a .45-caliber."

"Thank you, officer. That is very useful information."

Pam walked down to the stable's office to talk to the owner.

"I believe you board horses for an Alex Pipe. Correct?"

"We used to. Late yesterday afternoon, she showed up and checked out her horses. She came into the office and paid us up to date and bought some travel feed for her horses. She was obviously going on a trip, and I don't think she was planning on returning. Otherwise, she would have paid us monthly in advance as normal."

"Did she say where she was going?"

"No, nothing like that. There was no chitchat. She was all business."

Pam asked a few more questions and then left the office. Outside she called Tee on her cell.

"Tee, I think you better come out and take over this case. I believe the dead man is a TXA employee, and I believe that Alex Pipe may have killed him. We need to find out the identity of the dead man. I don't think I am going to convince the captain out here to let me take the case away. You will do a much better job of convincing him."

"Stay put, Pam, and don't let them take the body away. Stall them until I get there."

Pam went into the stable and looked at the chalk drawing of the position of the body. It looked like the gunman had been facing toward the back of the barn. *Arnold must have been shooting at Pam. He trapped her in the barn and was trying to kill her. I'll bet we find bullet holes in the walls and stalls. And I'll bet she was defending herself.* Pam thought back to Alex's shooting display in Dunstable. *Arnold, you watched her shoot and then you tried to gun her down. It's no wonder you're dead.*

Chapter 33

Pete's drive to Omaha took thirteen hours. Despite his identity change and different vehicle, he was on pins and needles, looking over his shoulder the entire trip.

It was 9:00 p.m. when he checked into a motel. He figured it was midnight back east, but Alex had not called him. *Maybe they caught up with her again and she's dead.*

Alex drove past South Bend to an overnight horse stable near LaPorte, Indiana. All she could think about was taking a hot shower and washing her hair. She still felt dirty after the dusty gunfight in the hay-filled barn. She turned on the hot-water heater on the horse trailer and had to wait for the water to warm. She then slipped into the trailer's tiny shower. It felt wonderful but not for long. The hot water tank was also tiny.

After she finished her shower, she sat on the bed with towels around her head and body. She told herself to call Pete, but she decided to rest for a minute first. She fell asleep. It was daylight when she awoke. She woke up hungry and ate granola bars and drank water until she got back to a truck stop on the interstate for coffee and breakfast.

After a big breakfast in LaPorte, Alex called Pete. Pete had already checked out and was driving toward Chicago. They decided to meet northwest of Chicago in Elgin. Pete said that he would be ahead of her several hours and would probably stop to see some old friends in Chicago.

A brief thought passed through Alex's mind that Pete might stop to see his ex-wife. *He is always talking about how much he misses her and still loves her.* She immediately recognized she was feeling jealousy.

This was a new feeling to Alex. She had always positioned herself in a relationship so that if anyone was jealous, it was the male, not her. She was not comfortable with this new feeling and mentally flogged herself for allowing such feelings. *You are being silly. One of the things you liked about Pete when you were first talking to him was his everlasting love for his ex-wife. It showed how sensitive and loving he was. But now that he might actually see her again, you don't like it. Stop this. You have no proof that he is going to see her. Alex, you are so screwed up when it comes to men. That is the one thing in your life you seem to have no control over.*

Alex left the restaurant, taking long strides, a determined look on her face. She jumped in her pickup and headed toward Chicago.

Pete was driving into Chicago from the west on I-88. As he drew closer to the city, he turned north on I-355 toward Elk Grove, his ex-wife's home. Despite what he had told Alex about seeing his old friends, he was really debating whether or not he should see Eve, his ex-wife. He had an overwhelming desire to talk to her. He justified it to himself because he needed to make amends for all the wrongs he had done to her in the past.

Pete had only one drink since San Francisco and was convinced that he would never drink again. He thought about the AA steps: *Make a list of all people we had harmed and make amends to them all, except when to do so would harm them or others.* There was no one he had harmed more than Eve. However, he still questioned his motivation to see her. Was he truly seeking to make amends to her or was he seeking to win her back, to have her again? The debate in his mind was endless. Should he call her? Should he ask to see her? Or should he drive past Elk Grove?

He pulled off at the first exit to Elk Grove and drove to a convenience store, where he pulled into the parking lot and sat in his car. Fifteen minutes went by, and he still could not make up his mind. He went in the store and got a cup of coffee. Pete got back in the car and drank the coffee. He needed a half tank of gas, so he drove over to the pumps and filled up. He sat in his car some more and then decided he needed something sweet. He went back into the store and bought a candy bar. While he was checking out, an older black man with pure white hair behind the cash register started talking to him.

"Looks like you got something on your mind, my friend."

"Yeah, I am trying to make up my mind about something."

"Indecision, indecision. It's usually about a woman, you know. Nine times out of ten. I used to be a bartender, you know, and I got to know people pretty well. Yes, sir, usually about a woman. But there is one way to make up your mind."

"What's that?" asked Pete.

"Just do it. That's all. Just do it." He had a big bright smile.

"Do what?"

"Do what you want to do. There is something you want to do, and you are talking yourself out of it. That's the confusion. Just do it."

Pete looked at the man for a moment. "Thank you for that advice. I think I'll do just that."

He walked out of the store and called Eve on his cell phone.

"Hi, Eve. It's Pete."

There was a pause on the other end. "Hello, Pete. How are you?"

"I'm fine, but I need to talk to you."

"Well, I have a few minutes, so go ahead."

"No, I need to talk to you in person. I'm in town," Pete replied. "I have something important to tell you."

"John is out of town on business. It feels a little awkward to meet you while he's gone."

"Eve, I won't be a bother, and it will take only about a half hour at the most."

"Well, okay, if you're not drinking, you can come over."

"I've quit drinking, Eve. That is part of what I want to tell you."

On the way to her home, Pete rehearsed what he wanted to tell her. Nothing sounded good enough to him, even though he had rehearsed it many times in the past. He arrived at her place and parked in the driveway. She lived in a beautiful suburban home, surrounded by shrubbery, trees, and flowers, but Pete's mind was elsewhere, worrying about what he would say, how it would sound. He rang the doorbell and stood in front of the door, shifting nervously from one foot to the other. She answered.

Eve was fifty years old, but her age was hard to guess. She was pleasant looking and pretty. Her face had age lines, but they seemed to blend together, as if she had always looked the same, ageless. She had a sophisticated presence, and slightly graying blond hair was swept back from her face. She was above average in height and slightly on the thin side. She smiled when she saw Pete and gave him a hug when he entered.

"It's good to see you again, Pete; it has been awhile. You look healthier than when I last saw you."

"Well, I am exercising again, and I am feeling a lot better than I used to. You look as beautiful as ever, Eve."

"Thank you. Come into the kitchen and sit down. Would you like some iced tea?"

"Yes, please. Your home is neat, clean, and well decorated as always." She did not respond and placed two glasses of iced tea on the kitchen table. She looked at him, smiled, and put her hands together and stretched her arms in front of her. "Well, I am glad to hear you have stopped drinking."

"I had a year's sobriety, thanks to AA, until one night recently, when I had one drink. But I'm back on track and know for sure I will never drink again."

He paused for a moment, unsure of how to tell her the purpose for his visit. "The reason I'm here is to make amends to you for all the harm and heartache I caused you when I was drinking. I can't undo what has already been done, but I can tell you how deeply sorry I am that I did all those things that caused our marriage to fail. I always loved you so very much, and it is difficult for me to understand why I would do things to hurt you."

Eve stared at Pete for a long moment. He anxiously looked back at her, waiting for her to say something.

"Pete, I never thought you would say that. I never thought you would get sober. I appreciate your apology. I waited and waited for years for you to quit drinking. I finally came to the point where I never thought you would. I gave up. The loneliness, the nights crying, and the wondering if you would make it home safely. I just could not take it anymore." Her eyes had tears in them as she spoke.

"Oh my God, Eve, I did not want to hurt you all over again. Please don't cry. I should not have come here."

"No, no. I am glad you came. The tears are both happy and sad. I am so glad you quit drinking. I am happy for you. I'm sad that it didn't happen when we were married. We had a wonderful marriage for quite a few years."

"I remember, Eve. I remember how wonderful it was. Do you remember the time we went out in that rowboat and I stood up and fell in the lake?"

"That was so funny," Eve responded. "Then you pulled me in after you, and we had a water fight. We were so much in love. Then we lay on the bank in our wet clothes and held hands."

Pete and Eve continued to reminisce about their romance and early married years. They both laughed until their sides ached, telling one story after another. There was no question that they had once been crazy about each other.

Eve got up to get some more iced tea. When she was at the refrigerator, Pete came up to her from behind. "I need a hug," he said.

She turned around and smiled. "I do too."

The hug started out quite innocently, but they began to hold each other tighter. The hug continued, and Pete wrapped his arms around her tighter and drew her close. Her perfume was intoxicating. Her hair smelled like lilacs. He thought she was going to melt into him, that they had become one. She finally drew back her head, looking up at him, still holding him tight, smiling. Pete started to put tiny kisses on her forehead, something he used to do when they were romantic. They were so close that their breathing interlocked, and they were drawn closer and closer to each other. It made Pete feel wonderfully dizzy, like he was in another world. Their lips touched, and they began to kiss, but she suddenly broke apart from him. She blushed and looked down. Pete's mind was fumbling for words.

"We can't do this, Pete. At least I can't do this. I am still attracted to you, as I have always been, but I have chosen a different life. You have your own life, also. I am sure by now you must have a girlfriend, and we need to think of our better halves. Our life together is over, and we need to go our separate ways."

"I really don't have a better half, Eve, but I know you do. I understand why you would want to remain faithful to him."

Eve walked away from him. "This was a nice visit, but I think you need to leave now."

"You're right. I should get going." They walked to the front door together. He turned to say good-bye, and they ended up hugging again.

"Eve. I have always loved you, and I always will." It was Pete's turn for the tears to well up in his eyes. He squeezed her, turned, and walked out the door.

"Wait," she said. He stopped and looked back. "I loved you once, and even today, though I am married and happy, I have a special feeling toward you. Please take care and stay in touch once in a while if for no other reason than to talk about the kids."

Pete drove to the interstate and eventually was on I-90 headed toward Wisconsin. He thought about Eve—her sweet smell, her soft lips, and the electricity between them. He regretted what he had thrown away and could not have back again.

#

The control center in California received a call. "Guess who showed up at his ex-wife's home?"

Ron Fenton had taken the call. "Well, well, well. Pete Oxwood. I'm not surprised. He just can't stay away from females. Which way is he headed?"

"He just left her house and is driving back toward the interstate. I am on his tail."

Chapter 34

Alex had intended to bypass downtown Chicago but got confused about the turnoff to I-94 and then I-294, so she stayed on I-90 into downtown Chicago. It was midmorning, and the traffic was heavy but not stop and go. Nonetheless, it took significantly longer then bypassing downtown. The traffic let up in the northwest suburbs, and when she got near Barrington, she pulled off to gas up, take a break, and walk the horses. She pulled into a gas station that had some grass around it. When she sat down in the restaurant, she ordered coffee and called Pete.

"Where are you, Pete?"

"Hi, Alex. I'm near a place called Belvedere in Illinois heading for Rockford."

"How is the trip going?"

"Nothing to speak of. I'm not being followed. So, it's going okay I guess."

"You're not very far ahead of me. What do you say we meet at Eau Claire, Wisconsin, late this afternoon? I know of a place to board horses just off the interstate near Eau Clair."

"Sounds good to me," replied Pete.

"Call me when you find a place to stay."

Alex hung up. She thought Pete sounded somewhat distant and like he didn't want to chat. She wondered if he had lost interest in her.

Pete decided to take it easy for the rest of the trip; he was ahead of Alex by a considerable amount. He thought about stopping at some grassy spot and doing some exercises. He had been an exercise fanatic in the army.

Each morning and evening he did multiple sit-ups and push-ups. If anything was available to hang on, he would do pull-ups. Anytime he had an extra half hour or more, he would jog or run. While he was driving, he would do isometric exercises, pitting one group of muscles against the other.

He pulled off the interstate at Eau Claire, Wisconsin, and began looking for parks or school grounds where he could exercise. When he pulled off the interstate, he noticed a silver Toyota pull off just after he did. As Pete drove around looking for a place to exercise, he noticed the Toyota several times in his rearview mirror. He was suspicious and decided to drive around rather than stop. *I wonder if TXA is following me again.* He remembered some evasion techniques he had been taught in his days as an army spook. Pete began to drive at regular speed around the same streets, retracing his path, continuing to look out his window as if he was searching for something and didn't know he was being followed.

Pete rounded a corner that he had gone around three times before and hit the accelerator hard, went a block, and made a hard right where he had turned left three times before. The Toyota driver turned the corner and turned left and drove for several blocks before he noticed Pete's car was not in front of him. By this time, Pete was three blocks away in the opposite direction and putting more distance between them.

Central control in California received another call. "I lost Pete Oxwood in Eau Claire, Wisconsin."

"Eau Claire. Let me look that up. Yes. The chief of police is one of us. I'll get the police to find Mr. Oxwood for us. Go to the police department and report that Pete has been following you. We will notify them about our fugitive from justice."

"Got it."

Pete found a restaurant to park behind and went in for coffee. It occurred to him that if he could get the driver of the Toyota arrested, he could buy some time. When he left the restaurant, he drove to the police department.

"Well I'll be damned," Pete said. The silver Toyota was parked across the parking lot from the front door. He drove past the building and parked in a parking lot nearby. He pushed the trunk latch and went around the car to the back. Reaching in, he pulled out a small laptop he had bought in Reno. He had Internet through his cell phone. Back in the auto, he put "Eau Claire County police scanner" into his web browser. He clicked on "Eau Clair County Public Safety" and picked up the police radio band.

After listening to police reports such as a compressor falling off of a pickup, an all-points bulletin informed officers to be on the alert for his auto with its Nevada license plates, specifying that the driver was armed and dangerous. *The TXA bastard beat me to the punch. I had better take side streets to the interstate.*

Pete knew that the interstate was generally south and east of his location, and he took off but at regular speed. He drove about five blocks, into a residential neighborhood, pulled over, and called Alex on his cell.

"Pete?"

"Yeah, Alex. Where are you right now?"

"About twenty minutes from Eau Claire."

"I've got a problem," Pete said. "TXA tailed me to Eau Claire, and the entire Eau Claire police force is after me."

"How would they know where you are?"

"I don't know. I have no idea."

"I'll bet they were waiting for you at your ex-wife's house. Right?"

Pete was silent and then said, "You're right. I was a stupid. I didn't think. Now I'm in real trouble... I am really, really sorry, Alex."

Just then, a patrol car went by headed in the other direction. Pete ducked down. "Shhhhh. A cop just drove by. I need to ditch this car and have you pick me up somewhere."

"What makes you think I want to pick you up?" Alex was amazed at her jealous reaction. *Alex, quit it! What is wrong with you? You don't really know him. Where did this jealousy come from?*

"That was not very nice of me. Of course I want to help you."

"Okay! Drive to those horse stables you mentioned," said Pete, "and wait for my call."

Pete saw another squad card pull up to the other end of the street. *Trapped! I will have to go on foot.* Pete grabbed his laptop and slid out the passenger door, staying low, taking his small laptop with him. The patrolmen in the squad cars could not see the passenger side of the car. Pete edged along the passenger side of several parked cars, keeping his head down. He got to a hedge and ran across the sidewalk, running the length of the hedge into the backyard. He had parked his car in front of a house that was apparently empty. There was a one-car garage on the alley behind the house. Pete broke into the garage looking for something to use to break into the house. He found a screwdriver and a small jigsaw blade. The house looked empty, but it was probably not abandoned; a Harley Road King sat in the garage.

The home was large, white, turn of the century, and two stories with an attic. It would be easy to break in. Within minutes, Pete was inside and ran up to the second floor. The furniture was gone except for miscellaneous items. It looked like it had been vacant for a long time. He ran into a bedroom fronting the street. Looking out the window, he saw six police officers and two sheriff deputies creeping toward his parked car, guns drawn. He opened his laptop and got back on the police channel. From the activity on the radio, it sounded like a BOLO alert had gone out to every law enforcement agency in the surrounding area.

Pete realized that when the officers found that he was not in the car, they would be looking for him on foot. *I don't think these policemen or the TXA guy know what I look like. The TXA dude following me probably picked up my tail at Eve's home, so it is unlikely he is one of the thugs from Palo Alto that has seen me in person.* Pete quickly ran back down the stairs and into the garage.

He found a piece of wire, cut it to be about nine inches long with a wire cutter still in the garage and hot-wired the Harley. He checked the fuel gauge. It was half a tank full. He turned the emergency fuel switch back and forth several times before he hit the starter and turned the throttle. The Harley's battery was weak and the gas old. Several times he tried to start it. Finally, it caught, and the Harley sputtered to life.

There was a full-faced motorcycle helmet sitting on the bike behind the driver's seat. It was a size too large, but he could strap it on, and it worked. He knew he had to move fast before they found out he was not in the auto out front. He heard a bullhorn blast out: "Get out of the car with your hands up." He opened the garage door and pushed the Harley out. No one was in the alley yet.

Pete turned the throttle and moved down the alley at a slow speed to keep from drawing attention. *Thank God this does not have the loud exhaust pipes on it.* He turned right and went two blocks down, two blocks over, and then back to the street he had parked his car. No one had followed him. There were police cars with flashing lights blocking the street. He stopped and pretended to be part of the crowd that gathered around the police cars, all gawking down the street where Pete had parked the car. No one paid any attention to him. He gunned the Harley and headed for a gas station near the interstate.

He filled up the Harley, which took only two gallons, but he wanted fresh gasoline in it. He called Alex on his cell.

"Alex. Pete here. I escaped."

"Pete. Are they following you?"

"They were and almost had me. I borrowed a Harley, and I'm near the interstate."

"Borrowed? Sounds like they might add vehicle theft to your crime list."

"Actually, my great-aunt Bertha from Eau Claire left it to me."

"Funny."

"Where are you?"

"I'm at Trinity Equestrian Center on State Route 37, west of the interstate."

"Great. I'm on Highway 37. I'll head west right now. See you in a couple of minutes."

Pete gunned the Harley and headed toward the stable. No one could see that he was smiling under the full-faced helmet. *God I love to ride.* He applied more throttle and started making small *s* curves in the middle of his lane, swerving back and forth. Next, he geared down and got a few small backfires before speeding up again. He was smiling even more.

A squad car pulled into the gas station about thirty seconds after Pete left on the Harley. They noticed him, but Pete didn't see them; he was too interested in the bike.

One of the officers glanced down the road at Pete on the Harley. "I saw that guy at the scene up on Third Avenue. He was in the crowd looking down the street. I remember because he didn't put his visor up when he was looking. I thought that was a little strange."

"Maybe that's our guy. The perp often returns to the scene of the crime."

"Why don't we follow him just to make sure?"

Chapter 35

Tee Scott had taken over the murder scene at the Marlborough stables. Tee had a way of taking over a crime scene that left little doubt in anyone's mind that he was in charge. He and Pam met briefly before she left the stables.

"Your Arnold's real name was Harry Misuriello, a New Jersey guy with a long and deadly rap sheet. He worked for TXA, according to the latest information we have on him. Alex must be as good with a pistol as you said she was. Do you have any idea where she is headed?"

"Alex is originally from Montana. From our intel, her family owns a ranch there," Pam told Tee. "I believe that Alex is headed to the ranch. She needs to put her horses somewhere, and the safe place would probably be her family's ranch. She knows she can't be on the run forever with those horses. They slow her down. She has to put them somewhere that won't cost an arm and a leg. Her family's ranch is the only logical place for her to go."

"Now if we can figure that out, the TXA bad guys will figure it out also," replied Tee. "We need to get to her first. This is the second time they have tried to kill her. They won't give up. Wherever she goes, they won't be far behind."

"She will have to travel by interstate; anything else would be far too slow," said Pam. "There are two interstate routes to Montana, I-90 and I-94. Both go through Chicago. If I were to fly to Chicago O'Hare, I would get there about the same time or earlier than she does. Plus, O'Hare is near those two interstates. When I get there, if our intel can pick up her approximate location, I can intercept her."

"Good plan," responded Tee. "I will pick a partner to go with you." The frown on Pam's face told him she did not like the idea.

"Partners slow me down. You know how much I hate working with a partner," replied Pam. "If it looks like there is going to be trouble, the Chicago office can assign someone to help. Anyway, I don't plan to get in a gun battle; I'm just going to meet with Alex and provide protection for her to Montana. She could be a valuable resource. I'm sure she knows some real dirt on TXA. We have been suspicious of them for a long time."

"I know you work very well on your own, so I'll let you go for now, but if I think things are too hot, I'll assign someone to partner up with you, not Chicago. We can't tell the Chicago office what we are doing. In the meantime, I will alert local and state agencies to be on the lookout for Alex and keep you informed. Unfortunately, we don't have much information to give them: a Dodge truck towing a horse trailer driven by a twenty-nine-year-old woman with dark hair. That's not much to go on."

Once Pam realized Tee was authorizing her to trail Alex on her own, her eyes twinkled, and a smile curved at the corner of her mouth. She looked like a little girl about to get into mischief. She stood up and saluted Tee and said, "Mon Capitaine. Je te suivrai aux fins de la terre et je suis ton meilleur agent de police judiciaire fédérale de jamais."

"Whatever. And don't call me captain either," he replied, looking at the ground and shaking his head as he walked away.

"Au revoir mon Capitaine."

Tee gave her a pretend dirty look over his shoulder and then grinned. He thought about how much he liked Pam and her antics. *Things would be dull at the office without her.*

Pam flew to Chicago. Tee had arranged for a rental car rather than getting one through the Chicago FBI office. When Pam got off the plane, it was too late to begin the chase, so she checked into a motel near O'Hare. The next morning, she had trouble gathering information on Alex's location. By the time she received the intel, Alex had driven past O'Hare. An agent from the Boston office gave her the bad news:

"As best we can tell, Agent Robinson, Alex Pipe drove past O'Hare field and got on the Jane Adams toll road. That highway ends about a mile south of the Wisconsin state line. You will be behind her, but you can probably catch up with her in a couple of hours, assuming that she stays on I-90."

The Jane Adams toll way was part of I-90. After Pam went through the first tollbooth, she drove as fast as she could. That way she could get the attention of the highway patrol, and they could help her by pulling Alex over. However, she wanted Alex to cooperate with her and tell her as much as she knew about TXA. If Alex was pulled over by the Illinois State Police, Alex might think she was being arrested for the shooting back in Marlborough. Any number of unneeded consequences could happen. Pam wanted to approach her in a nonconfrontational manner, so she slowed down to a more reasonable speed but was still exceeding the speed limit.

After four hours of driving, Pam believed she had narrowed Alex's lead to just minutes. She expected to see the horse trailer on the horizon soon, and within ten minutes she spotted a horse trailer behind a pickup. She sped up beside the pickup and saw that Alex was driving. Pam slowed down and got behind Alex's rig to a safe distance away. They drove on for another hour. Just before they approached Eau Claire, two semitrucks with trailers got between Pam and Alex. Alex turned off the interstate at an Eau Claire exit, and the trucks followed, blocking Pam's view. By the time Pam realized that Alex had taken the exit, it was too late to turn.

Chapter 36

Pam found the first place she could cross the interstate medium and drove back toward the Eau Claire exit on the opposite side of the interstate. At the end of the off ramp, Pam looked left and right but couldn't see the trailer in any direction. She turned toward the city and drove until she was convinced that Alex had not gone in that direction. She turned into a convenience store.

It occurred to Pam that Alex might stop at a horse stable to board the horses and asked the girl at the cash register if there was a stable nearby. The girl told her to turn around, stay on the same road, go under the interstate, and she would come to a stable in a few miles. Pam got back on the highway, went under the interstate bridge, and in a few minutes noticed the stable coming up on the left side of the road.

It was still light, and she could see Alex near the barn. Pam parked in front of the stable's office, keeping an eye on Alex while she formulated her plan. Once she figured out the best way to approach Alex, Pam walked toward the barn moving slowly, looking around like someone who had never been there before. As she approached the barn, Alex looked in her direction. Pam, trying to play the role of a friendly tourist, smiled and waved at Alex. She stopped and looked at the horses in a corral to her left and sauntered on toward the barn, in no hurry.

"Does that beautiful black horse belong to you?" Pam asked Alex.

"No, but that is a pretty black horse. My horses are in the barn."

"My name is Pam Robinson." She stuck out her hand to Alex. "I'm from Boston. What about you?"

"Nice to meet you, Pam." She stuck out her hand, and they shook hands. "My name is Alex Pipe. I've been living in and around Boston for ten years, but I'm really from Montana."

Pam put on her most disarming smile. "Actually, we have met before, in an unusual way."

"Oh, I'm sorry, but I don't remember meeting you before."

"We never met face-to-face. A few nights ago in Washington, DC, someone shot at you, and a car was chasing you as you drove away. I ran him off the road, and you escaped."

Alex was taken back. Her eyes looked startled, and her mouth came open. For a few seconds, her face froze in that position. "Why? Why were you there and now here? Are you following me?"

Pam let Alex absorb the news for a few seconds before she responded. "Don't be alarmed; I am following you, but I'm on your side. I know there are people trying to kill you. I also know you acted in self-defense at the stables in Marlborough."

Pam pulled out her badge and showed it to Alex. "I'm with the FBI, and I am here to try and protect you."

Alex looked at the badge and then back at Pam, still trying to absorb the totality of Pam's words. A noise caused them to look up. A motorcycle left the highway and headed in their direction driven by a man who looked like he might be Pete. The motorcycle quickly passed the two women and went behind the barn. Just then, a police car paused at the highway at the entrance to the stables with the officers looking around. *They are looking for Pete.* The patrol car continued down the road.

Alex started walking toward the back of the barn. Alex told Pam, "I was expecting a guy but not on a Harley. We agreed to meet here. His name is Peter Oxwood, and he is being followed by TXA also. We have only communicated by phone and e-mail. I have never met him in person, but I have seen many pictures of him on the Internet, and I know it's him."

Pete walked out from behind the barn and saw two beautiful women standing there looking at him. The younger one he recognized as Alex. She was more beautiful in person than any picture. The three met at the side of the barn in view of the highway. Before they could say anything more than hello, the police car had turned around and come back. The car was still on the highway about a hundred yards from the barn.

Inside the patrol car, the driver said to the other officer, "That kind of looks like our guy talking to those two women. The helmet is gone, but the clothes are the same. I am going to drive in. Call for backup." The officer waited a minute for the backup call to be completed and then drove slowly toward the barn.

Pete turned to the two women and said, "I stirred up a hornet's nest in town. The police are after me, but I didn't break any laws. As best I can tell, they were trying to help TXA capture me. They had me almost surrounded before I borrowed that Harley and escaped."

Pam turned toward Pete. "I don't have time to explain it now, but I am with the FBI. Let me handle this. Put your hands out." Pete hesitated. "Come on, hurry. Put your hands out." Pete complied. Pam put handcuffs on him. They turned toward the police as they walked up.

"We are here to take that man into custody," one of the policemen said. He stared at the handcuffs and wondered what was going on. "Why is he handcuffed?"

Pam flashed her badge at the policemen. "Pamela Robinson, FBI. I have already taken this man into custody. He is under arrest."

The area between the barn and the road began to fill up with police and sheriff cars. Their lights were flashing. Given the lights and number of law enforcement vehicles, the stables looked like the scene of a major crime.

Two heavyset men in uniforms with leather gun belts creaking as they walked approached Pam and the police officer. They were the chief of police and one of his deputies. The chief of police had a big mustache and looked a lot like Wilford Brimley, and the deputy looked like he had played fullback on the University of Wisconsin football team. They stopped and stared at Pam. Pam was standing next to Pete with her left hand on the back of Pete's right arm, as if she were holding him from escaping.

The chief of police spoke first. "My men tell me you are with the FBI. What jurisdiction do you have out here?" *My God, he even sounds like Wilford Brimley.*

"Chief, I was just going to ask you the same thing. This is the country, not the city. Your policemen don't have jurisdiction to arrest in the county since there was no imminent danger or a felony taking place."

Pam was actually guessing that the stables were in the country and outside of the city limits. She was concerned what would happen if she was wrong. A considerable number of police surrounded her.

"They were in hot pursuit."

"I saw the whole thing. You are stretching the definition of hot, Chief. That meandering around by the police car can hardly be called hot pursuit. Anyway, tell me what crime this man committed that allowed you to go after him to begin with."

"We put an all-points bulletin out on him."

"Who asked you to put out the BOLO on him? The state police? For what crime?"

"I am not at liberty to disclose that information."

"I wouldn't want to disclose the real source of the information either. Being a stooge for TXA is not good PR for your department, Chief, particularly when there was no crime involved."

"He did not come into Eau Claire on a motorcycle. That Harley has to be stolen. I'll take him."

"Not so fast, Sheriff. This man is under arrest for national security reasons. That trumps anything you tag on him, particularly since I arrested him first and you have no proof that the motorcycle was stolen."

Pam grabbed Alex behind her arm with her right hand. "I am going to get in my car with these two and leave. Please get out of my way."

"I want to see your identification."

Pam showed them her badge.

"Call dispatch and have them check this FBI agent number to see if it is valid."

"What about the girl?" the sheriff asked. "Is she under arrest also?"

"Yes. She is involved in the same case as Mr. Oxwood."

"I don't think so. I have reason to believe that her name is Alex Pipe and she is wanted for murder back in Massachusetts," responded the chief.

Pam knew that the information about the shooting in Massachusetts could not have come to the chief from anyone except TXA. Tee Scott had taken jurisdiction of the case in Massachusetts from the local law enforcement groups. The cops there would not have had enough access to the crime scene to determine who the killer was. Only Tee Scott would have such information, and she knew that Tee Scott would not put out a BOLO on the case. TXA knew they had sent their man,

Harry, to Marlborough to eliminate Alex. The only group that would think Alex was a murderer was TXA. Pam reasoned that TXA must have the chief on their payroll. That was the only logical conclusion.

Pam had to think fast. "Only TXA says she is a murderer," Pam responded. "That company is not a law enforcement agency. I am sure my people in Washington are going to be interested in the fact that TXA bought you off, Chief."

The chief looked at her, wondering how Robinson would know about TXA and the payoffs.

"Everyone out of my way," yelled Pam as she stepped toward her car with Pete and Alex on both sides. Police and deputies glared at her. No one was getting out of the way. *Oh boy, what a mess I'm in now.*

Chapter 37

"Chief, her agent number checks out okay," a policewoman yelled.

The chief and deputy walked away so they could speak in private. The chief whispered to the deputy, "How would they know anything about TXA? The only people who are supposed to know about it are the two of us. We could be in trouble if the TXA plan falls apart."

The sheriff nodded. "Let's let them go. We should go back to the station and speak with TXA about this. I'm getting nervous."

Pam saw the police and sheriff's men part as she pushed toward the car. It brought to her mind the parting of the Red Sea in the Bible. She was praying that God would keep the sea walls from collapsing on her. Had she bluffed them well enough? Tee Scott did not know exactly where she was, and neither did any other law enforcement agency. The chief and their men could eliminate her, Alex, and Pete. No one knew where they were, except TXA. Pam's stomach was in her throat as she put Alex and Pete into the backseat of her car.

"Okay, boys. Let 'em go," yelled the chief.

Pam drove through the group of cops and bystanders out to the road and turned right toward the interstate.

#

The control center in California got a call from Eau Claire.

"This is Jeff. We had them, and the cops let them go."

"Slow down. Who is we, and who is them?"

"The Eau Claire police had Pete Oxwood, Alex Pipe, and a lady FBI agent surrounded at the barn outside of town and they let them leave."

"Why?"

"The FBI woman said that the feds knew her location and knew about the cops' connection to TXA. That scared them. They let her go, and I don't think they want to play ball anymore."

"We have informants inside the FBI, and they don't know about anything going on in Eau Claire. I would have heard about it immediately if there was."

"What do you want me to do?"

"We will have a man by the name of Poker Jack meet you in thirty minutes in front of the police station. I want you to kill all three of them."

"Even the FBI lady?"

"Yes. Our men inside the FBI are high in the organization. We had them put a stop to the FBI investigation of TXA, so the lady is either pretending to be an FBI agent or she is a rogue agent. Either way, we must get rid of her permanently."

#

Pam was able to drive to the interstate without incident but kept an eye on her rearview mirror. She turned south toward Chicago. The backseat was small, and Alex and Pete were crammed together. Alex thought Pete was the most handsome man she had ever seen. She didn't mind being pushed up against him. Pete felt the same. After a few minutes of driving in silence, the group felt safe enough to talk.

"If I hadn't borrowed that motorcycle, I'd be dead," Pete said. Pam and Alex did not respond but nodded as if in agreement, though both thought that "borrowed" was not the proper description.

Pam looked at the two of them in the rearview mirror. "I don't think it will be long before they are after us. I'm going to call in my location, and then we will think of something." She called Tee Scott and told him the story.

"What did I tell you about having a partner? You are going to cost me my job one of these days," said Scott. "How do you always talk me into skating on thin ice?"

"I know. I know. I'm sorry. But look at the bright side. I made it out safely. I'm here in one piece, and I have Alex Pipe and a guy by the name of Pete Oxwood, who is being chased by TXA also. Ne devrais-j'obtenir une médaille pour actes de bravoure?"

"If you are asking for a medal, forget it. Nevertheless, I am glad you are okay. Now, how do you expect to get out of Eau Claire County alive?"

'Ne t'inquiétes pas. Je suis en train de formuler une idee maintenant et je te rappellerai." For once, she interpreted it for him. "That means: Don't worry. I will call you back with my plan."

Pete and Alex overheard Pam's phone conversation with Tee Scott. Pete spoke up. "Speaking of French, I learned to speak French in the army. Je suis—"

"Hold it right there," said Alex, instantly jealous. "You two start speaking French to each other, and I won't know what you are talking about. I'll crown both of you if you keep it up."

"Mais je voulais flirter avec Pete en français parce qu'il est beau," replied Pam.

"I think I know what you said," Alex said, looking at Pete. She was pretending to be more upset than she actually was. Pete turned red. Pam smiled.

They were headed south on Interstate 90. It was getting dark outside. Pam was thinking about a way they could get to Montana. Alex perked up in the backseat. "I have a plan." She then crawled over the seat into the front.

Alex looked at Pam. "Have you ever hauled anything behind you with a pickup?"

"I used to haul a boat behind the family car when I was a teenager."

"Good. Let's go back to the stable. We'll hitch up the fifth wheel, load the horses, and you will drive out. Tell anyone guarding it that you are impounding the rig because espionage was conducted with it."

"What if they are waiting for us?" asked Pete.

Pam replied, "I don't think local law enforcement is a problem. But I'm not sure about the TXA guy. He might be there. But we outnumber him three to one. I vote we carry out the plan."

"Aye."

"Aye."

Pam turned around at the next exit and headed north again toward the stable. Alex and Pete were checking their firearms. Pam was thinking about hers. *I have never shot anyone. I wonder if I could do it.*

Jeff and the other man sent by TXA huddled together in front of the police station. "I was told to look for a Jeff."

"That's me."

"Call me Poker Jack. Where do you think we can find them?"

"I am pretty sure they will show back up at a local stable to pick up Pipe's horses. Alex is her name, a real beauty. Maybe we can have a little fun with her before we finish her off."

"Lead the way." They got into Jeff's car and headed toward the stables.

Pam drove up to the stables. It was now dark outside. Alex got out and went to her truck, backing it up toward the horse trailer. Pete followed her and directed her. As soon as they were hitched, Alex ran to get her horses with Pete following close behind. Alex took Hank and gave Duke's reins to Pete. They ran them to the trailer, and Alex loaded the horses and secured the back door.

Pam was standing in front of the truck. Alex and Pete were still running when they approached her. "If they are going to come after us, this would be the time to do it," said Pam. "We are all standing together and are easy targets in the barn light, even though it is weak. We need to get in the truck and go. You two get in the truck while I scan the area."

Jeff and Poker Jack had walked to the barn from the road. They watched as Alex and Pete got the trailer and horses ready. Jeff told Jack to circle around on the other side and they could shoot from both directions at the group. Jack was to whistle when he was in place, and Jeff was to immediately fire first. Jack took a long route to stay out of the barn light. Jeff was getting impatient for him to get into place. He stood up and tried to see where Jack was on the other side. In the process of moving around, he stepped in a hole and fell down. He hit the ground hard.

Pete and Pam were just starting to move toward the truck when Alex heard the noise from Jeff falling. She immediately threw herself on the ground while pulling her pistols. She yelled, "Get down." Pete hit the turf, pulling Pam with him. He pulled out his 9-mm. Pam pulled her 9-mm Glock.

Nobody moved. Alex, Pam, and Pete were partially hidden by the dark shadows falling across the barnyard. Pam had noticed movement after Jeff fell down and was staring at the spot in the dark while staying as close to the ground as possible. Jeff was very nervous. Poker Jack had not whistled yet, and he was beginning to think that he had walked away, leaving the odds one against three. He tried to fit in the hole he had fallen in, but it was too small. Finally, he heard Jack whistle.

Pete and Pam were near the right front tire on the ground. They were looking at Alex, who was in front of the truck but on the other side. When Jack whistled, Pete instinctively rolled to his right and shot at the placed the sound came from. Jack returned the fire, missed short in front of Pam, and threw up dirt in her eyes. As soon as Pete saw the flash of Jack's gun, he fired directly at the spot of the flash. He heard a groan. Jeff fired at Alex. She immediately fired at the flash point. Alex felt her upper left arm burning. She reached up to her shoulder with her right hand, and it felt wet. The hand came back covered with blood.

Chapter 38

After checking out her wound, Alex believed the bullet had grazed her arm. The wound was superficial but bloody.

Pete yelled. "Alex, are you okay?"

"Yeah, what about you guys?"

"We're fine. I think I got the guy on this side, but he might just be wounded and still a threat."

"I don't think I missed this one over here," Alex yelled back. "But I'm not going to hang around to find out. We need to leave now. Someone is going to report the gunshots. Let's crawl back to the truck and get the hell out of here."

No shots were fired at them as they got back to the truck and left the scene. Alex and Pete felt confident that the two TXA goons were dead or seriously wounded. Pete had done night fighting in the service and believed he was a good shot. Virtually all targets shot at by Alex were hit dead center. *I couldn't have missed at that distance,* she thought.

Pete patched up Alex's shallow flesh wound with tape, gauze, and globs of antibiotic cream. Alex always carried a first aid kit in her trailer for both horses and humans. "Do you think it will leave a scar?" she asked Pete.

"Perhaps, but you can wear it as a badge of honor. You can tell your grandkids that you won the battle at the OK Corral,"

Pam thought about the gun battle. She had not fired a shot. She had never fired a shot. She had always felt that a gun should be used to deter a problem that could lead to injury or death rather than to be used to cause it. She wondered if she could shoot a person if the need arose.

\#

"We haven't heard from Jeff or Poker Jack all day," said Ron Fenton at the TXA control center. "We better check on them. Trixie call the chief of police in Eau Claire and see what he knows."

"Chief, this is Trixie with the TXA control center. One of our people named Jeff was following Pete Oxwood into your city, as you know. Then we sent out a guy named Poker Jack last night to help Jeff out."

"I'm aware of all of that," replied the chief. "We saw Poker Jack slinking around outside the station last night."

"We haven't heard from Jeff or Jack, and we wonder if you can help us out."

"We found Jeff dead this morning. And, no, I will no longer help you out. You people didn't tell the truth to us about what we were supposed to do to help you. Breaking the law and killing people does not fall within our definition of helping out. You told us that the FBI was part of the movement. However, we ran into a real, live FBI agent. We don't like messing around with the FBI. Also we don't like messing around with innocent people that you say are murderers when they aren't."

"Okay, calm down. What happened?"

"Apparently, your two thugs went back to the stable and tried to ambush the FBI agent, Oxwood, and Pipe. It didn't work. Jeff is dead, but we don't know about the other one."

"Didn't you notify the state police or anyone about these murders?"

"No, the way I figure it, it looked like self-defense. We will report it that way. I think that those three are well out of the state of Wisconsin, and we can't remember any of their names. By the way, don't you or any of your kind ever call here again."

\#

Alex drove her Dodge truck toward Minneapolis St. Paul. They were in Minnesota, and she was doing seven miles over the speed limit. She had driven the speed limit in Wisconsin. She did not want to get picked up by the Wisconsin Highway Patrol. Now she was making up for it. The three had decided to drive straight through to Montana taking turns driving. They would change drivers at every gas fill up, which was about every three hours. One of them would try to get a nap on the bed in the horse trailer while another would ride shotgun. Normally "riding shotgun" was just a way of saying they would ride in the passenger seat. In this case, the term was used closer to its original meaning.

Pam asked Alex and Pete if they had their cell phones on. Both did. "Turn them off and take out the batteries. TXA can track you otherwise. I can keep mine on. They can't trace an FBI cell."

Chapter 39

Alex figured it would take fifteen hours to drive to the family ranch in Montana if they didn't have the horses. But it would take closer to twenty-four hours nonstop with the horses.

Pam sat in the passenger seat first, and Pete napped in the trailer. This would be the first time the two women had a chance to talk about anything other than their immediate survival. Alex now had the chance to tell Pam everything that had happened. She told her about her job and her and Pete's discovery of secret information in the TXA files.

"When I saw Jimmy Montgomery leave Phil Frane's office, I was certain that I was being watched and that my phones were probably bugged. I am sure that the phone bug is how TXA found out about my trip to DC."

Pam listened and interrupted from time to time. "I followed you and Renata from your apartment to the airport and caught the next flight to DC. Agents there told me where you were staying, and I checked into your motel. I then followed you around DC."

Alex explained in detail the information that Carl Jones had gathered and the disk she had in her possession.

"What it boils down to is UPA is using political contributions from defense contractors and others to fund the shipments of military products by the defense contractors to military bases. The many Z corporations are a way to hide and confuse what they are doing. The most prominent defense contractor is TXA. They are shipping products to Malmstrom Air Force Base in Great Falls, Montana, and to other bases, but Malmstrom is the most notable."

Pam explained in more detail why she got involved in the TXA case. "I was investigating TXA because of the arrival of Dmitri Zakhar and Jimmy Montgomery at TXA. These two are always on the other side of whatever our government favors. Wherever they show up, there is usually armed conflict being planned or actually taking place."

Alex replied, "Jimmy Montgomery was handsome and a smooth talker. I was completely fooled by him. Dmitri is a different case. I never liked the man."

Pam injected more detail. "I was following Jimmy Montgomery the night he picked you up for a date. For a while after that, our Bureau office thought you might be involved. I was assigned to start following you after that. I watched you practice mounted shooting in Dunstable. Harry Misuriello, the man you shot, was also there watching you."

"I had no idea I was being watched. And all because of a stupid computer file."

"I followed Harry, who I had nicknamed Arnold, back to Marlborough. He gave me the slip near there. I figured that you were not part of the Zakhar scene and TXA was following you. The question in my mind was why they were following you. About that time, my boss told me that someone up the line had called off the TXA investigation."

"Why would they do that if Zakhar was such a potential threat?"

"The only thing I can figure out is TXA or someone bought off a high-level FBI administrator. It ties into the fact that TXA bought off Eau Claire law enforcement. If you think about it, Eau Claire is an insignificant part of law enforcement in this country. The number of people around the country on TXA payroll must be staggering. Anyway, my boss let me go rogue and follow you."

Alex asked, "Why didn't you think I was in with Zakhar?"

"Two things. Harry gave me the slip, and he didn't fit the image of a law enforcement officer. Second, you just don't look the part, even though you are good with a gun. It was just my gut instinct."

"I'm lucky you had that instinct," said Alex.

Pam tilted her head back in thought. "Where were we? Oh yes, I was following you around in Washington... I checked into the same Holiday Inn as you did. The night of the shooting, I followed you back to the Holiday but lost track of your car after you went into the parking lot. I waited and waited to see if you were going to go into your room but finally gave up and went to the lobby. I then saw you come in and take the elevator up to your room."

"We knew that someone was following us," said Alex. "I waited in the car to see who it was. Then I saw a woman cross the parking lot to the lobby. Of course, I didn't know that you were with the FBI and were also following us. I figured that the people following us had something to do with Clancy McCleary's murder. We had just met with Carl Jones. He told us we were heading into dangerous waters and mentioned one of the Z corporations and United Patriots of America."

Pam continued. "I sat in the bar and had a drink at a table so I could watch the lobby. A little later, Renata stuck her head out of the elevator and then ran across the lobby looking scared to death. You ran out a few minutes later. I left my drink and went into the parking lot. Renata was almost to the car when the shot rang out. You ran up to Renata and put her in the car. I ran to my car while shots still hit your car. Then I noticed that the person shooting was in another car in the parking lot. When you peeled out, the shooter's car pulled out behind you and was following you. I followed them. In that isolated stretch of road, they were trying to drive up beside you and force you off the road. I knew that you were in danger and forced them off the road. I was a little shaken up, and the bad guys disappeared before I recovered. After that, I lost track of you and went back to Boston."

Alex thought for a moment. "Thank you for saving our lives. When I saw you bounce them into the ditch, I was so relieved. We were on our way to a location where I could get an identity change and Renata some help before she bled to death. The place was owned by Renata's father, Dominic Russo."

"Dominic Russo? Do you mean *the* Dominic Russo?"

"One and the same."

"If I had shot Russo's kid and killed her college roommate, I would go out and start digging my own grave. When he finds out who they are, they will wish they had never been born.

"So he also owns an identity change business?

"Yes. They said they run their own witness protection program."

"It's no wonder we can't get much information out of most of them by offering our protection program. They know they can get one anyway."

Alex continued. "Mr. Russo may be the head of a crime organization, but he has been so very nice to me. He put me up in style in Boston. We visited Renata. He bought me wonderful meals. I loved the Italian sausage. He gave me a laptop so I could study Carl Jones's disk, and he had his men steal my truck back."

"There is probably a good side to most everyone," said Pam.

"Then I did a stupid thing. I went to my bank and withdrew a bunch of cash. That's what tipped them off on my location. Their eyes and ears are everywhere. Anyway, I drove as quickly as possible to get my horses. They must have put Harry on my tail rather quickly because he showed up before I could leave. He caught me in the barn and used the shadows to hide. He fired at me before I shot him. It was self-defense. It really was."

"I believe you, Alex. Actually, I figured that out at the scene of the shootout. When I heard of a murder at a Marlborough horse stable, I immediately figured it had something to do with you. I also figured you would head back to Montana to put the horses back on the ranch and then disappear. All roads to Montana go through or near Chicago. I flew there and picked up your trail the next day."

"Yes, I love my horses. I couldn't leave them. I knew that could lead TXA to Montana, but they don't know Montana or our ranch. Also, I could drop the horses off on the outer reaches of the ranch and not get close to home. The horses know their way back to the horse stables."

"We still may have to do just that."

Chapter 40

A conference was taking place at the control center in Palo Alto. A group of employees had rolled their desk chairs to the middle of the room, and others stood and listened.

"We have a few Minnesota state troopers on our side," said Trixie Bloom. "We could use them to pull over Alex and Pete."

A man with a ponytail and arms full of tattoos spoke up. "But we don't know where those two are. They must have turned off their cell phones and taken out the batteries. And we lost them on the spy satellite and can't pick them up again until daylight."

"They have to be heading to Pipe's home in Montana," said Ron Fenton, "which means they are on the interstate headed toward Minneapolis and then Fargo."

"That's a lot of interstate to cover with very few troopers," said the man with the ponytail.

"What's the most logical stopping place to gas up after Eau Claire?" asked Fenton.

Trixie spoke up. "St. Cloud, Minnesota is a logical place. It's about three hundred miles from Eau Claire."

"We will have to use Minnesota troopers," said Fenton. "How many do we have on the payroll?"

"Maybe a hundred total, scattered all over the state," replied another man.

Fenton looked at Trixie. "Have a few hang out around St. Cloud and see if Pipe stops there. We still have a couple of hours to get them in place."

#

After a couple of hours on the highway, Alex's rig pulled into a truck stop in St. Cloud to gas up and allow everyone to get a bite to eat. Pete was groggy. He was rubbing his eyes and a little unsteady on his feet.

"I had trouble sleeping. The horse smells were overwhelming. How can you put up with that, Alex?"

"I like the way the horses smell, and I don't even notice the manure smell. Just something I'm used to I guess. You get to drive next, so drink some coffee."

They ate like hungry wolves. It seemed like forever since their last meal. While they ate, they scanned the crowd for any suspicious characters that might be following them. They checked the parking lot as they walked back to the truck. There was a state trooper's car parked in the lot. No one could see any troopers, however. They got into the truck and got back on the interstate.

Alex slept in the trailer, and Pam rode shotgun while Pete drove the next leg of the journey to Montana. Pam expected that the Eau Claire police would have radioed ahead to the Wisconsin and Minnesota State Police to have them pulled over. She had practiced a story she would tell the state troopers if they were pulled over. She would tell them that she had two fugitives wanted by the FBI and was taking them to the Billings, Montana, to federal authorities for unspecified crimes related to national security in that jurisdiction. She had put a pair of handcuffs in the sleeping area of the trailer. That way, if they were stopped, the person sleeping in the trailer could emerge in handcuffs. She hoped that there were no holes in her story.

What if TXA sends out more goons or bought off cops and tries to pull us over? They may not want to make a big scene on an interstate highway. They may wait for us to stop before trying anything.

#

A police radio call went into the California control center.

"We have sighted the perps at a truck stop in St. Cloud. They are getting back on the interstate. They have another person with them—a woman."

"Why didn't you apprehend them?"

"I thought we were just supposed to find out where they are, not take them into custody."

"They need to be picked up and held long enough for us to send out a man to take them off your hands. Go after them. They are headed for Fargo."

"We can't leave this general area without jeopardizing our jobs."

"Damn it. Okay. We'll have someone look for them near Fergus Falls. Out."

#

Pete and Pam had a pleasant conversation as he drove. Pam found him to be very engaging. He had a way about him that made her feel very comfortable, as if she had known him for years. Despite their troubled circumstances, their conversation was about life in general, relationships, and their past experiences. She was very attracted to him. His magnetism pulled her toward him as if she had no control over her emotions and did not want to have any. It occurred to her that they were about the same age; both were attractive and looked younger than their actual years. *We would make an attractive couple.*

Pam's relationship with her husband had grown stale over the years. Ever since the last child left home, there had been little interaction between them and no romance. They lived together and usually got along without fights or arguments. When there were fights, they were big, and Pam usually ended up leaving home and sleeping in a motel. She believed they loved each other, but that was as far as it went. He had his own life revolving around his job as a professor that did not include her. Pam suspected that he was too interested in some of his female students. If he arrived home late, it usually ended up in a fight between them.

But then again, she thought, her husband was not included in her FBI life either. For the most part, they were like two ships passing in the night, saying hello to each other as they passed. Pam had not felt the kind of passion she felt around Pete for several years. Passion had been dormant in her, and suddenly it was back. It was thrilling and confusing at the same time, and Pam was not sure how to handle it.

It appeared to Pam that Pete seemed totally unaware of the effect he was having on her and continued to chat without even a hint of flirting. *What do I have to do to let him know I am interested? Should I try?*

Pam broke out of her reverie as Pete turned into a truck stop in the Minneapolis area. She was suddenly ashamed of her attraction to Pete. *Pamela Robinson, what has gotten into you? Are you trying to step between Pete and Alex? What a mistake a triangle relationship would be in the midst of this TXA mess. Calm down, girl.* She shook her head and started to fan herself with a magazine from the front seat.

The truck stop was busy even at this time of the morning. Alex got out of the trailer and paid for the gas, getting a cup of coffee to go and a Snickers bar. Pam went to the trailer, and Pete moved over into the passenger's seat. They were back on the interstate within minutes and driving toward Fargo.

The conversation between Pete and Alex got off to a slow start. Alex had grown quite fond of Pete during their Internet and phone romance. She liked his ideals and believed he had a good heart. However, his subsequent bout with the bottle and his visit to his ex-wife were blows to her feelings. They had not had a chance to talk since he had driven to the stables on the motorcycle. When she first saw him, Alex was taken back by his good looks and charisma, but her feelings had been sobered by his revelations.

Pete broke the silence. "How did you know that guy was out there in the dark when you warned us to get down?"

"I heard movement and figured that, considering the sound and area it was coming from, it could only be made by a human."

"How did you know he was an enemy?"

"If the person making the noise was a friend, he or she would have identified themselves from the dark. There was no warning except the sound of someone stumbling and falling down. It could not be the police because the police would not sneak up on us. We had no allies or friends there. It had to be the TXA guy that was following you earlier in the day."

"We would probably all be dead if you hadn't warned us; you certainly are good with a gun."

"I learned to shoot when I went hunting as a young girl. I exhibited a talent for it, and my parents didn't stop me in developing my talent. I always thought guns were sporting goods, to be used in different shooting events. I have won many trophies, but I have killed two men within days of each other, and I don't feel very good inside."

"I had to kill when I was in the military. It took me awhile to get over the feelings. Whether the person I shot back there is dead or not, I don't have any feelings other than I am glad it was him and not me."

Alex couldn't hold back any longer. "Why did you go visit your ex-wife when you were going to meet me the same day? I thought we had developed a pleasant, warm bond between us. It hurts to think that you didn't feel the same way."

"I didn't do it to hurt you. I felt compelled to get a lot of guilt off my chest by apologizing to her for breaking up our marriage."

"That sounds logical. But it is the timing of the whole thing that bothers me. I thought we had this wonderful relationship even though it was long-distance. We are then thrown into this life-threatening series of events with both of us being chased and both of us trying desperately to help each other get out of the mess. I don't see how you could have been distracted by the need to apologize unless there is something more."

"I don't know what to say, Alex. I am a weak but passionate person. There are times I give in to my feelings without thinking about the possible consequences. Despite this, I still have the feelings toward you that I did before, and I hope we can develop something more together."

Pete continued, "I want you to know how deeply sorry I am that I disappointed you by my actions. Please forgive me. Perhaps we can start over."

The sincerity of his apology moved Alex. "I forgive you. I never have been jealous about any other man."

"Thank you, Alex. By the way, you are more beautiful than I ever imagined. Your pictures do not do you justice."

"I could say the same thing about you, Pete."

They both smiled, and Pete reached over and put his hand on Alex's shoulder. She put her hand on his and smiled lovingly. A feeling of sexual excitement welled up inside her, but then she remembered they were on the run.

Dawn was approaching as the Dodge approached Fargo. Alex spotted a highway patrol car following her.

"Pete, we're being followed. There's a state trooper right behind us." Pete looked but couldn't see the car because of the trailer.

"If I have to pull over, get out and run to the trailer to wake up Pam."

Chapter 41

Pete reached into his shoulder holster and got his gun. His face was scowled in anticipation; his eyes were narrow slants.

Alex had a decision to make if the patrol officer tried to pull her over. *I can't outrun him. They will set up roadblocks if we don't pull...*

Before she could complete her thought, the state patrol car turned on its siren and pulled into the left lane, accelerating. Alex's grip tightened on the steering wheel as she drove, looking in the rearview mirror.

The sirens from the state patrol car woke up Pam in the trailer. She immediately sat up and grabbed her Glock. Alex began to slow down and drove toward the shoulder.

"I don't think we have any choice but to pull over, Pete."

The patrol car screamed by Alex's rig at high speed and continued on the interstate toward Fargo.

"Unbelievable! What a relief!" exclaimed Alex.

"Yeah," said Pete. "It certainly got my attention."

"I don't know how they could have lost track of where we are, except that it's still dark. Pam must be right about turning off our cell phones. We have had no trouble since we left Eau Claire, other than that scare. I keep waiting for the other shoe to drop. TXA seems to have awesome surveillance capabilities."

By that time, they were near the Fargo/Moorhead area. Fargo, North Dakota, and Moorhead, Minnesota, are only separated by the Red River. Dawn was approaching. Alex drove the truck through Moorhead, over the Red River and through Fargo, pulling off I-94 at a truck stop on the west side of Fargo.

"I've heard of the Red River Valley, but this is all flat. Where are the sides of the valley?" asked Pete.

Alex responded, "North Dakota is so flat that they don't have any valleys, so they made one up."

"Yeah, sure."

Alex laughed. "In Montana, people tell North Dakota jokes. But other places do the same thing. Arizonians tell Montana snowbird jokes."

While the truck was being gassed up, everyone grabbed a danish or donut and coffee and got back into the rig. Alex drove out into the country off the interstate. She let the horses out to walk around in the grass next to the road. Pam and Pete stood in the bright morning sunlight sipping coffee from to-go cups. Pam was grateful for the warm sun. The temperature had fallen to forty degrees during the night, and she was cold despite a blanket on the bed. It was Pam's turn to drive. She had not slept well in the cold. She was thinking about having missed her hot morning shower.

The three held a conference before heading out on the next leg of their journey. They agreed that surveillance of the truck and trailer by TXA from the air was a strong possibility. "We better stay off the interstate highways," said Alex. "TXA is less likely to be looking for us on the side roads, and there are many pickups with horse trailers in North Dakota. It will be the safest thing to do." Everyone agreed.

It was Pam's turn to drive, with Alex in the passenger seat and Pete in the trailer. They took the back road toward Bismarck. The roads were all straight and flat. Alex was sipping on a cup of coffee trying to relax. She had had only three hours of sleep and felt tired.

Pam was the first one to talk. "I've been waiting for TXA to surprise us again. It's like waiting in suspense for the other shoe to drop. I keep wondering when and where. I almost had a heart attack in the trailer when the sirens started. I was startled out of my sleep and hit my head on the low ceiling when I sat up to grab my gun."

"I agree, it's nerve-racking waiting for them to strike," Alex responded. "I feel like a sitting duck out here in plain sight in the wide-open spaces of North Dakota. They must not have enough manpower to find us. They couldn't have bought off every state patrolman in three states."

Pam responded, "I think they can buy off a large number of people—cops, FBI agents, politicians, you name it. Big corporations like TXA make huge amounts of money. TXA made $40 billion last year, about the same as Exxon. Paying off a few cops is pocket change to them."

"How does buying off politicians and police make money for them?"

"It's what the politicians can do for them to make more money," answered Pam. "During Prohibition, the police and politicians were bought off so the criminals could make more money selling booze."

"So whatever they are doing, they must think there is a pot of gold waiting for them," said Alex.

"Yes," Pam said. "We have to figure out what they are up to. It normally doesn't make any sense for two everyday citizens to be chased across the county for making a few waves. What you and Pete have done is a major threat to them even if it appears to be innocuous on the surface. Do you or Pete have any idea what their end game is?"

"We don't really know," Alex responded. "We know they are tied in with UPA and that military products are being shipped to some of our military bases. But we don't know what the exact products are or why money from UPA is going to shell corporations, which buy the military products that get shipped to our military bases."

Pam shook her head. "Why the elaborate cover-up?"

"That's what we hope to find out in Great Falls," replied Alex.

"Speaking of Great Falls, TXA undoubtedly knows I am headed to my hometown, but they don't know we're going to Great Falls. As long as we can drop the horses and trailer on a remote spot on my folks' ranch and not go into town, we can relax a little at the ranch and on our way to Great Falls."

"I'll relax if we are driving at night," said Pam.

Alex stretched out her arms and legs and put her hand on the back of her neck, rubbing out the tired. "Once we get to Great Falls, what are your thoughts on getting into the air force base?"

"I have gotten onto many military bases but always had a meeting previously set up with the provost marshal," said Pam. "I have never gotten entry without telling them who I was going to see. Sometimes they will announce my arrival before they let me through the gate. I always have to get a temporary pass."

"How do we get Pete and me on the base also?"

"I'll do the same thing as before and tell them you are under arrest and are my prisoners. I think that's better than putting you both in the trunk."

"But we don't have a trunk," answered Alex.

Pam smiled. "I just had a vision of you and Pete in a trunk."

"Trapped in a trunk with Pete could be interesting." Alex laughed.

"Once we get inside Malmstrom, we'll want to find out what happens to the shipments from TXA. I think we need to find out when the shipments normally arrive at the base from Nevada and get to the gate just ahead of that time. Then we will follow the truck and observe where the truck is unloaded. We'll have a much better idea of what TXA is doing."

Nothing was said for the next several miles. Alex broke the silence. "Pete was an officer in the military in a black ops unit, but he doesn't seem to want to take charge in this situation we're in."

Pam thought for a moment. "You have a strong personality, Alex. You are a go-to girl. I think Pete has let you take charge because he doesn't want to upset you."

"But how did he climb the ranks in the military?"

"I think Pete is very well liked by everyone, and he needs that attention. He is the type who is a great leader as long as he has orders from someone else to carry out. He works at pleasing almost everyone. If he is rejected by someone whose attention he likes or needs, I'll bet he would try to move heaven and earth to get the person back under his spell."

The two were silent for a while. Finally, Alex turned to Pam and asked, "Do you think Pete is handsome?"

Pam wanted to use the right words and paused for a moment. "I think he is a handsome and charming person. You are pretty interested in him, aren't you?"

"Yes, but I have my reservations sometimes. In your experience as an older woman, do you think he is the kind of man that would cheat?"

"Older woman? Are you calling me an old lady?" Pam asked with a quizzical smile.

"Oh, no. I meant a more experienced woman."

"He likes women, but he is rarely the aggressor. I think what you have to watch out for are other women. I don't think Pete's will power is strong. If a woman really goes after him, I don't believe he can resist.

Les femmes sont attirées par Pete comme c'est un papillon à une flamme de feu."

"What does that mean? I only understood the word Pete."

"Nothing new. Just the French version of what I said in English." Alex didn't believe her.

Before Alex could say another word, the loud noise from a helicopter vibrated throughout the truck cab. Looking up out of the passenger side window, Alex saw a two-person helicopter overhead to her right. Leaning out the glass bubble of the copter, a man was aiming a rifle at the pickup. Alex yelled at Pam, "Trouble overhead! Vary your speed. Take evasive maneuvers. They are aiming at us."

A bullet shattered the windshield in front of Alex. After she realized she was not hit, she rolled down the passenger window, pulled out her pistol, and fired three rapid shots at the tail rotor of the copter while another bullet hit the passenger door. The copter wobbled, shook, and veered away from the road.

The three shots had disabled the rear rotor.

Pam yelled. "Are you hit? Are you hit?"

Alex yelled back, "No. I got the SOB. I got him. He's gonna crash."

Pam slowed down to a stop, got out, and ran around the front of the pickup to inspect the right side and Alex. Pete hustled out of the horse trailer. They were in a rural area without traffic. Pete and Pam inspected Alex for signs of blood and then looked at the sorry state of the right side of the pickup cab. Alex dusted small pieces of glass off her clothes.

"Are they coming back?" asked Pete.

"I doubt it," replied Alex. "I saw pieces fly off the rear rotor, and it looked like they were having trouble keeping it in the air. But I didn't hear a crash."

"I vote we get out of here," yelled Pam as she rounded the front of the pickup and got back behind the steering wheel.

"Hell yes," said Alex.

"You're damned straight," said Pete. They piled into the cab, and Pam floored the accelerator, leaving small pieces of glass beside the road in a dry and desolate area in rural North Dakota.

Chapter 42

The pickup truck approached Bismarck where the three would go through the ritual of the two previous stops. It was nearly noon, and they needed food. Everyone was anxious because of the helicopter attack, and they ate and moved rapidly, looking at everything and everyone around them. They wanted to get away from Bismarck as soon as possible.

Pete and Pam occupied the cab for the next leg of the journey, and Alex said she would get some sleep in the trailer. Although it had been cold the previous night, the temperature at noon in Bismarck was over ninety, and the sun was relentless in heating up everything it touched. Ninety degrees in the sun felt like it was over a hundred. The trailer was boiling hot. Alex opened every window in the trailer and gave extra water to the horses. She knew from experience that sleeping in the trailer would be difficult in the heat and decided to try to sleep in the backseat of the air-conditioned pickup cab. The three headed toward Beach, North Dakota, with Pete driving.

The tireless, unchanging Dakota countryside did nothing to help the three tired travelers. A motel room with a shower and air-conditioning sounded good to all of them. As they neared Montana, the North Dakota Badlands offered a welcome change in scenery.

When they pulled into a truck stop near Beach, North Dakota, Alex got a cup of coffee and got into the driver's seat. "We have two ways we can travel. One is west on the interstate to Glendive, Montana, and then north to the ranch. The other is north on a North Dakota state highway and then west to the ranch. The state highway route takes an hour longer in theory, but with the agriculture traffic and oilrigs, it will take even longer. The disadvantage of going the faster route is that TXA would expect us to take that route. What do you two think?"

Pam responded, "I thought I heard some truckers talking about a Montana Highway Patrol check point on the interstate at the Montana border. I called Tee Scott in Boston to have him check it out. He called me back, but he could not get a good answer from anyone. There's definitely a roadblock, and they are stopping everyone."

"I think we need to avoid any roadblock," Pete said. "Even if it is legit, one of them could report our position back to TXA."

Alex responded, "I agree. We will get to the ranch well after dark taking the slower route, but I know my way around that area."

Before they left, they spent some time standing near the trailer drinking coffee. Pete perked up. "What is that nice smell?"

"If you look across the prairie in the direction of the wind, you will see clouds on the horizon. The dark under the clouds is falling rain. That's a thunderstorm quite a few miles away. The wind blew the smell of the rain on the prairie in this direction. I really love the smell. It's so clean and fresh."

The drive from Beach to the ranch would take them more than five hours. Once they were underway, Alex took a few minutes to tell the others about the ranch.

"We're going to stay in a house that was built fifty years ago by my dad and grandfather. It was built for a ranch manager and his family. I've seen several managers come and go. The present manager has a home in Nashua, the town nearby, so he doesn't use the house. I use it in the summers when I visit. I don't like being stuck in Glasgow away from my horses."

She continued. "I'm not going to contact my folks; when the ranch manager comes out, I'll swear him to secrecy, not only with my folks but with everyone else in the area. Pam, you could help out by flashing your badge and telling him that it is a matter of national security that he keep quiet about us being on the ranch."

As they drove north on North Dakota state highway, the three chatted about any subject they could think of to keep their minds off the danger they were in. At one point, Alex told them that in rural Montana and North Dakota, an overwhelming percentage of vehicles on the roads were pickups. "Have you even seen a car since we left the interstate?"

Pete said, "Maybe not, but that looks like one headed south toward us."

"Here I am telling you we have not seen a car, and one pops up."

"I'd say he's moving toward us at very high speed," Pete offered. The car sped past.

Looking in the rearview mirror, Alex saw the car's break lights come on, and the car make a sudden and fast U-turn in the middle of the highway.

"It looks like we have trouble," warned Alex. Pam and Pete tried to look out the rear window of the truck, but the trailer blocked their view.

"Hold on," said Alex as she pushed the accelerator toward the floorboard.

The car moved toward the pickup and trailer at high speed. Soon it was able to pull along the driver's side the pickup. The car slowed down to the pickup's speed and started making small turns back and forth. It seemed clear to Alex that the car was going to try to force them off the road.

"Brace yourselves," yelled Alex. Pete and Pam could clearly see the car drop back toward the road edge and then accelerate toward the front of the pickup.

Alex anticipated the auto's first thrust at the pickup and turned the truck into the car as it moved toward the front bumper of the truck. The truck and car hit with a loud impact. The vehicles bounced off each other and swerved from side to side but stayed on the highway.

Within a minute, the car again tried to push the truck into the ditch, and again Alex anticipated the move and turned the truck into the impact. Again, the vehicles stayed in the road. Again and again, the car moved into the truck. Repeatedly, Alex slammed the truck into the car.

Alex's temperament in a crisis was obvious to Pete and Pam. She had a fierce determination. It reminded Pam of Alex in the mounted shooting practice she had witnessed in Massachusetts.

Keeping the trailer on the road was difficult. With each turn into the car, the weight of the horse trailer caused the trailer to fishtail, making it even more difficult for Alex to keep the rig on the road.

"I need some help," yelled Alex. "Someone shoot the tires on that car."

Pam was closest to the back door window. She rolled down the window and took her 9-mm from her shoulder holster. The truck was rocking back and forth as Alex tried to keep it on the road. It was difficult to get a good aim on the car's tires. The car dropped back slightly, as was its habit, and then took another run at the front of the pickup. Pam was able to keep her aim on the right rear tire and fired four times rapidly. At least one of the bullets pierced the tire, causing the driver to lose control of the car. The car dropped back and was swerving back and forth across the highway as the driver tried to maintain control. Alex and Pete watched as the car went into the ditch, flipped, rolled over several times, and came to a stop on its top.

Alex pulled over and stopped the truck, halfway on the highway. All three got out of the truck and looked back at the overturned car. It looked like someone was struggling to get out of the car. All three reached for their guns. Suddenly the car exploded, sending a big ball of fire into the air. They could feel the shock waves. They stared in amazement at the burning vehicle. No one could have escaped the explosion. Not a word was spoken between the three. They stood in awe of the spectacle.

Alex went to the trailer to check on the horses. She climbed into the trailer and checked each horse carefully, petting and talking gently to each. Soon she closed the trailer doors. "The horses are shaken up but are not hurt," Alex said as she walked past Pete and Pam toward the driver's seat. "Let's get out of here."

Chapter 43

Alex drove her pickup into Nashua, Montana, the closest town to her family's ranch. Glasgow was another twenty minutes west. Alex hoped TXA did not know about the ranch and would concentrate on her parents' home in Glasgow.

From Nashua, they turned north onto a dirt road and drove about five miles. It was pitch-black outside. The headlights created a narrow tunnel of light surrounded by the dark through which they passed. All they could see was the dirt road and, now and then, barbed-wire fences to the side of the road. Alex turned the rig into a road blocked by a gate and stopped. She had driven the road to the gates hundreds of times and gave it no thought, but to the others, it was an unfamiliar place in the dark. They had no idea where they were. Alex cut the lights and engine off, and they sat in the dark.

Alex whispered to Pam and Pete. "So far so good. Let's sit here awhile and let our eyes get accustomed to the dark. Let me know if you see or hear anything, anything at all."

The group grew silent and peered into the dark, listening for any noise. A faint howl was heard miles away. "Coyote," whispered Alex.

"Do you think they're waiting ahead to ambush us?" asked Pam in a low voice.

"I don't know. I've been trying to figure out the probability that TXA would know about the ranch. The ownership of the ranch is in the name of a close corporation, an entity allowed under Montana Law for ma-pa businesses. My parents own the corporation. TXA would have to know the name of the location of the ranch or the name of the corporation or both. There is no database that connects corporate names with the location of real property. I would say the probability is low that they have connected me with this ranch property. But I still want to be careful.

"Pete, the way it works out here in the west, the person in the passenger seat opens the gate and closes it after the truck pulls through. You should get out and close the gate after I drive through."

Pete acknowledged his role as gatekeeper, and after closing the gate and running toward the rig, he noticed that it was completely black except for the taillights on the trailer. *No lights, no houses, no vehicles. Middle of nowhere. I have never seen it so black.*

The road into the ranch was across flat ground but was full of bumps and ruts and slow going. "Dad needs to blade this road," Alex said. She had not turned on the headlights. She knew the ground more or less and felt her way along. Finally, she turned on the parking lights. They could then see then saw a dim outline of a house, which became more distinctive the closer they got. Alex drove near the front door and turned on the truck lights, which made the front door visible. It was temporarily blinding. The house was a simple ranch-style home, built years ago but not rundown. Alex bounded up to the front door, turned to her right, reached under a rock, and found the key.

She opened the front door and went in slowly. She walked around the inside of the house, turning on lights and looking in each room. Satisfied that it was safe, she returned to the front door and waved for everyone to come in. Pete turned off the truck, and he and Pam walked up a couple of steps on to a porch and then into the door.

Pam said, "That felt like the longest trip I have ever taken. I hope there is a shower in here."

"Yes, there is, and even an indoor toilet," Alex laughed.

"I have a problem... I don't have a change of clothes. Pete doesn't either."

Pete said, "I'll save you the embarrassment and go nude along with you." He smiled.

"You men! Here I am feeling sweaty and dirty, and you only think about..." Pam acted put out but grinned.

"Pete! Be good or you'll sleep in the barn," kidded Alex. "Pam, I have clothes you can wear until we can get to a store. You are desperate for a shower, so you go first."

"Do you think we need a sentry tonight?" Pete asked Alex.

"TXA may not know their men spotted us on the road. I don't think they had time to talk to TXA in the short period of the encounter. Anyway, I'm sure there is no cell phone coverage in that part of North Dakota. My best bet is that they have people stationed in Glasgow waiting for me to drive up to my parents' home. Word might spread that we are out here at the ranch but not by tomorrow morning. The house can't be seen from the road."

"None of us are rested enough to do sentry duty anyway," said Pete.

"Okay, we all sleep tonight," said Alex. You can have the bed over there in that bedroom that used to be used for our managers' children. I'll sleep on the couch, and Pam can have the master bedroom."

While Alex took the horses to the barn, Pam and Pete took their showers and searched the home for sheets, blankets, and food. The temperature had dropped into the fifty-degree range, a swing of more than thirty degrees. They each made their beds and were quickly asleep. Alex came back from the barn, turned off all the lights, and lay down on the couch with a blanket and a pillow.

The little house stood in the vast prairie in the black of the night, its occupants wrapped in their blankets, falling deep into sleep.

Chapter 44

After a couple of hours of sleep, Alex woke up with an aching back. The couch was very uncomfortable. She tried stretching and changing position, but nothing seemed to work. Alex wondered if Pam would mind some company in her queen bed. Alex quietly moved down the hall to the bedroom door and tried to open it. It was locked. She tried calling out in a loud whisper and tapping on the door, but nothing woke Pam up. Alex went back down the hall and looked into Pete's room. He was sound asleep. There was plenty of room for both of them in the bed. She pushed on Pete to see if he would wake up but got no more than a snort out of him. Believing he would not wake up, she got her blanket and pillow, slipped into bed, and was soon asleep.

During the night, they had rolled into each other quite by accident, but neither woke up. Out of instinct, Pete draped an arm over Alex's sleeping body. They spent the rest of the night snuggled together, each in their own dreams. Early in the morning, while it was still dark out, Pete awoke and found Alex wrapped in his arms, her face on his chest. She looked so pretty, he thought. He was unsure whether to wake her. He did not want her warm, nesting body to pull away. His brain was still foggy, and he was still in that dreamy state somewhere between sleep and consciousness. He pulled her tighter against him and nuzzled into her hair. He lay there with her and slipped back into sleep unknowingly, still holding her in his arms.

Alex woke with a start, one eye open, trying to focus. The reality of being in Pete's arms was confusing to her. She pulled back, waking him up. She was not mad. Sleeping against him had felt secure and peaceful.

"What did we do last night?" she asked Pete in a sleepy voice.

"Nothing. I think we just gravitated together during the night. I thought it was very pleasant."

"It was very nice but don't get any ideas," she said dreamingly.

Her words were not very convincing. She looked sleepily down at him for a brief time and then slipped back under the covers next to him. He took her into his arms again and looked down at her snuggled into his chest. She had a pleasant half smile on her face.

The sun woke Pam up at six. She put on her same dirty clothes and headed down the hall toward the kitchen. Pete's door was open, and Pam could see Alex buried in Pete's arms. They looked so comfortable together. Pam stood and stared for a moment and wondered how it felt to snuggle up to Pete. She suddenly shook her head and headed for the kitchen. There was coffee in the cupboards, sealed up in a mason jar with the lid closed tightly on it. Pam set about making a pot with the gusto of someone preparing a gourmet breakfast.

The window off the kitchen looked out on the vast prairie. The sun coming in the window was extraordinarily bright. The air felt fresh and clean and was invigorating to Pam. She wanted to go out and walk into the fields with the sun warming her face. While the coffee was perking, Pam went for a walk outside. She walked around the house and then east into the sun. The air was chilly, but the sun was warming. The air was so clear it sparkled like crystal. It seemed to Pam that it was so clear she could see hills in the vast distance out on the ends of the earth.

The little house seemed even smaller in the vastness of the plains spreading out in all directions. *Was this the way it was in* Little House on the Prairie? The romantic west fascinated Pam, who felt a romantic twinge at all she saw and felt. She thought about Pete and wondered why she felt this great passion for him. She was, after all, married with grown children and a husband back home. She still loved him, but the passion she felt for Pete made her realize that the passion for her husband had long ago left the marriage. Her passion for Pete was unexplainable. She really didn't trust him and felt like she should warn Alex. On the other hand, maybe she should keep her mouth shut because maybe she was jealous of Alex and the attention she got from Pete. Her distrust of Pete and her lust for him were pulling her in opposite directions, and she could not identify the reason for either one. Rather than dwell on the unexplainable, she turned to soak in the beauty around her.

Pam realized that the coffee was probably ready and headed back toward the house feeling happy and full of energy for a new day.

The smell of the coffee must have been the deciding factor in waking Alex and Pete. They came straggling into the kitchen with blankets around their shoulders, their hair a mess, and sleepy looks on their faces.

"Good morning, love birds," said Pam to the two.

"It was the comfortable bed. That's the reason I was sleeping there. Pete stayed on his side of the bed all night," replied Alex.

"Sure, sure. It looked comfortable in there but not because of the bed," Pam replied with a grin.

"Spying on me?" Alex pretended to be mad. "Don't answer that!" She laughed. "Give me some coffee!"

The three sat around the kitchen table drinking coffee and planning the rest of the trip. "The TXA goons have to be in Glasgow expecting us to show up. It won't take them long to find out about the ranch, so we can't camp out here very long," Alex warned.

"Agreed," said Pete. "The first thing I want to do is get some food in me."

"And I want to buy some clean clothes," said Pam.

Just then, there was a knock at the door. Alex jumped up and peeked out the window.

"It's Harold Strand, the ranch manager," announced Alex as she went to the front door.

"Hi, Alex. You didn't tell me you were coming."

"Good to see you again, Mr. Strand. My friends and I are on an important trip, and we need your help."

Alex and Pam told Strand that their trip was one vital to national security and must be kept secret; they were leaving and would be back in a couple of days but asked him not to tell anyone that they had been there, not even Alex's parents.

"How much danger are you in, Alex?" asked Strand.

"Enough to have been in two gun battles."

"This sounds like pretty serious stuff. But I'm not surprised that you and your forty-fives survived gun battles. I'll keep my rifle ready and my mouth shut. Don't worry. If I see any strangers, I'll scare them off."

Strand went out to the barn, and the group continued planning. "I think we should drive to Wolf Point, the last small town we went through on the way here. It is in the opposite direction of Glasgow, and TXA won't expect us to go there. We can eat and buy clothes there. In addition, I need to buy some ammo. I've had enough coffee. Let's get going!" Pam asserted.

Alex asked Arnold Strand, the ranch manager, if she could swap trucks with him for a few days. Stand's truck was a Ford F-350 dually, four-by-four diesel with four doors. "Your truck looks in pretty bad shape, Alex. I hope you're not planning any more road battles."

"Please, Arnold. They know what my truck looks like, and they will try to kill us. I really need something new to drive."

"Okay, but be careful, for God's sake."

They piled into Strand's truck and drove off the ranch toward Wolf Point. Alex had on her cowboy hat and boots, and she wrapped up a change of clothes in a small bag along with toothbrush and other toiletries. They stopped at a local restaurant, ate big breakfasts, and drank more coffee.

In eastern Montana, the biggest clothing stores were the ranch supply stores that sold livestock feed, fence posts, dinner place settings, western wear, guns, ammo, tools, boots, popcorn, Christmas cards, western belt buckles from Montana Silversmiths, and practically everything else. Alex always thought that ranch supply stores had a unique smell she associated with Montana and home. She browsed while Pete and Pam bought jeans and shirts. Pete also needed some all-terrain boots, and he found some with a western style. Pam already had her FBI-recommended all-purpose shoes.

Pete decided to buy a cowboy hat. It was the finishing touch to his new cowboy appearance. Alex thought that he looked very handsome outfitted in his western wear. He didn't look like a dude, like so many who came to Montana for the first time and dressed like cowboys. He walked up to her and tipped his hat to her. "Howdy, ma'am."

"Hi, cowboy! You sure look handsome in your new duds." Alex gave him a big smile.

Pam walked up in a new cowgirl shirt and jeans. "Nice outfit, but you should get a cowgirl hat," said Alex. "You would be the only one of us without one."

She pulled Pam over to the hat section and started putting hats on her head. "I feel silly wearing one of these."

"No you don't. Try this one."

Pam looked at herself in the mirror. "That's not too bad."

Pete went to look at belt buckles. Pam turned to Alex. "Pete sure looks handsome in that outfit."

"Yeah, but I think he would probably look good in anything," Alex replied.

Pam paused for a second. "Or nothing," she said with a grin and a twinkle in her eye. Alex playfully hit her on her shoulder.

Pam left Alex looking for Pete to show off her cowgirl look. Alex was looking for ammo. Her thoughts were on Pam. *I wonder if Pam is sweet on Pete. She talks about him a lot.*

Alex looked back at Pam showing off her outfit to Pete. Pete had a big smile on his face and was obviously telling her she looked very good. Pam was a bit flirty it seemed to Alex.

Alex told the group, "We don't know what kind of problems we will run into. I think we need to stock up on ammo. I'm down to seven shells." The group bought sufficient ammo for several battles, plus a reserve.

They all walked out of the store in cowboy hats and got into the truck. Many of the men in town were dressed the same way, as well as some of the women. Everyone wore jeans. The little group blended in well.

"We're off to Great Falls," said Alex as they piled into the white Ford pickup. Alex turned around and headed back toward the ranch to the road across the Fort Peck Dam and then turned south. The trio's Great Falls adventure was off to a solid start.

Chapter 45

The route to Great Falls took the group south on Mt 13 S. After forty-five minutes, the Ford turned west onto Mt 200. That highway would carry them all the way to Great Falls some six hours away. This part of Montana was sparsely populated. All the towns along the route were small; several consisted of a post office and a bar in the same building.

The countryside was varied. There were places that looked like badlands, while others were lush with crops. Many of the places along the way were cattle ranches with huge fields dotted with cattle. The fields alternated between being green to brown, depending on irrigation. It seemed like most of the cattle were black.

"Black angus," said Alex. "They're bringing the best prices."

Several times, Alex pointed out across the fields and told Pete and Pam to look at the antelope.

"Where?" Neither could see any.

"It takes awhile for someone from the east to develop the eye for seeing them," Alex told them.

The biggest town on the route was Lewistown, which looked like a major metropolis compared with the tiny towns, but it had only 5,900 people. It was a regional trade center for farmers and ranchers. There were far more doctors and lawyers than 5,900 people could support, but the tiny towns and ranches over such a huge area added up to quite a few additional people who spent their money in Lewistown. The trip to Lewistown took a little over four hours. It was midafternoon when they pulled into a gas station.

Alex loaded up on diesel fuel for the two large tanks in the big Ford. They looked around for a place to eat nearby and ended up at one of the ma and pa restaurants; their specialty was broiled chicken. The food was great, but the decor's best feature was red-and-white plastic tablecloths.

Alex, Pam, and Pete sat for a long time after they finished eating. All three were staring into space, drinking sips of coffee now and then. Everyone was tired. They had all been on high alert for TXA henchmen after the high-adrenalin conflicts. The morning drive had been uneventful. They had not felt this safe since their trip began, and the lack of adrenalin was exhausting.

"Maybe we should all take a nap," said Alex. "It doesn't look like any of us are in good enough shape to drive."

"I agree. I am really feeling my age," said Pete. "I would be worthless if we got into another gunfight. I need to sleep. Let's check into that motel down the street."

They checked into the motel. It was small but clean. They weren't looking for luxury, just sleep. Pam and Alex took one room, and Pete got a room with a single bed. They were asleep in minutes.

The trip to Great Falls took only a couple more hours. They got up early the next morning and were in front of the gate at Malmstrom Air Force Base at sunup. They parked the truck among a number of cars and trucks in a service station very near the base's main gate on Goddard Avenue. They sat in the truck, hidden from suspicion by many vehicles surrounding the Miracle Mile Service and Repair station. They could easily see who entered the gate. Pam got into the driver's seat and turned to Pete. "Put on these handcuffs and sit behind me when we go to the gate." Alex sat next to him. "I don't have another pair of handcuffs so put your hands down between your knees like you have them on. Both of you need to try to look guilty and stupid."

After several hours of watching, they noticed a large truck with Nevada plates pulling into the gate. "There's the TXA truck from the Nevada plant," said Alex. "The information on the disk was accurate. But what's in that truck? What are they shipping and why?"

"Get in the back, Alex," said Pam. "Let's go find out!" Pam put the Ford in gear and arrived at the gate while the big truck was still stopped at the gate.

When the truck pulled through, Pam quickly flashed her badge to the guard. "I'm Pam Robinson. FBI. I have two prisoners that I need to house in the brig for a day."

The baby-faced security guard wore a blue beret. He looked like he was sixteen years old, not even old enough to shave. He looked at Pam's ID. He turned to his companion in the gatehouse. "Is this normal?" The other guard looked puzzled and shrugged his shoulders. The young guard turned back to Pam. "Why don't you house the prisoners in one of the local jails? This does not seem like air force business."

Pam looked sternly at the guard. "Son, this is not a normal situation. This is a matter of national security, directly concerning the military, and local law enforcement is suspected as accomplices."

"I'll call the provost marshal's office and have them lead you there."

"I know my way," Pam lied.

Pam immediately drove away, watching carefully as the big freight truck was turning a curve in the distance. Pam had to speed to catch up. The truck continued on Goddard Avenue for some distance and turned off to the right into the lot of a warehouse building. Pam pulled as far off to the side as she could and watched the unloading dock. The airmen on the dock quickly unloaded the crates and piled them on the dock. As soon as the truck was unloaded, it pulled away from the dock and went back the way it had come in. The crates on the dock were left outside. A guard with a rifle stood near them.

Pete said. "Well, that guard is a good sign those crates are filled with something other than cans of pork and beans."

"Let's wait to see what they do with the cargo," said Alex. They continued to watch the crates on the dock for about an hour when a smaller truck with Montana plates came into the lot and backed up to the loading dock. Airmen came out on the dock and began loading the crates on the truck. The driver got out of truck cab. He was short, in his fifties, with a beer belly, balding head, and white pasty skin. He acted as if he knew the airmen loading the crates.

When the loading was close to finished, Pam suddenly opened the door. "I'm going to check this out," said Pam as she got out of the Ford. She walked across the parking lot and approached the short, balding man. "I'm Pam Robinson. FBI." She flashed her badge. "Could I see some identification?" The man was startled. He started to reach for his wallet but turned and yelled toward the dock. "Sergeant, could you come here please?"

The burly sergeant jumped down from the docks and walked over. "What's going on, Frank?"

"This lady says she is from the FBI and wants to see my ID. Can she do that?"

The sergeant turned to Pam and asked to see her FBI badge. Pam gave it to him. He looked at it and handed it back to her.

"Mrs. Robinson, would you mind telling me what you are doing here?"

"I am here on a mission of national security. It is very important. I want to know what this man is doing and what is going on here."

"Mrs. Robinson. You have no jurisdiction here. The 341st Security Forces are in charge on this base. I am going to have to ask you to leave. Now."

Pam looked up on the dock. Eight members of the 341st stood looking at her in their blue berets with rifles pointed at her.

"I said leave *now.*"

Pam knew she should leave but she stood defiantly staring at the sergeant. She glanced at his name badge. "Sergeant Jarrett, I am going to report this to my superiors in Boston."

"If you don't leave, Mrs. Robinson, we will ship you back to Boston in a pine box."

Pam turned on her heels and walked back to the pickup. She could feel ten sets of eyes on her back and hoped no one had an itchy trigger finger. She jumped into the truck. Alex was behind the wheel. "Gun it." The pickup truck's wheels squealed as Alex tore out of the lot and back on to Goddard Avenue toward the main gate.

Alex said, "I figure that the sergeant will tell his superiors about you, Pam. If he is on the TXA payroll, the goons will be after us again."

Pete looked out the window behind him. "They're not following us. Let's go back to Miracle Mile Service Station and hide the pickup in all those cars. We'll wait for the truck to come back through the gate and follow it."

#

Sergeant Jarrett called the security forces office. "There was an FBI agent by the name of Pamela Robinson snooping around down here at loading dock a few minutes ago. The TXA shipment came in, and we were loading onto Frank Smith's truck when she came up to us."

"Did you catch a license plate number?"

"No, the truck was too far away, near the edge of the lot. All I could tell is that it was a white F-250 or F-350 Ford dually diesel with Montana plates. There were at least two other people in the truck. The truck had four doors. I saw a man in the backseat and another woman driving."

"Did Robinson say what she wanted?"

"She said she wanted to know what was going on and that it was a case that involved national security. Do you think the FBI is on to us?"

"No, we have carefully placed people on the inside at the FBI that are steering agents away from any investigation. Still, this is strange. I better pass this up the line and see what they want us to do."

#

Alex parked the Ford in the service station parking lot and waited for the Montana truck to drive back through the gate. They only had to wait five minutes. The truck went through the guard gate and continued straight ahead. The street changed name after it left the base to Second Avenue N. The truck passed directly in front of the Miracle Mile Service Station and Alex's pickup. "We can't follow very close," said Pam. "That short, paunchy truck driver saw the pickup." They slipped in two cars behind the truck. It turned left at Fifty-Seventh Street S. They continued to follow at a safe distance. The truck turned left again on Tenth Avenue S, which was also Mt. Highway 200, the same highway that the trio had used in traveling to Malmstrom. "He is headed back east the way we came," said Alex.

Mt. Highway 200 followed the same route as US Highway 89 and US Highway 191 for quite a few miles until each turned south at different locations. The Montana panel truck did not turn south on either highway, so it was clear to Alex that the truck was headed for Lewistown where they had slept the night before. They followed it into Lewistown where it stopped at a truck stop for gas. Alex decided to pull over down the street at another gas station so that the driver would not recognize the pickup. She got some more diesel fuel in case the TXA truck led them on a long journey.

While she was fueling the pickup, Frank Smith turned and looked back toward Alex. Alex froze.

Chapter 46

The phone rang in the control center at TXA. "This is Col. Howard Judah at Malmstrom Air Force Base. May I speak to the person in charge?"

"Hello, this is Ron Fenton. What do you have?"

"An FBI person was snooping around here not too long ago down at the docks. Her name is Pam Robinson with the FBI Boston office."

"Robinson? Did she have anyone else with her?"

"Yes, our entrance gate reported her driving in with two prisoners to put in the brig overnight," said Judah. "But we don't think they were prisoners. The so-called female prisoner drove the truck away from the dock."

"They have surfaced again," said Fenton, addressing no one in particular. He turned back to the phone. "How long ago did they leave?"

"It has probably been twenty to thirty minutes," replied the colonel.

"Shit." Fenton was frustrated. "Why so long to report this?"

"The sergeant at the dock called my lieutenant immediately, but it took awhile for the lieutenant to track me down."

"Do you know which direction they went?"

"No."

"Keep me informed, damn it." Fenton threw his phone across the room.

Fenton walked over to Trixie at her terminal, trying to cool down. "Where was Pam Robinson the last we knew?"

"She got in Alex Pipe's pickup along with Pete Oxwood in Eau Claire, and they took I-90 north to Fargo and then west. We were sure they were headed to Alex's home in Glasgow, Montana, but they never arrived. The last we knew, they were headed north from I-90 along the North Dakota/Montana state line."

"Didn't we dispatch some locals down that road?"

"They were found dead in a burned-out car along the road," replied Trixie. "So we don't know if they saw Pipe's pickup truck or not."

"Her pickup is a bland-colored Dodge Ram pulling a horse trailer, right?"

"Yeah. So?"

"Her bland-colored pickup is probably following our delivery truck. I don't know if it is pulling a horse trailer. If not, what did they do with the horses? Okay, Trixie, use the satellite to find a bland pickup probably pulling a horse trailer. And when you locate it, use our assets to stop them permanently."

Trixie advised the camera operator on the spy satellite to turn their cameras on to Mt. Highway 200 out of Great Falls. When she was notified that the camera was positioned on the highway, she used her controller, which looked similar to a video game controller, to zoom in the camera on the highway. She had to guess how far along the road they would have traveled from Great Falls in the lapse of thirty minutes or so and concentrated on vehicles in that area first. She spent fifteen minutes scanning vehicles without success. There were too many pickups on the road, some with horse trailers and some without, and a number of them were light colored. *Does anyone drive a car in that state?* She didn't realize that according to statistics, every other vehicle in Montana was a pickup.

Frustrated, Trixie decided to try to find the TXA truck first and see what was following it. There were only a few medium-sized trucks on the highway, and she soon found a truck she felt was the TXA truck. There was a bland-colored pickup some distance behind it without a trailer, but the closest pickup was white. After an hour and a half, she gave up and switched her headset to phone, brought up a list of names on her screen, and clicked on "Poker Jack."

"Jack here."

"Trixie here. What is your location?"

"I am sitting with my thumbs up my ass in nowhere-ville wondering why I am still working for you guys," replied Poker Jack. "It is a good thing you all are paying me so well; I don't take a bullet in the head for just anyone. My head hurts like hell."

Jack had a bandage around his head covering a bullet wound caused by Pete Oxwood's 9-mm. The shot had grazed his head but was close enough to knock him out and leave a nasty wound. Even without the bandage, Jack normally looked like a guy who had just gotten out of a knife fight. The bandage made him look even more dangerous. At a poker table, any other player at the table would hesitate bluffing a guy who looked like he had a switchblade up his sleeve and wanted to use it.

"I want you to drive to Lewistown, Montana, and start looking for Alex Pipe's bland-colored Dodge Ram three-quarter-ton pickup," said Trixie. "It might be pulling a horse trailer. We feel sure that Pete Oxwood and Alex Pipe are in the truck, and there is another woman with them. These are probably the same three people you battled in Eau Clair. You are to take them out—all of them. Our delivery truck is about an hour and a half from Lewistown heading east on Highway 200. We feel sure they are following that truck."

"Okay. I should be able to get there in an hour and a half. It will be a pleasure to take them out."

#

Throughout the drive from Great Falls, Alex had closely monitored her rearview mirror for any hints of being followed. It surprised her that no one had followed them from Great Falls. She had envisioned a hoard of military vehicles on their tail. While pumping diesel into the borrowed one-ton pickup, she kept a vigilant eye on vehicles passing along the main drag, particularly those coming from the east. She noticed an auto coming slowly from the west that had two men in the front seat. The car was new and clean and looked like a rental car, which was out of place in central Montana. The man on the passenger side had a bandage around his head and tattoos appearing from under his T-shirt. Both he and the driver were looking intently at pickups they passed. The driver of the vehicle had a scar on his face and looked directly at the big white Ford and at Alex but showed no sign of recognition in his eyes. They continued to look around without slowing down.

Alex finished filling up the tanks and got back in the pickup cab. "I didn't like the looks of those guys in the Chevy that just passed. They aren't Montanans. They don't dress like Montanans and aren't wearing hats. Mean-looking dudes. I think they are TXA goons, but they didn't seem to notice us."

Pete turned around in his seat and looked out the back window. The Chevy was pulling into the gas station where the TXA truck was being fueled. "Why didn't they recognize us?"

"They must be looking for my Dodge pickup, and I didn't look like my picture in this cowboy hat," replied Alex. "You two were hidden in the truck."

"TXA must have figured out that we are following their truck. They know we are here but don't know what we look like. Ironic," said Pam.

"Put back on your cowboy hats," said Alex. "We will look like local ranchers, and they won't pay too much attention to us."

They watched the Chevy at the convenience store gas station. The man with the bandaged head got out and walked toward the TXA truck. Pam, Pete, and Alex didn't know that the man was Poker Jack, the man Pete had wounded in Eau Claire. The truck driver was finished pumping, and the man approached him.

"My name is Jack. I work for TXA Corporation. Has anyone been following you?"

Frank Smith was suspicious. "How do I know you work for TXA?"

"This knife says I do. Answer my question. Have you seen anyone following you?"

"Okay. Okay. You don't have to get nasty. What kind of vehicle?"

"A Dodge Ram 2500 pickup, bland in color, we believe. But we want to know if anyone has been following you."

"I don't think so. I saw a white vehicle a couple of times, but I couldn't tell what kind it was."

"A white vehicle, eh? That sure narrows it down," Jack said sarcastically. "Look, we are going to follow you the rest of your trip to see if anyone is tagging along, but I want you to keep an eye out also."

"I don't think you want to follow me all the way in that car," said Frank. "You probably need a four-wheel-drive vehicle for the place we're going."

"I'll chance it," sneered Jack.

Smith got back in the truck, pulled out on the highway, and continued east with Jack following in the Chevy car. Alex, Pam, and Pete pretended to be in a conversation as the TXA truck pulled back onto the highway. Alex did not get back on the highway immediately. "We don't want to follow very closely."

Alex knew the highway and knew there were very few main roads the TXA vehicles could take except straight east. This would allow her to follow them and stay almost completely out of sight. Alex waited until they could no longer see the truck and Chevy before she pulled onto the highway.

Not far outside the city limits, Alex looked in the rearview mirror and saw the Chevy following them. "Trouble! They're on our tail. Don't look back."

Alex kept an eye on the Chevy in the rearview mirror. "Quick, look for a ranch entrance." They drove a few more miles and then noticed a ranch archway coming up on the left. Alex put on her turn signal several hundred yards before the turn off and started to slow down. "I can't see a ranch house from the road. That's good. We will be able to drive out of sight on the ranch road. It will look like we are headed home," Alex added. She turned onto the dirt road and passed under the ranch archway.

Poker Jack eyed the white truck slowing down. He guessed this was the pickup truck he was looking for, even though it was not a bland-colored Dodge. He had figured that the first pickup following the TXA truck out of Lewistown was a prime suspect. Jack had directed his driver to pull into a side street and wait to see who followed the big truck. "That's them," he had told the driver. But now that the white pickup had turned onto the ranch road, he was not so sure. That white Ford F350 might belong to whoever owned the ranch. A sign hung down from the archway stating, "Circle T Ranch." He looked at his scar-faced driver and said, "Pull over and let's watch the truck."

Alex drove the pickup at a normal speed down the dirt road, not knowing where the road would lead. Once she could no longer see the main road, she pulled over. "Pete, run back there and see if that Chevy is still in view." Pete worked his way slowly back toward the road, keeping low. He reached a vantage point where the main road was clearly in view. He saw the Chevy sitting on the side of the road. He reported back to Alex. "It's there. They figured out who we are."

"Don't jump to conclusions," Alex stated. "If we don't go back down that road in a few minutes, they will think we are local ranchers, and they will pick up the tail on that TXA truck again. Go back and let us know when they leave." Pete went back to his vantage point. A few minutes after he started his surveillance again, he saw the Chevy pull back on the road and head east. In the meantime, Alex and Pam were throwing dirt and mud from an irrigation ditch onto the truck.

Back at the truck, Pete told Pam and Alex that they were gone. "They could play the same trick again," Pam said.

"Yes, they could, but as it stands now, they'll have to drive like hell to catch up with the TXA truck," Alex replied. "Let's go."

Alex accelerated back to the highway, turned left, and sped east. It was quite a few miles before they could see the back of a car. So few cars used this highway that Alex knew it had to be the Chevy. She slowed down and stayed well behind the car.

The group approached the town of Jordan, Montana. Alex knew that Highway 200 would curve north into Jordan and that another road branched off and headed south. On the other end of the tiny town, she knew that Highway 200 turned back east and that at the junction where Highway 200 turned east, a dirt road headed north, and yet another road went west. Alex would have to get dangerously close to the Chevy to find which road it would take. She accelerated through the curve and sped into town. As soon as she looked down the main street, she saw the Chevy pulled up behind the TXA truck in the middle of town. She hit the brakes and turned right onto a side street.

Alex turned around, drove back to the main street, and stopped at the corner. Pete got out and peeked around a building at the corner. He saw the truck driver and the men from the Chevy talking. *I wonder why they stopped.* Suddenly Alex was at his side. "We need to see if they turn left or right or drive straight ahead. We can stay put until we know." They watched as the men got back into their vehicles and drove straight ahead on the dirt road that headed north. Alex was surprised. "They are going up Hell Creek Road into the Russell Wildlife preserve."

Pete looked at Alex. "Why are you so surprised?"

"That's a gravel dirt road into the wildlife refuge. It ends at the Fort Peck Lake. It's a dead end. The only way out is to turn around and come back down this same road. There are only a few small buildings at the end of the road, just fish and game offices. And no building in between. So I can't figure why they are taking Hell Creek Road. That's the last direction I thought they would go."

Pete was puzzled. "If there are no buildings, where are they going to put the stuff in the truck?"

"Good question. Let's get going."

The trip on Hell Creek Road was rough and dusty, but it was easy following the cloud of dust left by those they were following. "Depending on where that truck goes, the Chevy is going to have trouble with getting high centered on some parts of the road. And some of the branches off the main road have loose dirt on them that a two-wheel-drive car can't climb."

Pam looked at Alex from her seat as shotgun. "So what are we going to do when we meet those guys walking away from their stuck Chevy?"

"The same thing we'll do if they turn around and drive out—have our guns ready."

Alex noticed that there was no cloud of dust ahead. "They stopped." She drove on. "Gun up."

She drove the white pickup several more miles, kicking up its own cloud of dust, but there was no sign of the TXA truck or the Chevy car. "Where did they go?" asked Pam.

"They could have turned onto one of the side roads, but we should have seen their dust trail," replied Alex. "Let's run around and see if there are any tracks onto side roads."

"Wait, look over to our right," said Pete. "That road has some tracks that look fresh." Alex turned the pickup onto the road. It went downhill. At the bottom of the hill, the tracks stopped.

At the bottom of the hill, the tracks stopped in front of a big rock.

"Those tracks could have been made by someone driving up the hill from this spot that was parked here last night," offered Pam.

"Must be," replied Pete. "Otherwise, anyone driving down the hill just evaporated into thin air."

Chapter 47

They drove back up the hill and checked out all the other roads and trails in the area; the TXA truck and the Chevy car could not be found. "I don't know how it's possible, but we lost them," said Alex. "It's getting dark. Let's head back to the ranch and scout around tomorrow."

They drove back toward the ranch. At Jordan, they turned east on Highway 200 and retraced their path back to the ranch. They arrived well after dark and went immediately to bed. This time Alex made no pretense of sleeping on the couch but went directly into Pete's room. She cuddled up in his arms. "Wanna play around?" asked Pete.

"Too tired," she said and immediately went to sleep.

Pam watched Alex go into Pete's room and felt a rush of jealousy. The tug-of-war inside her about Pete and her marriage and Alex started again. *I just don't understand myself. Why do I feel this way? It makes no sense. I love my husband. At least I think I do. But he doesn't show any affection toward me anymore. When was the last time we made love? Can't even remember. Alex is so young and beautiful. You can't compete with her. Admit it, Pam. Admit it. You want to fuck Pete. You don't care about making love to him. You just want to screw him. Why him? Why now? Damn. Damn. Damn. Go to sleep. Go to sleep.*

The next morning, Pam was the first one out of bed and made coffee. She peeked in on Alex and Pete. They looked very comfortable together. *I wonder if they did it last night or this morning. Come on, Pam. Don't get started in your head first thing. Let it go. Damn. If anyone could hear these thoughts, I would just die.*

Pete came out first and headed for the coffee pot. He sat down at the table with Pam. He put some sugar in his coffee and looked across the table at her. "You look very nice this morning, Pam."

"Thanks. A shower and a hairbrush can do wonders. You look pretty good yourself." *You are getting very bold.*

Pete had not had sex with Alex. He woke up feeling aroused, but Alex was still asleep and not interested. When he put his arm around her, she had turned over the other way. When he got his coffee and looked at Pam, there was sexual tension in the room. He noticed that Pam's robe was open at the top, and he could partially see her breasts peeking out from the edges. She leaned over the table and got the sugar. Her robe opened more. It was as if Pam was letting him see her breasts. She was not being shy. He took a sip of coffee and looked at her across the table.

"Pam, you are turning me on."

"Well, you turn me on too." She got up from the table and walked into her bedroom, glancing and smiling back at Pete. Pete got up from the table and walked into her room. She was standing next to the bed. He grabbed her and kissed her passionately. She threw caution to the wind. She had to have him. She kissed him back, hard and long. She let his hands roam under her robe. She had nothing on underneath to stop his probing fingers. She gasped as his fingers touched her in the right places. Suddenly, there was a sound in the hall. They broke apart quickly. Pete left the room. Pam stayed behind, catching her breath. She heard Pete's voice. "Good morning, Alex," he said.

Alex replied, "Good morning. How are you this morning?"

Pam was flushed and feeling very guilty. *There really is something wrong with you, Pam. Why did you do that?* She waiting until she was sure that Alex was in the kitchen before she came out of the room.

Alex had noticed Pete walking toward the kitchen from the general direction of Pam's room but gave it very little thought. She was groggy and needed coffee. She noticed that there were two cups of coffee already on the table. She had taken a couple of sips of coffee when Pam entered the kitchen. "Good morning," said Pam.

"Good morning, Pam," replied Alex. "I see you two beat me to the coffee."

Pam sat down and took a sip of her coffee. She wondered if Alex had noticed anything. Pam felt rather sheepish and did not know how to respond.

Pete picked up the conversation. "Pam was the first one up. How long have you been up Pam?"

"Only about an hour," Pam answered as she stared down at her coffee cup. She dared not look Alex in the eye. She was sure that if she did, Alex would figure out what had happened.

Pam's reluctance to join in the conversation and her unwillingness to look at her alerted Alex that something was out of order. She glanced at Pete and then at Pam. *Neither one of them was in the kitchen when I woke up. I wonder where they were.*

Pam knew that things were getting a little tense around the table. She had to figure out something to break the ice. "Pete, I am sorry, but I am going to have to leave you again. I still don't feel too well and need to lie down again. Sorry, Alex. I am sure I will be better in a little while."

"You do look a little flushed, Pam," said Alex. "Have a nice nap."

Alex felt a little ashamed for having suspected that something was going on between the two. She thought she better talk about the day ahead. "I am going to go on the rez today and ask around for some help from somebody who knows that area well and can help us figure out where that TXA truck went."

"Do you need any help?" asked Pete.

Alex was going to say no but hesitated. *That would leave Pete alone with Pam.* "Yes I would. Unless you would rather stay here and take care of Pam."

Pete hesitated for a second. He had always had trouble understanding women. He was actually almost insensitive to their feelings, at least on an emotional level. He could not tell if Alex was testing him about his feelings for Pam or if she was concerned about Pam's health. He instinctively took the smart way out. "Oh, I really want to be with you."

They gave Mr. Stand back his Ford, got into Alex's banged-up Dodge pickup, and headed east. In less than five minutes, they arrived at a rundown ranch house. Alex jumped out and walked up to the door. Pete watched as an older male Indian came to the door. He gave Alex a hug like they were old friends. Alex said something to him, and he began to gesture and point to the southeast. Alex got back in the truck. "He gave me the name of a hunter that knows the area well. His home is about ten miles from here. They drove east, turned south on a dusty road, and came to a stop in front of what looked like a rundown shack. However, there were some good-looking horses in the fields behind the home. Alex knocked on the door. An old Indian woman came to the door. Pete watched Alex talk to her for a few minutes, and then she came back to the truck.

"He is in Wolf Point."

"Who is in Wolf Point?" asked Pete.

"Max Iron Cloud. He is a hunter that is supposed to know the area where that truck disappeared. That was his grandmother back there. She said she thinks he is drinking again. I hope not."

They drove into Wolf Point. It was still before noon. Alex stopped in front of a bar and went in. She came out a few minutes later and almost ran into a man on the sidewalk. "Have you seen Max Iron Cloud?" The man replied he had not. Alex continued down the street and went into the next bar. In a few minutes, she came running out and waved for Pete to follow her. She ran to a third bar and asked the bartender which one of the men in the bar was Max Iron Cloud. The bartender pointed across the room to a man sitting at a table holding a coffee cup. Alex walked up to him. "Are you Max Cloud?"

"That's me," said Max. "Why does the pretty lady want to know?"

"I have a job for you if you're sober," replied Alex.

"I'm sober. This is coffee in this cup. What kind of job?"

Alex sat down at the table. Pete came up to the table and pulled up another chair. "He's with me. His name is Pete Oxwood. My name is Alex Pipe."

"I know who you are, pretty lady. I remember you at powwows with your father twenty years ago. Also, you won every shooting contest you ever entered. You are pretty famous on the rez."

"Thanks, but I need to talk about you scouting for us. Are you familiar with the northeast side of Hell Creek Road up on top before you go down to the lake?"

"I hunt there all the time. I know the area very well."

"We were following a truck yesterday, and it disappeared near there. We want you to help us find where the truck went."

"I saw a truck disappear into the side of a hill in that same area just recently. I can take you right to it." Max was excited.

"This could be dangerous. You should bring along some fire power," said Pete.

"Can you meet us at my father's ranch before sunup tomorrow morning?" asked Alex.

"I'll be there with my horse Midnight before light," replied Max. "You should bring your horse too, Alex. That's rough country around there."

Chapter 48

Alex and Pete returned to the ranch. It was still early. Pam was walking outside and said she felt better. She and Pete made some coffee and sat in the kitchen drinking together. Alex decided to spend some more time looking at Carl Jones's disk. She had not had any opportunities since she left Boston.

Pam and Pete looked across the kitchen table at each other. Pam smiled at Pete and then glanced down and stirred some sugar in her coffee. Pete got up and walked behind her. She tingled in anticipation of what he might do. He started to massage her shoulders. His hands felt alive and magical. Warmth radiated through her body. "Oh, Pete," she whispered. His hands began to slip down inside her blouse. She stood up, smiled at him, and went out the back door. Pete followed. Pam walked out toward the main barn. Pete watched her until she went inside one of the barn doors. He then walked to the barn.

Alex did not take a break from her study of Carl Jones's disk. She finally quit and went to the bathroom. When she went in the kitchen, Pete and Pam were there chatting.

"Hi, guys. I have been studying Carl Jones's disk and believe that UPA may be supplying weapons to someone who is trying to overthrow our government. The shipments to the military bases always are shipped from the military bases to other locations. The shipments to the bases are just a front for where the military hardware is actually going. The money that is going to the defense contractors from the Z corporations is to buy military weapons. UPA gives tax-free contributions to the military contractors through the Z corporations in the form of orders for military hardware. It looks like ordinary sales by the military contractors to our government, and it completely hides what's going on."

"Why are the US military bases allowing the shipments to come into their docks and then turning right around and shipping them to someone planning a coup?" asked Pam.

"Apparently, UPA has brought off key military personnel to ensure that the shipments enter and leave the bases without anyone raising questions. It is clear that TXA and other defense contractors are in bed with General White. The list of people on White's payroll is huge. There are high-ranking FBI and Homeland Security personnel being paid, as well as many law enforcement and military personnel. I never realized that these big corporations had so much money."

"It's no wonder that I was told to stop the investigation of TXA," said Pam. "Tee Scott felt like something was wrong and let me go rogue because of it. And I am certain that the police chief back in Eau Claire was on the payroll as well as the airmen back at Maelstrom Air Base," said Pam.

"Carl Jones's disk should be enough to stop this coup. Let's get the disk to your boss, Pam, and he should be able to report it," injected Pete.

"Report it to who?" asked Pam. "How would he know who to trust?"

"He wouldn't know what to do if he got this disk out of the blue," added Alex. "If we had not decided to investigate this, it would have taken us forever to figure it out just from the disk. I think we need to find out exactly what is in that truck and report that. It would be hard, tangible evidence of what these guys are stealing from the government and what they plan to do with it."

Pete stood up at the table. "To find out exactly what is going on, we need to find that TXA truck."

"Hold up, Pete," said Alex. "We need to wait until early tomorrow morning when Max Iron Cloud will be here to help us. We don't quite have everything ready to go. We need to clean our firearms and load up with ammunition tonight."

The three sat down and the table and continued to talk about information that Alex had obtained from the disk. "I was able to find out who ordered Clancy killed and who ordered the shots at me that hit Renata."

"Who was that?" asked Pete.

"Lt. General Preston White."

"How did you find that out?" asked Pam.

"They recorded all their phone conversations digitally. They are on the disk. Stupid, wasn't it? Reminds me of Richard Nixon's tapes."

"Alex, how did General White know you were involved?"

"Renata and I visited the crime scene. One of White's henchmen saw us there and called General White, who immediately ordered that we be taken out. I previously thought that Harry Misuriello was ordered by Dmitri Zakhar to take me out, but Harry lost me in the DC traffic. He was surprised when he was told that someone shot at me and hit Renata. Dmitri thought Harry shot Renata and was upset because she is the daughter of Dominick Russo."

"So the guys I ran off the road are General White's henchman!" exclaimed Pam. "Why didn't they shoot you when they saw you at Clancy's old office?"

"As best I can tell from the recordings, they didn't yet have White's orders to kill me," replied Alex "They called White from their car, and he must have told them to kill me at that point—while I was driving back to the hotel. I was taking evasive tactics, and they probably drove straight to the motel or arrived just after Renata and I got in the room. They knew where we were staying."

Pam added, "When I got to the motel, I sat in my car quite awhile waiting for you to come out of your car. Finally, I went to the lobby, and that's when you came in and went upstairs. A while later, I was surprised when Renata ran from the elevator to the front door. Then you came down and ran out too. That's when I know there were problems and went straight to my car."

"I was too busy trying to get away, so I did not notice any cars following me until a little later," said Alex, "and that's when I saw you come up beside them and run them into the ditch."

"White's men got out of the parking lot first, and it took a minute or two to catch up with them. I knew they had to be the shooters and that you were the victim. Even when I was following you around Massachusetts, I really didn't think you were in with Zakhar and Jimmy Smith."

"Okay, guys, let's stop reminiscing about the good old days," said Pete, with a grin. "We have work to do."

Chapter 49

Light was just barely appearing on the horizon when Max drove onto the ranch. Alex, Pam, and Pete were in the kitchen drinking coffee when they saw the headlights of his truck pierce the twilight and move toward the little ranch house. They got up and got their guns and ammunition. Alex put her two forty-fives in her holster and tied the leg tie to her thighs with the leather strings on the bottom of each holster. She pulled the hammer thongs over the triggers of her pistols and went out the door.

The previous night, Alex and Pete had put her two-horse trailer on the back of the one-ton Ford pickup and loaded her tack. She put Hank in the trailer. Max unloaded Midnight from his trailer to Alex's. The group piled into the pickup with Alex driving and drove back to the main road in the increasing twilight.

The trip back to wildlife preserve was uneventful, except they were all on the edges of their seats in anticipation of the adventure before them. They reached Jordan, turned right, and headed north toward Fort Peak Lake. It was a bright, clear morning. There has been an early snow during the night, just enough to keep the dust down, but it made the road slick. Alex was forced to slow down. The roads became slicker as they progressed. Alex was having trouble driving, and when they reached a turnaround point, she turned the rig around and pointed it back down a hill.

"We can't go any further in this truck," said Alex. "A lot of rigs get stuck up here when it's wet. We need to stop at this point where we can still get out without getting stuck. This is the best place. Let's take the horses from here."

"But Pete and I don't have a horse," replied Pam.

"I know. Why don't you and Pete stay here for a few minutes while Max and I scout around?"

Alex and Max unloaded their horses and saddled up. "We will be back in a few minutes," said Alex as they rode off.

Pete was upset. He did not like the idea of standing around. He turned to Pam. "I think I remember where that truck disappeared. I'm going to walk there and see if I can find it on foot. Are you with me?"

Pam did not hesitate. "I'm ready to go," she said. "I didn't come here to stand around."

Pam and Pete walked down the hill on the grass beside the road. It was too slick to walk on the dirt.

Alex and Max arrived at the point that Max had seen the truck disappear into the hillside.

"You see this big rock," Max said to Alex. "Almost anyone can roll this out of the way." He proceeded to push the fabricated rock from the trail. Alex walked up to the rock and shook it back and forth to see how light it was. She then walked toward the hillside.

"The hillside goes almost straight up," she said. "There has to be a big sliding door in the rock if a truck drove in." She examined the grass and shrubs on the hill. "This is very clever, Max. Do you see that the shrubs immediately in front of us are a different color than those to the sides?"

"Yes, that sage brush was planted and died. The grass is also dead. And look, there is a netting material holding the ground in place. It's really hard to see."

"The dirt must be too shallow for the brush to take root, and it died over time. I can plainly see the outline of the door. It is huge. But if you weren't looking for it, you'd never see it. Amazing."

"The door has the dirt and foliage on top of it, and there must be enough clearance that it does not scrape off when it opens and closes. I wonder how they open it."

"I doubt they have an opener outside," said Alex. "Probably if you want the door to open you have to radio in a request, and they operate it from the inside. If that's the case, there has to be another entrance for a person to go in to operate the big door when no one else is inside."

"Let's ride to see if we can find it," said Max.

Alex and Max rode up the side of the hill where it was not very steep to the top of the hill over the door. The horses could sense the excitement of their masters and were kicking up their heels when they could.

Pete and Pam had reached the top of a hill and were headed down toward the point where Pete last saw the truck. Pete noticed something different off to his right. He stopped and stared at a big circle in the snow. "That's unusual," Pete said to Pam. "Why would there be a big circle in the snow out here? Let's go look."

The circle looked like a place where someone had dumped branches and limbs from clearing the land. Pete stepped onto the edge of the circle. It seemed like it was going to give way. "Don't step out there, Pam. It is unstable."

Pam knelt down on the side of the circle and tested the dead limbs. She was able to crawl out a small distance before she felt it was unstable. She stopped. "Pete, there is warm air coming up through the branches."

"Warm air?" questioned Pete. "That means there must be a heated cavern or man-made enclosure below. This could be an opening to vent air. The warm air is melting the snow."

Pete walked around the opening. He thought he heard a noise coming from under the brush. He knelt down and listened. "That's a circulation fan blowing the warm air out of this vent. This reminds me of something I saw before when I was in Army Intelligence. I think we are standing on a missile silo."

Chapter 50

Max and Alex sat astride their horses at the top of a hill. Attempting to locate Pete and Pam, Alex and Max rode down and then across a plateau. The breeze in their faces felt good, their cowboy hats protecting them from the blistering sun. Max spotted Pete and Pam. "Alex, look downhill."

"I didn't think they would sit still very long," said Alex.

They rode down to Pete and Pam. Everyone started to speak at one time, excited to relate their findings. "Hold it. Hold it," said Pete. "I think we're on top of an abandoned missile silo."

"That makes sense. Maelstrom built missile silos all over Montana back during the fifties Cold War with Russia," replied Alex. "A lot of them have been abandoned."

"Why would that TXA truck be hauling something to an abandoned missile site?" asked Pam.

"The TXA missile manufacturing plant in Nevada ships missile parts to Maelstrom," said Alex. "It appears innocent enough since Malstrom is a missile defense base. But since the parts were redirected to this silo, it has to mean that this silo has been secretly reactivated."

"Why would the government secretly reactivate a Silo?" asked Max.

"They aren't," said Alex. "But TXA is. It all makes sense now. TXA, General White, and UPA and their followers are behind this. I think they want to take over the government."

"It's no wonder they want to kill anyone who finds out about it," said Pete.

"I don't think we have much time," replied Alex. From what I gathered off the Carl Jones disk, this coup will happen very soon. I think we need to find our way inside and deactivate the silo."

"We don't know how many armed men may be in there," said Max.

"We just can't stand out here and not do something," said Pam. "We need to try to stop this."

"I agree," said Pete.

"Max and I were looking for a back door to this place," stated Alex. "Let's all go back up the hill and look around."

The group reached a plateau at the top of the hill. They searched the area for nearly two hours without success. They finally decided to rest in a treed area overlooking the plateau. Alex and Max tied up their horses and sat down. They rested against the trunks of the trees, drank water, and ate jerky, which Max had in his saddlebag.

Alex noticed movement on the plateau. A couple hundred yards away, she saw a group of men walking in their direction. She grabbed her binoculars from her saddlebags and stared at the group. She noticed that they were climbing out of a trap door, which was in the area they had searched, but it had been well camouflaged.

"There are armed men coming out of the rear entrance we could not find. It looks like there are about twenty-five of them; they are coming in this direction."

Both Pete and Max took turns looking through the binoculars. "Those guns they are carrying look like hunting rifles, not military weapons," Pete said.

Alex looked again. "They look like a group of ragtag Montana hunters. Why would they be in a missile silo?"

"They don't look like much of a threat, but there are a lot more of them than there are of us," said Pete.

"I think I know how to find out," said Alex. "Everyone, find a good hiding place."

When the group was about twenty-five yards away from the trees, Alex whispered to Pete. "Pete, yell at them and tell them to drop their guns and put their hands in the air. Tell them it would be stupid to try anything."

When the group was about twenty-five yards out, Pete yelled as instructed. Everyone was amazed when the entire group immediately dropped their weapons and put their hands in the air.

Alex yelled at the group. "A couple of us are coming out to talk. We will have our weapons shouldered. Don't try anything. There are a lot of guns pointed at you from these woods."

When Alex and Pete approached the group, she recognized the man in front as the truck driver they had followed.

Pete spoke up. "What are you men doing here?"

The truck driver looked at the ground and spit out some chewing tobacco. "We don't want to have anything more to do with this."

"Anything more to do with what?" asked Alex.

"Aren't you with TXA?" asked Smith.

Pete and Alex looked at each other, puzzled. "No. We used to be."

"You aren't here to stop our escape?" Smith asked.

"No, we're just wondering what is going on here," said Pete. "Put your hands down and tell us what is going on."

"My name's Frank Smith. We're a group from the Montana Militia. We were upset with our socialist government and were recruited to help a takeover of the government. It was supposed to be a grass-roots uprising to restore the country to the way things used to be. There are similar militia groups around the country involved. We were to guard this missile silo and to bring missiles and parts to the silo from Great Falls. But we were fed a pile of shit. There are all types of foreigners involved—Arabs, Muslims, Mexicans, and Russians taking over."

"Are they here?"

"Yes, an initial group of about twenty cutthroats who can hardly speak English. They are mercenaries with military weapons and battlefield experience. And more of them are to come over the Canadian line tomorrow. We were told that the coup was supposed to be a bloodless takeover. We were told that the government would back down when they saw how many of its own people were taking up arms against it. The president would resign, and the leaders of the revolution would appoint a new government based on conservative, God-fearing principles. That's not what is happening. It looks like there will be a bloody takeover by troops from other countries, and I'll bet that companies like TXA are planning to run the government."

"How many are inside?" asked Pete.

"Like I said, there are about twenty heavily armed mercenaries and probably ten or so technicians and support people for the missile launching and the communications center. There are also about four, maybe five TXA employees."

Alex looked intently at Smith. "We are here to stop this coup. We want you to help us."

"That's impossible. They have too much firepower. They will kill us all when we go through the doors."

"Maybe so," replied Alex. "But my plan is to draw them out in the open. Your deer rifles could pick them off one by one at a range their guns can't shoot."

"That sounds good, but how do you plan to draw them out in the open?"

"We could smoke them out if you can show us the location of the air intake vent." Smith responded that he could.

Alex turned to Pete. Do you think you could start a fire over the intake vent?"

"With Max's help, we can figure a way."

"Frank, I want you to divide your men in half and put one half in front and one in the rear of the silo. Find shelter at least 150 yards from the entrances. After Pete starts the fire, they should come out shortly thereafter. Your men can pick them off one by one. Pete, after you start the fire, take Max with you to the front of the silo. When they stop coming out, you and Max go in the front and shoot your way to the control center. Pam and I will do the same from the rear."

The Montana Militiamen were delighted at the thought of shooting the hated foreign mercenaries and were eager to take up positions. They found cover behind various rocks and trees. The opposition's assault rifles would not be very accurate at 150 yards, but the 30.06, .243, and .257 hunting rifles with scopes would be very accurate in the hands of Montana hunters.

With everyone in position, Pete and Max gathered brush and piled it on the air vent's opening. Max took out his lighter and put it in the kindling. The fire started slowly and gathered strength.

Chapter 51

Alex and Pam took cover in the pine trees above the escape hatch along with Alex's horse Hank. Half of the Montana Militiamen were scattered out behind rocks and trees facing the rear exit of the missile silo. They watched the fire on the air intake duct to the silo. Instead of the smoke rising in the air, the circulation fans below were sucking the smoke down into the operational areas of the silo.

It seemed like an eternity, but finally the escape door opened, and a soldier in battle fatigues stumbled out, coughing and gasping for air. Two others followed him. The militia gunners took aim. Six bullets hit the first soldier; four hit the second one, and the last man out got two slugs. Someone in the group starting yelling, "Coordinate, coordinate!" After that, the men alternated shots. Surprisingly, some of the soldiers survived and got behind rocks and trees. Some lay down in the exit door. They sprayed bullets from their assault rifles at the militia. The shots were ineffective.

After a while, no one came out. Shots could be heard at a distance from the front of the silo, but they were few and far between. There were only three remaining mercenary soldiers facing the militia, Pam, and Alex.

"Pam, get up on Hank behind the saddle! We are going for a ride."

Pam put her foot in the stirrup and flung herself up into the saddle. Then she put her hands under her and pushed herself behind the saddle. Alex didn't even use the stirrup. She could jump and throw her long legs over the horse into the saddle.

Pam yelled at the militiamen. "Hold your fire." She then took off to the left and out of sight. In a few minutes, she appeared down the hill to the left and behind the soldiers. "She's flanking them," yelled Frank Smith. The militia stopped coordinating their shots and fired as rapidly as possible at the remaining troops. The volume of bullets distracted the soldiers' attention away from Alex. She was behind them with Hank running at full speed and shooting before they recovered. All three died within five seconds.

Alex brought Hank to a halt and jumped to the ground. "Pam, get off. We are going in."

The women entered the silo escape hatch. The smoke coming out of the door had lessened considerably. There was a metal staircase going down. Pam and Alex paused at the top with their guns pointed down the stairs. "Let's go down to that landing one at a time. That way they can't shoot us both at the same time."

They went down the stairs cautiously and were surprised to meet no resistance. They went from room to room until they heard voices speaking in foreign languages. Pam recognized two soldiers speaking Russian and then heard one speaking French. Pam whispered to Alex. "They survived inside by going in the kitchen, closing the door, and turning on the ventilation fan over the stove."

Then they heard Pete and Max yelling instructions to each other from another room. The soldiers turned their backs on Pam and Alex and rushed to the rear door, going out the other way. Alex stepped in behind them and fired at their backs six times. All the men fell except one who escaped out the door and was immediately shot by Pete. Alex and Pete met in the middle of the room. "Are there anymore out here?" asked Alex.

"I think there are. I heard some other voices to the right."

Pam stood behind them. She had yet to fire a shot. She was dismayed at the thought. *I am the only law enforcement person here. Why am I the only one not shooting?*

Pete led the way toward the place he heard voices. Pam started to follow, but almost immediately shots rang out and a gun battle ensued. Pete and Alex jumped behind metal support beams. Shots from an automatic weapon sprayed out toward them. There was a pause, and Alex peeked around the beam and fired one shot and ended the gun battle.

Max, Pam, Pete, and Alex met in the middle of a large room and decided to fan out in twos to search every room in the silo. As they moved from room to room finding no one, Alex and Pam became separated, until they were each wandering into rooms alone. Pam walked into a room and saw Alex looking at three unarmed people cowering in a corner. Across the room behind Alex stood an evil-looking man with a bandage around his head and a pistol pointed at Alex. Pam immediately recognized him as one of the TXA men she had seen in Lewistown. Poker Jack yelled at Alex. "Die, bitch." Alex started to turn around. A shot rang out. Poker Jack fell dead. Alex saw Pam with her gun pointed at the fallen man.

"Oh my God, Pam, I didn't see him. Thank you. Thank you."

"That's the first time," said Pam.

"What?"

"It's the first time I ever shot anyone."

"You couldn't have picked a better time to start," replied Alex.

Pete and Max entered the room. "Smith said there were four TXA employees here," said Pete. "That one with the bandage on his head only accounts for one. The driver of the Chevy is another one. I wonder where the other two are located? My best guess is we find the communications center."

Pete walked from room to room looking at the ceiling. It soon became obvious to the others that he was following overhead cables. "Something I learned in the army," Pete said. Finally they reached a room with a metal door without a door handle. "It's an automatic door with a control panel. See that metal box to the right of the door? That's the control panel." Pete examined the box. "It requires a card to activate. We're going to have to shoot it off. It's probably a 'fail open' system, so shooting it will cause it to open."

Everyone stepped back as Alex shot the control panel. Pete pushed on the door, and it swung open. Immediately a shot rang out, and Pete retreated. Alex got on her knees by the edge of the door and placed her hat halfway into the room. A bullet went through the hat. Quick as a cat, Alex looked around the door and fired one shot. A scream and the sound of a falling gun followed.

Alex walked across the room with her pistols pointing toward three men. One was on his knees, gun on the floor, holding his shoulder. Alex recognized him as the driver of the Chevy and also recognized the other two.

"Don't move an eyelid," ordered Alex to the men. Pam moved up next to Alex, her 9-mm pointed at the cowering men. "Pam, I believe you have read these men's dossiers, but you have not met them in person. Let me introduce you to Dimitri Zakhar and Jimmy Montgomery."

"Enchante," Pam said with a smile. "It's a small world, isn't it, Alex?"

"Alex," said Dimitri. "Alex Pipe. I almost didn't recognize you in that cowgirl outfit. I suspect you think you are going to stop us, but things have gone too far. Disabling this site won't stop all the other actions we're taking. What do you think, Jimmy? Do you think this sweet little thing in her cowgirl outfit will bring us down?"

"Not hardly," replied Jimmy. "Alex, those guns don't scare me one little bit. I should have taken you down on that date we had in Boston."

"Jimmy, you wouldn't have succeeded then, and you won't now. Both of you are going to tell me exactly how to stop this coup, and you are going to do it now."

"Fat chance of that," said Jimmy.

"I guess you never heard of the Annie Oakley of the Fort Peck Indian Reservation," replied Alex. "I hate to brag, but I can split a playing card in half at fifty paces."

"That's not so difficult."

"It is when the card is turned sideways," Alex retorted. "Unless you start talking, I will put a bullet into every part of your body where it won't kill you but will cause considerable pain. Quite honestly, gentlemen, given my high esteem of you, that would make my day."

"Don't believe me?" In a flash, Alex fired four quick shots. Both Dimitri and Jimmy screamed with pain. Blood poured down from their ears.

"Those are just creases," said Alex. "I can do better. How about creases in your temples? What if I try that from way across the room? Then we can try direct hits to your kneecaps. I hear that's painful."

The defiance on the men's faces lessened. Alex paced backward to the opposite wall. She put her pistols in her holsters. "Let's try for the temples from a quick draw position."

With lightning speed, Alex's right hand moved to her right holster, and Dimitri screamed and fell to the cement floor, with blood gushing from his temple. Dimitri screamed something in Russian at Alex, undoubtedly profanity.

"What about you, Jimmy?" asked Alex. "Do you want to take a chance?"

Jimmy looked down at Dimitri. "We don't owe this damn country anything. Hell, this place isn't worth dying over. I don't really give a crap about General White and his American flag and patriotism and all that shit. I'm out."

"Mother Russia will have me back," said Dimitri. "I'm with you. What all do you want to know, Alex? Just put down that pistol."

After a few questions, Dimitri and Jimmy told everything they could think of about the coup, including who was involved and the locations of each potential attack.

Pete looked at the controls and monitors in the communications center. There was a clipboard with codes on the top paper designating locations that could be contacted. Among the coded locations were the TXA control center, General White's office, and facilities near military bases around the country. He typed the code for TXA communications control. The monitor blinked and then typed out "TXA Central Control" followed by "Go ahead." Pete typed, "Hold on. I will be back to you in a minute." He then typed in the code for Edwards Air Force Base. The same kind of message appeared. He typed, "Need status update." The screen scrolled through a long report with references to "Zero Day" and "Zero Day + 2."

Pete yelled, "I think they are two days from launching their attack. Alex, could you run up to the truck and get the computer and Jones' disk for me?"

Alex rode Hank to the truck and was back in fifteen minutes. While she was gone, Pete contacted his former army superior officer via satellite phone. His former superior was now a general at the Pentagon with considerable authority. Pete asked him for the communications address for the General's most secure computer center.

When Alex returned, Pete plugged the laptop computer to the communications computer by USB ports and readied the laptop to transmit the contents of the disk to the secure link at the Pentagon. He hit the enter button, and the data streamed away.

Pete then created a file containing the location of each potential hostile attack site and transmitted it to the Pentagon also. He then got back on the satellite phone and told the general everything that had been happening, what was on the disk, and what was in the file he had just transmitted.

#

Lt. General White sat in his closed Washington office looking out the window. The sun was almost below the horizon, and the automobiles scurrying about had started putting on their headlights. He knew the coup had failed and that the authorities were on the way to arrest him. They had just been at his house, and he might have fifteen minutes before they arrived. Reports were coming in from all over the country. Ron Fenton had been arrested in California, and Butch Butler in Washington, along with many of their comrades. Dmitri and Jimmy had escaped, and their whereabouts were unknown. Alex was particularly upset about their escape. It looked like they rode away on her horse Hank.

Many thoughts went through his head. He had almost pulled it off. *We almost did it. Only two days short… but not all is lost. I will be the hero of the people and a martyr for our just cause.*

White heard a noise at the door. Looking up, he saw a large man standing in the doorway. In a deep voice, he said, "My name is Dominick Russo."

"I know who you are; you don't scare me. If you were going to kill me, you would have sent your henchmen. Why do you care about what's going on? You're just a common criminal."

A pistol suddenly appeared in Russo's hand.

"Hey, what are you so hot about? I didn't do anything to you."

"You shot my daughter and killed her best friend, Clancy McCleary."

"That stupid redheaded cunt? She was poking her nose into my business. She deserved what she got."

"Did my daughter deserve to be shot?"

"Collateral damage. It happens in time of emergency."

"Emergency? Your ego is getting in the way of common sense. Your ego distorts everything to justify your desires. Even in this time of defeat, I know what you're thinking, General. You want to make the world your stage during your high-profile treason trial. The cameras and the microphones will carry your message across the globe. You want to die a hero, a martyr. Don't you, General?"

"Nonsense," yelled White. "Get out of my office. You petty criminals are the scum of the earth. Get out!"

"No, General. You and your corporations are the criminals. Your corporations want to run this country and eventually the world. What you want is power. Evil, deadly power."

"You have power, and you kill people," replied White. "What makes you think you are superior to me?"

"Yes, I have power, and I make money but only on my turf. Your corporations are never satisfied. They aren't really capitalists. They take and take and take. If they can eliminate competition, they will. That's hardly free enterprise, not when there is no one left to compete with. I like the old version of American capitalism where everyone shares in the wealth. Everyone makes a little money. Everyday people with all their faults, warts, and sins band together and share. That is America. You and your true believers are actually fascists."

"Fascist? How dare you call me a fascist."

"Oh, but you are. My papa was raised in Italy during the time of Mussolini's rise to power. He warned me of the evils of fascism. Benito himself defined fascism for us: 'Fascism should more appropriately be called Corporatism because it is a merger of state and corporate power.'"

"Get out of my office, you low-life Guinea pimp. Or, better yet, stay in my office. The feds are on the way to arrest me, and they would love to find you here."

"I am not going to let you die a martyr, General. There will be no trial and no stage on which you tell your warped story."

Russo shot White in the chest five times. A silencer muffled the shots. The gun was dropped. Russo disappeared down the back stairs. Ten minutes later, the federal officials arrived to arrest White. But he was dead.

Chapter 52

Fall comes early in northern Montana. The cottonwood trees along the streams and rivers change color from green to gold. The days are warm and sunny, the evenings cool and crisp.

The sun rose over the prairie. It was still very cool. The horses' breath created small clouds from their nostrils. Alex and Pete rode toward a small herd of cattle. Their purpose was to move the herd to a different pasture.

As the sun rose higher in the sky, the sun's rays warmed everything they touched. The combination of the cool air and warmth from the sun invigorated Alex's senses, causing the prairie to smell fresh and alive.

Alex watched as Pete dismounted to open a wire gate. They had been living together on the ranch since the coup by UPA and TXA was foiled. Alex, Pam, and Pete did not receive any gratitude in the news for their efforts in toppling the corporate conspiracy. The government expressed their eternal gratitude but kept a tight lid on publicity. The coup was an embarrassment to the government.

Alex had fallen in love with Pete. But something about him or their relationship did not seem right, and she could not put her finger on it. She watched Pete's fluid motions dismounting and opening the gate. It created a stir of passion within her. But she was somewhat cautious about giving him her complete love and devotion. She was torn between being too cautious and abandoning caution all together. She realized that her relationship with Pete was as close as she had ever been to true love, but she was still reluctant to give in completely.

Pete drew back the wire gate and stood to one side, holding the gate while Alex rode through leading Pete's horse. Pete's feelings toward Alex were mixed. He truly enjoyed being with her on the ranch, learning the ways of ranch living. He realized one day that he had never enjoyed a job as much as he did as a ranch hand. His lovemaking with Alex was spectacular, but he wondered if it was the sex or if he truly loved her.

The two rode out to small herd and began driving them back toward the barn and main house. The horses they rode were experienced at driving cattle. If one cow moved away from the herd, either horse would stomp their closest front leg into the ground, and the cow would move back into the herd. Pete was amazed. *This horse makes it look like I know what I'm doing.* They got the herd into a corral near the barn, put up their horses and tact, and walked back to the house. *I really love doing all this ranch stuff.*

Alex had spent a lot of time thinking about her past and future. She had talked to Renata several times. They had many laughs together. Renata was still man crazy, and every other sentence, it seemed, had some sexual innuendo. Renata had taken over Alex's old apartment and wanted Alex to come back and live in the apartment again. However, the last time Alex talked to her, she learned that Renata had run into her old flame Carlo, who was now divorced, and she was in love. Alex didn't want to be a third wheel in that.

Alex could have returned to work at her old job after all the bad apples were purged from TXA. She wrestled with the idea, but her memories of the corporate life were negative. She saw that too much power and money in a corporation could change a good company into one lacking socially redemptive values and could become more evil than good.

She had toyed with the idea of forming a detective agency with Pam Robinson. They had also talked often on the phone. Pam had retired from the FBI, despite her boss's pleading to stay. She also was in the process of getting a divorce. It seemed that her college professor husband liked to entertain his female students. After she returned home, Pam learned that he had been seeing the young girls for quite a few years. It was no wonder he had not made love to her in years.

When she arrived home, she caught him in a compromising position and immediately asked him to move out. Pam now had a life of her own. She had a good retirement income, month-to-month rent on a little apartment, and plenty of time to do anything she wanted. Pam was really quite interested in the detective agency idea that Alex mentioned.

She thought about it a great deal. She also thought about Pete a great deal. When she had met Pete in the barn at the ranch, Pete had a change of heart, and nothing really happened between them. She nonetheless had fond memories of her feelings toward him.

Alex finally came to the conclusion that she should stay on the ranch. She was a Montana girl deep in her heart. She had missed Montana a great deal when she lived in Massachusetts. She enjoyed the ranch work and thought maybe she could do part-time detective work.

Pete had been in touch with his children, and one day after several months on the ranch, he got a call from his son.

"Oh my God," said Pete on the phone. "When did it happen? Have you talked to your mother? How is she holding up? Has a funeral been arranged yet?" The conversation continued with numerous questions before Pete hung up.

"Who died?" asked Alex.

"My ex-wife's husband was killed in an automobile crash last night. I am going to have to go down and help her with the funeral and her finances. She just does not do those kinds of things well."

"Why don't you have your children do all that?" asked Alex.

"They are no better than their mother at those kinds of things. I am the only logical person for the job."

"But you aren't married to her anymore; it's not your job."

"I know. I will only be gone a couple of weeks. It's not like I am moving back there."

Pete hustled to the bedroom to pack his belongings. It did not take long. Alex tried to talk to him as he packed, but he was too distracted and in a hurry. The only thing he said was, "It's a good thing I bought that used pickup a month ago." He clamored out the door and jumped in his pickup, throwing his bags on the small backseat.

He started the engine and told Alex he would be in touch soon. He gunned the engine and headed for the highway.

He didn't even kiss me good-bye. She watched as the truck's wheels left a cloud of dust on the way to the highway. He was driving fast. When he reached the highway, he spun out before he got traction and accelerated east toward Chicago. Alex watched until the truck was no longer in sight. She wondered at that moment if she would never see him again. She felt in her heart that Pete was going back to his ex-wife and that she would take him back now that he was sober. She sat for a long time on the porch thinking about her troubled history with men. The sun was going down rapidly, and it was getting dark, but she continued to sit there staring toward the road.

Alex got up and took a deep breath. She went in the house and closed the door. It was quiet and lonely in the house. A single tear went down her cheek.

About a month after Pete left for Chicago, Alex was throwing some hay to Hank and Duke in the barn. She started to brush them down, talking gently to them. During these mindless tasks, she thought about Pete. She missed him very much and had come to the conclusion that her past inability to give herself completely to the relationship was her failing, not Pete's. *Why have I always been so afraid to really love someone?*

Someone knocked on the barn door. Alex turned and saw the outline of a cowboy in the door, his face in the shadows. "I was wondering, ma'am, if you could use some help on the ranch. If so, I'm willing."

Alex burst into joyful tears and ran into Pete's waiting arms.

Epilogue

"Welcome, Comrade Zakhar," a Russian general said enthusiastically, grasping Dmitri's hand with enthusiasm. "Welcome back to Mother Russia."

"Thank you, Comrade General," replied Dmitri. "It is good to be back in Moscow among my countrymen. Do you remember Jimmy Montgomery? He was on assignment with me in America."

"Yes, yes. I remember you, Jimmy. From England, correct?" replied the general, without waiting for a response as he shook Jimmy's hand. "Welcome to the Kremlin, Jimmy."

The general escorted them into a conference room. "I read the FSB report on how you escaped the missile silo in Montana; very interesting. By the way, Jimmy, in case you did not know it, FSB is the old KGB."

Jimmy smiled. "It was rather interesting. We are lucky to be alive. That Montana cowgirl Alex Pipe is lightning fast with a pistol and deadly accurate. Unbelievable. She damn near shot our bloody ears off. It was just enough to make us bleed profusely without knocking us out. But I still wondered if I was going to die. We sought medical help, and when the person treating us turned his back, we simply walked out the door with bandaged heads. When we got outside, there was a horse tied up right there in front of us. We rode the horse north to the Canadian border."

"Was it one of those cowboy horses with a big saddle with a horn and a lasso tied to the side? And saddlebags?" asked the general with considerable enthusiasm. It was obvious to Dmitri and Jimmy that the general had seen too many American cowboy movies.

"Yes," replied Dmitri. "I think it belonged to the cowgirl Alex Pipe."

"The FSB report said that it was easy to cross the border into Canada," said the general.

"Very easy," Dmitri asserted. "The Canadian border with Montana is not protected in many places. The border goes through hundreds of miles of rural area. Once we were in Canada, we added some facial hair and used one of our many passports to eventually get to Moscow."

The general changed the subject. "There will be several others joining us from the FSB and from our Cyber Espionage Group, part of Russia's Foreign Intelligence Service." A number of individuals began entering the room, some in uniform and some in civilian clothes. One of them had a commanding presence and voice and was dressed immaculately in an expensive suit and tie. He opened the meeting.

"Comrades and Mr. Montgomery, I am Lev Brazin from the President Executive Office. I am here on behalf of and at the direction of our president, Vladimir Putin. He sends his greetings to all of you, and he sends his special commendation to you, Dmitri Zakhar, for your efforts to infiltrate the corporate structure of the United States and to help in the attempt to overthrow the government of the United States."

"Thank you, Comrade Brazin," replied Dmitri. "Tell President Putin I appreciate his commendation."

Another man in civilian clothes addressed Dmitri. "I am Alexei Leskov, head of the Foreign Intelligence Service. Sitting on my left is Feliks Stepankov, my director of the Cyber Espionage Group. Feliks worked closely with Ron Fenton, one of our assets assigned to the Palo Alto operations center. It is unfortunate that he was arrested, but he will not talk. Before he was arrested, his staff escaped. It is fortunate that all evidence of a connection with Russia was destroyed. Mr. Fenton also was a dual citizen of Russia and the United States. We had assets hidden in many places and embedded deeply in American society. Places you would never dream of."

Lev Brazin was growing impatient. His condescending attitude permeated the room. He picked a piece of lint off of his expensive suit and interrupted Alexei before he could continue. "We learned a great deal about how billions of American dollars can be diverted to numerous purposes under the guise of political contributions. We will continue to use this money in our next campaign, which we will discuss shortly. And, of equal importance, we learned that American cyber capabilities and cyber security is very weak."

Brazin took a few steps and opened the conference room door. "Come in," he said. A balding man wearing glasses with very thick lenses and black rims entered the room with a smirk on his face.

"Gentlemen, I introduce you to Mr. Carl Jones from the United States, a cyberexpert. We have hired Mr. Jones to help our Cyber Espionage Group in our new espionage operation against America."

A number of men around the table greeted Jones as he moved toward an empty chair. "At the same time that we introduce Mr. Jones, we must ask Mr. Montgomery to leave the room. This operation is only on a need-to-know basis."

After Montgomery left the room, Brazin continued. "President Putin has decided that we will not support another coup attempt in America. Instead we will accomplish the control of the government of the United States with a less direct approach. It will be called Operation Hammertoss."

The men around the table leaned forward. Carl Jones continued his smirk as if he had already been briefed. Between Jones and Brazin, it was difficult to tell which man had the most condescending attitude.

Brazin continued. "Operation Hammertoss will be a broad cyber attack on American institutions with the purpose of weakening the fabric of American society and its democracy. We will flood the social media sights and news services with misinformation from now until the American elections next year. The misinformation will increase in intensity and reach a crescendo on Election Day. Our ultimate purpose is the election of a president of the United States who is pro-Russian." An audible gasp arose from the conference table.

"There is no cyber security in America that we cannot compromise. Mr. Jones is very familiar with the most sophisticated cyber security in the United States, including the CIA and FBI."

All eyes turned toward Jones. Jones's smirk increased. Brazin condescendingly picked another piece of lint from his suit. He continued. "Americans are angry, particularly white men. They are frustrated by the attention given to minorities and by the loss of manufacturing jobs. They are looking for a strongman, someone who unequivocally says he will bring change. They don't really know what they want exactly, but we know that they want a strongman with a strong image of change. We will create that man. We will undermine anyone or any organization that gets in our way. We will amplify discontent and incite the American public to demand radical change."

"Who would this American strongman be?" asked the Russian general.

"We have not decided yet, but there are a number of billionaires and corporate executives who do a considerable amount of business with Russia. We are grooming them. We plan to pass out special rewards and generate positive international news about them. We need someone as president who is friendly toward our foreign policies in the Ukraine, Syria, and the Crimea. He must also be against NATO."

The men around the conference table applauded Brazin enthusiastically and expressed their support in loud voices.

"But what if the strongman becomes president and does not follow through on Russia's behalf?" asked the general.

Brazin smiled broadly. "We always have insurance against such actions. The information and videos we have gathered about our prospective American presidents is quite incriminating."

Brazin addressed Dmitri again. "Dmitri, we need to get a change of identity for you and forged papers to get you back in the United States. You need to take over Ron Fenton's group. We will reassemble it in the same location. We need boots on the ground, so to speak, in addition to our use of the Internet from Russia."

"I am happy to help in any way I can. America has grown weak, but there are still some strong individuals we have to overcome," said Dmitri. As he rubbed his temple, he said, "In that regard, I hope I don't have another encounter with that cowgirl Alex Pipe."

Printed in the United States
By Bookmasters